The Plague of Dreamlessness

M. Reese Kennedy

SUNKEN
GARDENS
PRESS

www.sunkengardenspress.com

PART ONE

PLAGUE

For several decades in what is thought to be an age of advanced science, the Plague of Dreamlessness drifted between imagination and foreboding, more apparition than affliction, a quirky but ominous whisper from the not too distant past. It was contemporary mythology just intriguing enough to plant itself in the imagination, just menacing enough to hold it there, and just credible enough to stand the tides of skepticism. It was folklore at its most compelling, regional in nature, knowledge of the sort passed primarily along family lines.

When the Plague became official, begrudgingly acknowledged more than fifty years after its disappearance, it remained unsolved and highly elusive, a construct of epidemiologists presented, rather abruptly, with a cluster of inexplicable case histories. With no associated fatalities, no proven qualities of contagion, and no evidence of bacterial or viral origin, the phenomenon would not logically qualify as a "plague" at all. And with the modest number of cases and the passing of so much time, the extent of the investigative ardor was, perhaps, more than might have been expected.

But thirty-six incidents of unexplained and prolonged coma, all impacting males, all transpiring more or less simultaneously in one unremarkable American city, were bound to attract a certain amount of attention, even if it were all a thing of the past. And while nothing resembling a recurrence had been flagged over the five intervening decades, a strange and unlikely confluence of events drove this wisp of a Plague, belatedly but inexorably, into the limelight.

REMEMBRANCES

The Saint Madeleine Sophie Barat Academy of the Sacred Heart, named for the French-born founder of the Society of the Sacred Heart, has opened its doors to Catholic girls in old Omaha since 1873. Gnarled trees with pitch-dark trunks crowd its circular drive, cracking and heaving the pavement with the upthrust of hellish roots. Four stories of darkened brick form hulking outcroppings and fitful setbacks, each face an assault of conflicting elements – cornices, balustrades, arches, friezes, parapets. The windows are cruelly narrow and set unevenly, as if in afterthought. A portico on squat brick columns casts perpetual shadow over the double doors beneath.

Just inside, an imposing set of marble stairs ascends steeply to something unseen, evoking a sense of penance, unworthiness, and self-abnegation, silently affirmed by the tread wear of decades. The summit reveals a cavernous central hallway, running the length of the building past several heavy wooden doors on both sides. Ornately framed religious paintings and icons collected in three centuries crowd the walls in a clash of genre and form. The chapel entrance is just beyond.

The college function is long gone, but in those years Omaha girls could cloister on that campus from kindergarten well into their childbearing primes. That would mean seventeen years of schoolgirl skirts below the knees, nuns swishing in the halls, atavistic Catholic rituals at every turn. My three older sisters – Mary Martha, Mary Margaret, and Mary Monica – were Barat Academy grade schoolers. My older brother Drew, like most normal Catholic boys in our neighborhood, was at Saint Martyrius, the local coed parochial school. For reasons unclear to me then or now, Barat leadership thought it prudent to experiment with the enrollment of young boys, and the call went out for a handful of eligible first graders. I was of kindergarten age, but my father, a pillar of Catholic leadership in a very Catholic city, had me jump the year to join the inaugural coed class.

I'm all for breaking barriers — would have had no objection to attending a primarily girls college, for example — but Barat was stony ground for the seed of my boyhood. I slicked my hair with VO-5, clipped on the required navy blue bow tie, and marched up the marble steps and down the tiled corridors, past endless streams of giant girls, past carven images of writhing saints and the suffering Jesus, and on to my first grade classroom.

PLAGUE

On December 7, 2025, the National Institutes of Health raised the official curtain on the Plague of Dreamlessness — and concurrently launched a firestorm that would result in the sacking of its entire management team. In what had promised to be an uneventful and unenthusiastically attended press conference, NIH Director Donald Cyr folded one unusual announcement within a string of bland updates, perhaps in hopes that no one would really notice. The Institute was releasing detailed records of a number of unexplained comas that had occurred in the late 1960s, not in some far-away third-world country, but smack in the US breadbasket, in Eastern Nebraska, primarily Omaha. The geographical concentration suggested a localized contaminant or infectious agent, but the pathology had been unresolved at the time — and remained so fifty-six years later. In response to questioning, Cyr reported that the documents showed no sign of official medical inquiry, and when pressed further on the point he acknowledged that the lack of such an inquiry did seem irregular.

Press coverage the following morning focused not only on the bizarre nature of the medical phenomenon, but on its equally bizarre treatment in the hands of the NIH. The NIH, after all, had uncovered a menace to the public health in a completely ludicrous manner, matter-of-factly releasing records it had held and neglected for decades. It was unclear what Cyr had expected, but he suddenly had a problem on his hands. Hard evidence of the shadowy epidemic had taken over five decades to surface, but within a week follow-up stories documented an aura of longstanding and long ignored local legend: grandchildren and great-grandchildren recalled their forbears' strange afflictions; retired nurses and orderlies described the rash of comas that had arrived without cause and vanished without comment.

Journalists were asking the tough questions: Given the information it held at the time, why hadn't the NIH either announced the outbreak or investigated it? Did its long silence and inaction constitute gross neglect, hideous misjudgment – or worse? How far had any decision to conceal the outbreak migrated up the management hierarchy, and how many generations of subsequent management had knowingly complied? And was it simply a case of withholding information, or had the NIH played a more active role in suppressing inquiry?

The scandal seemed to strike a national nerve. Competing tabloids dubbed the story "Comaha!" and "Omacoma." Coma grabbed at our collective imaginations, evoking the fairy tale spell of Sleeping Beauty and the enchanted sleep of Rip van Winkle. But it was inextricably tied to the all-too-real tragedy of brain trauma, and to a host of other medical horrors. Perpetual sleep embodied the very essence of the unknown, more mystical than scientific. The unreachable, unwakable sleeper: Was there a chance he was dreaming, hearing, processing? Could he feel a touch, or a lover's kiss? Would he awaken in time, returned from the distance still whole of mind and body? Would he emerge too late, a damaged shadow of himself? Or would he simply never return? The combination of the ever-ethereal coma, in a mysterious and localized outbreak impacting only men, all under a shameful administrative shroud, was like a derailed train on the side of the road; drivers-by had little choice but to brake and gawk.

PALM TUNNELS

Henry Cleverby, who'd been living in a holding pattern, waiting numbly for a share of his grandfather's money, finally got his wish. As fate would have it, Jeremy Cleverby, the aging and distinguished Democratic Senator from Nebraska, a widower who had repeatedly refused more modest and manageable accommodations, teetered in the worst possible location. He pitched and tumbled spectacularly, down the long grand staircase that formed the architectural centerpiece of his twelve thousand foot West Omaha mansion. Broken and alone, he lay through the night pressed in hideous orientation against the bottom step, contorted on the hardwood and soaked in his own effluvia. He hissed his final expiration at dawn's first light.

Henry had returned permanently to Omaha a year earlier, after three listless semesters at college. His parents had moved to Houston during his first term away, a spectacular piece of good luck in his view. Any doubt on the point was permanently expunged when they returned for the Senator's funeral. Their haranguing and hounding, in conjunction with the tiresome string of memorial observances, made for a truly unbearable stretch of ten days. But at its merciful end Henry was back to his own devices, and greatly supplemented with the two assets his grandfather's will had allotted him: the modest but mortgage-free Dundee house he'd grown up in, and a money fund sufficient to cover his remaining five semesters.

While the inheritance itself was somewhat less than he'd hoped, the actual passage into ownership – the physical taking of the house and the sudden and felicitous control over the money fund – seemed somehow to turn a switch within him, igniting a feeling that his life was now, for the first time, officially underway. As if awakened from a long dream into a state of uncharacteristic rationality, he began to contemplate his next steps in the panorama unfolding with sudden clarity before him. He had the benefit of an insight, well beyond his years, into four important realities: he would never return to college; his arrogant and unpliable personality made him virtually unemployable; money was an ongoing requirement; and the money fund he'd just come into wouldn't last forever.

And so Henry Cleverby slept on it, contemplated and pondered, philosophized and considered, and came at length to a pivotal resolution: he would buy a business with his newfound capital, a business he could parlay into a lasting and lifestyle-friendly annuity. Such a business needed to be of a type he could run in relative comfort, without having to get up too early in the morning, put in a lot of face time, tax his brain, or curry anyone's favor. If it were mildly interesting that would be even better.

He contacted a few business brokers, but, in spite of his distinguished lineage, none of them seemed to take him seriously. He combed the internet, the newspapers, trade publications. He spent hours driving the city in search of posted sale notices. Fast food outlets, car washes, convenience stores – nothing grabbed him. But as so often happens, the answer appeared within his own small circle. An old grade school classmate mentioned over drinks that his entrepreneurial but unsettled older brother was headed into substance abuse treatment; he was desperate to sell his midtown tattoo and piercing parlor. Plenty of tattoo artists would have been thrilled to take on the enterprise – it was well regarded in those circles – if only it had come with the benefit of owner financing. But the transaction in question required ready cash. And ready cash was now Henry's strong suit. Tony's Twilight Tattoo was soon Henry's Twilight Tattoo, for less than the cost of one semester's tuition.

PLAGUE

The more Donald Cyr floundered in his public appearances, the more the storyline became set against him: the rash of perplexing comas, long rumored but never seriously discussed in any medical forum, had been secreted away from the public by the very body charged to protect it. The embattled director announced an in-house committee to investigate the outbreak. But the initiative was almost universally panned as a cynical cover, a johnny-come-lately, a feeble afterthought. The committee members were not only ridiculed, they were effectively dysfunctional, hopelessly divided in their approach. Squabbling led to resignations, and before long the director's appointees had melted away completely, supplanted by another committee, this one charged directly by Congress.

In fact, neither of the sanctioned groups had much of an edge on the science writers, medical notables, and other self-appointed dabblers who squared their shoulders at the trough. The NIH documents were fully declassified, nestled in the realm of public domain. Independent researchers, self-promoters, and rogue academics all sifted through the same files as the official committees, joining in the general rush to serve the public curiosity, hunting for clues, scratching at the medical implications. The more engaging of these experts became minor celebrities, regulars on news and talk shows. They discussed salient tidbits from the medical records of the thirty-six men, ran background pieces on coma and its range of forms and origins, and speculated broadly as to the cause of these particular cases. Was it some lurking environmental hazard? Was it an infectious strain? Was it some unknown shutdown mechanism within the brain? The Plague of Comas, as it had then come to be called, had become a piece of medical mythology almost overnight.

In time the Congressional committee delivered its muddled report – 386 pages of fingerpointing, sidestepping and circumvention. The report did nothing to enhance anyone's understanding of the Plague, but it did seem to signal an irresolvable futility; in its wake the story cooled. The newly crowned celebrity experts reached the same dead end as the more faceless public health officials: they were stumped. Their many diagnostic theories came to be seen as grandstanding and guesswork. The NIH cover-up, while generally believed to have occurred, had never been quite substantiated. The news cycle was reduced to the increasingly tiresome political squabble over the agency's restructuring, on the unspectacular grounds of ineptitude.

But even as the Plague of Comas waned in the topical spotlight, a certain mystique seemed to cloak it, a faint glow, a nimbus both quirky and endearing. Allowed a quiet return to the shrouds of history, the curious Plague took on a retrospective allure, a nostalgic tinge reflecting the passing of decades. Campy Plague of Comas tee shirts popped up in the most eclectic and offbeat shops. A notable catchphrase was spawned; one surrounded by dimwits was said to be trapped "in a plague of comas." And musical acts sprung up with derivative branding; The Kings of Coma (formerly Death by Decibel) and Visions of the Plague both went platinum.

REMEMBRANCES

Barat nuns wore black habits that flowed to their ankles. As they whisked shapelessly down the hall you could just catch a glimpse of their no-nonsense black shoes. Silver crucifixes hung on chains from their necks. These were not simple lower-case tee crucifixes, but detailed models the size of my fist, with realistic three-dimensional Jesuses. I was most curious about the starchy white headgear that dug up under their nunly chins and wrapped around to cover their ears, foreheads and necks. It looked like a knight's helmet without the face shield. Did they have crew cuts underneath?

As if through divine dialogue, this question was answered almost immediately, with the release of "The Sound of Music" in 1965. Julie Andrews' hair was short-cropped and yet appealing, stylish and blonde. Granted, she looked nothing like the nuns at Barat, most of whom had puffy pink faces bursting out from their tight white collars. Our first grade teacher, Mother Teshima, from what little I could see, was an exception; she was actually slim, and relatively young, with nice skin. But she wore granny glasses, and gave no indication that she could strum a guitar, or dance, or sing. And, oddly enough, she was Japanese, quite likely the only Japanese nun in the State of Nebraska.

Our class was tiny – two other boys and six girls. We toed the line in and out of the classroom, such comportment mandated not only by the ominous nun-to-child ratio, but by the ever present threat of Prime. At the all-school Prime assembly, held weekly in the chapel, each student presented herself before the very altar to receive a quite public assessment of her most recent school behavior and spiritual devotion – the two were inextricably linked. This was done with an eye to visual effect, by the presentation of one of three possible pocket-size cards – blue for Tres Bien, yellow for simply Bien, and red for Assez Bien (literally "rather good," but at Barat "sinful" or "horrific"). The mood was somber and deathly serious. I began a long and extremely timid run of Tres Biens.

We spent a lot of time in that chapel. I contemplated the fourteen Stations of the Cross along the walls and the full-color crucifix hanging overhead and wondered why some crucifixes showed a separate spike for each foot and others showed the feet crossed over for a single spike. Or why some showed a support wedge for the feet and others had the feet flat on the cross, forcing bent knees and providing extra agony as I imagined it. Shouldn't this all have been uniform, in keeping with the actual historic occurrence?

The holiest day in the Barat school year was the day of our Blessed Virgin Mary. For that occasion one special girl was given the high honor of becoming the Petite Marie. The school body would gather in the chapel, the all-nun choir ringing from on high, for the procession culminated by the Petite Marie, who in this case happened to be my sister Mary Margaret, walking slowly and demurely down the aisle, as if proffering herself as a child-bride to Jesus, or simply a sacrifice on the pyre, a pre-adolescent girl with an unwavering sense of purpose and duty, eyes downcast to show long angelic lashes, with a delicate white veil pulled off her face, and bobby socks and a simple pastel dress in a soft Easter yellow. She wore a broad blue ribbon diagonally over one shoulder, in vaguely military fashion – somewhat suggestive of the young Jeanne d'Arc – but the particular robin's egg hue was unmistakably the color of the Blessed Virgin, the only saint to my knowledge with a proprietary theme color. Shafts of sunlight pierced the decorative stained-glass windows as the Petite Marie moved past my pew, hands clasped perfectly in prayer. Perhaps she too could achieve immaculate conception.

PLAGUE

To be fair, those in pursuit of this medical oddity from a bygone generation had very few resources at their disposal. They lacked the rigorously constructed data a timely scientific inquiry would likely have produced. While the fifty year-old hospital records uniformly mentioned the curious lack of trauma, toxic poisoning, or advanced disease normally preceding the onsets of coma, they varied widely from there. Some merely said no more, as if the doctor's job did not include further speculation; others provided synopses of the patients' reported conditions prior to the comas, but in a halfhearted, defeated tone implying full awareness that none of it made sense. Only a handful of doctors made official note of their bewilderment.

Post coma notations were similarly unsatisfying, scattered and sparse; one can suppose doctors have enough work without trying to figure out why a patient is suddenly well. With none of the thirty-six victims – nor their spouses, nor the doctors primarily responsible for their treatment – still living, original sources for the reporters and medical researchers stalking the Plague were generally of a nature they considered second-rate. In time it became apparent: there just weren't enough pieces to solve the puzzle.

So the trail had grown cold when the NIH made public another batch of pertinent materials. This second release, eighteen months after the first, was essentially an act of public expiation for the NIH. Its new management team was freshly installed in the wake of the congressional hearings and the resulting, and quite comprehensive, wave of resignations and dismissals – Donald Cyr among the latter. The new group, led by Director Nate Howard, sought to reposition itself as both proactive and forthcoming, and the perfect opportunity presented itself almost immediately.

Newly hired personnel, undergoing standard orientation on a random Wednesday afternoon, discovered fresh Plague-related files in poorly labeled archives. These were quickly passed on to the office of the director, from there to the public relations department, and then to the public.

Within these secondary documents sat an unpublished article based on a series of survivor interviews conducted by an obscure freelance journalist, an Omahan by the name of Wesley Grassford. Grassford had apparently been rejected by at least six local and regional medical publications, possibly because he was young and uncredentialed (his *Remembrances* would be published only posthumously); possibly because the article was stale-dated – Grassford appears to have made his submissions almost nine years after the last coma victim had awakened; and possibly because of its excessive length – the article ran over 40,000 words. Perhaps several or all of those factors were in play; the rejection slips on file provide no explanation. Just as likely, the various editors may have, with some justification, considered Grassford himself to be slightly unhinged. What is certain is that with Grassford's rejections had gone the last and best chance at prompting an official investigation of the Omaha outbreak in anything near real time.

But many decades later, at the dawn of Nate Howard's NIH reign, Grassford's long-delayed contribution was something of a godsend to Plague buffs. The author was alive and well, still residing in Omaha, when his unpublished article made front-page news. He became the subject of great journalistic interest, holed up in something the press called "a wind-scarred shack" and "an unkempt relic" north of the city along the river. Grassford reluctantly confirmed his authorship and allowed that he, quite remarkably, still held his original source material, the interview tapes and transcripts. In the years following the Plague he had somehow identified and contacted twenty-three survivors. Every one of them had recounted a peculiar condition preceding the onset of coma: a string of barren, dreamless sleeps, with subsequent bouts of lethargy, disorientation, and malaise.

REMEMBRANCES

Understandably, most people think of Omaha as flat and treeless. In fact, old Omaha, the eastern section nearest the big brown Missouri River, which separates Iowa from Nebraska, is chock-full of walk-your-bike hills; and at least in my early days here, before Dutch Elm disease ravaged the city, it was heavily shaded with stout elms and helicopter maples.

From my vantage point, old Omaha was split into three distinct sections. South Omaha had the zoo near the river, the ballpark, and the stockyards. North Omaha had the airport along the river and the black neighborhoods a little further to the west. Between them, along the river, the ten city blocks of Jobbers Canyon (handsome turn-of-the-century brick warehouses looming a hundred feet over matching brick streets) gave way to downtown, and then to the white residential neighborhoods. One of those was Dundee.

Dundee was bisected north to south by Happy Hollow Boulevard, which, as it ran through our neighborhood, was actually two roads wrapping a narrow park with heavy-trunked hardwood trees running down both sides. Presumably too insignificant to carry an official name, this park went by "Sunks" in the neighborhood. The name seemed owing to the park's hollow or sunken nature – it was a three-block-long narrow bowl, dipping sharply from both arms of the boulevard. On the north end its sloping sides were pronounced enough to provide a nice little kids' sledding run, short but enhanced with a bump in the middle – enough to cost my brother a front tooth when he rode the Flexible Flyer on his belly with my sister on his back. The south end held enough flat space at the bottom of the bowl to provide a very passable playing field.

Some speculated that the park had once carried the more flowery title "Sunken Gardens," suggestive of a bygone era when municipal attentions might have been more given to beautification – plantings and flowerings perhaps having predated the trampled grass and packed dirt familiar to us. But most likely "Sunken Gardens" was just a sarcastic title my brother or one of his friends had made up.

The sledding end of Sunks is bordered by Cuming Street, which, along with Burt and Izard Streets on either side, forms a part of "Governor's Strip," a run of streets named after Nebraska's territorial governors prior to statehood. In our early years, free outdoor time was restricted to our little block on the hill bordered by Cuming, Burt, Happy Hollow and 52nd Streets. There were six houses in all, big-family three-story houses on smallish lots. Ours, the middle one facing Cuming Street, was built of red brick and draped with a dreamy green coat of large-leafed ivy that would ripple up the side of the house in the slightest breeze. The house was fronted by two big elms spaced just right, a square-trimmed hedge, two postage stamps of a yard, and a terra cotta porch that was generally in some state of disrepair. My sisters would hang me over the porch wall, my head sunk in the spruce bush, and razz my ears until they burned a bright crimson – I would run inside and dip them alternately in cups of cold tapwater.

The Klosner house, directly behind ours and facing Burt Street, had two boys, five girls, a wide blacktop play area, and a dug-in trampoline. When my mother rang the cowbell to call us home for dinner this was typically where we'd be. The trampoline was the only one of its type any of us knew about anywhere. It was dug right out of the Nebraska topsoil – several feet of rich stoneless dark earth – with the heavy gauge steel frame and the jumping surface directly at ground level. It was a huge neighborhood attraction, known throughout Dundee, but Mrs. Klosner, a goodly but tired-looking woman who seemed to struggle keeping up with her housework, managed an impressive vigilance against intruders, limiting the jumpers to an elite few. As immediately adjoining neighbors, we were privileged to jump there as we liked, our only intercession from Mrs. Klosner being the constant enforcement of the One-Jumper-at-a-Time edict. But from the elevated sightlines of her kitchen window she conducted a relentless vigil to shoo away unfamiliar kids who would slink up her driveway hoping for a turn. They would no sooner poke their heads around the corner of the house than she would crash out the door and rout them to flight.

But all hell broke out one week every summer when the Klosners left for vacation. Bigger kids, high school kids, would show up from all over Dundee and beyond, jumping eight, ten, twelve kids at a time, short-bouncing kids off onto the grass, or worse, just off the edge so their legs would gouge awkwardly into the gaps between the springs. (I couldn't help slinking over to watch, a cowed stand-in proprietor, keeping my distance and hoping not to be noticed.) Sometimes they would stuff a kid into the pit through the large corner gap in the springs. He'd tumble to the lowest point, where he'd be forced prone in the dirt so as not to be completely trampled under all the jumpers. But with enough jumpers he'd be trampled anyway, emerging long minutes later with filthy clothes, dirt-crusted lips, matted hair.

Mr. Klosner operated Karl Klosner's Pub in South Omaha, which did a fair weekday lunch trade and a substantial bar business seven days a week, mid-afternoon to late night. He was an imposing man, broad around the chest and broader still around the stomach, with menacing black eyebrows and thick black hair on his brutish forearms, but we hardly ever saw him. Far more often we would hear him, in our living room, in our bedrooms, as his voice boomed unkindly through the neighborhood on those rare occasions he was home. On fall Saturdays the smoke from his half-smothered leaf fires would settle thickly over the whole block, choking out the sun and ghosting through our screen windows.

17

Karl Junior was the one of seven Klosner children closest to me in age, a noisy heavy-set kid and a bombastic jumper whose signature move was an impressive seat-drop he called the "Thunderbutt." Sledding in Sunks late one winter when we were still very young, when thaws had pooled a foot of water at the bottom of the bowl only to freeze again on the surface, Karl rode his sled to the bottom in an upright sitting position, came to a complete stop, then broke through the ice, sinking and hollering and soaking his bottom.

PLAGUE

Omaha, not unlike any other American city, had no dream tracking, or public record keeping of any sort in the field, more than a quarter of the way into the twenty-first century. For all of man's progress – through the Renaissance, the Ages of Reason and Enlightenment, the Scientific Revolution, the Industrial Revolution, the Computer Age – dreamwork as an academic matter, let alone as a matter of public health, remained ignored and undeveloped. As a scientific field with significant application potential across many disciplines, it was essentially undiscovered.

There were certainly fits and starts of crude dream harvesting during the heydays of Freud and Jung and in the ripple of excitement that followed their work. But when they took their first baby steps they were centuries behind their peers in the other sciences; they could barely be considered to be rubbing two sticks together. At best, the early work in the field was sporadic, the methodology so ungainly, inconsistent, and regionally dispersed as to defy the entire notion of statistical analysis. Virtually all of it resided in the private sector or at the very fringes of academia. What little survived was so primitive and so piecemeal as to be dismissed by researchers as ineffectual and unavailing. Only years later, when the events linked with the Plague were at least partially understood, did dreamwork explode in the public mindset and become entrenched in the medical sciences and in our global approach to public health.

So when dozens of Omaha men drifted into unaccountable coma between August and December of 1968, it is not hard to imagine that medical teams of the time had absolutely no idea where to begin. Without the slightest notion of dreamlessness, much less of its connection with a host of other health constructs, they were hopelessly adrift. It simply defied logic that perfectly healthy men, men with no trace of tumor, stroke or trauma, no sign of poisoning, infection, or disease, were suddenly unwakable, lost in comas stretching into weeks and longer.

As one would expect, the NIH files contained some snippets of perplexed commentary. "At least the fourth case of unexplained coma in this hospital in the last five months," scrawled one exasperated Omaha physician in perhaps the most telling entry, dated December, 1968. Fragmented documentation reflects puzzled communications between individual MDs, and between MDs and department chairmen. But such pondering gathered little headway; it floundered and died in its adolescence, at intermediate levels in the greater medical hierarchy. The files show no evidence that anyone on the local level understood the scope of the outbreak, despite its regional concentration. Communication between unaffiliated hospitals was not formally structured. Consolidation of data at any level was fundamentally problematic in that pre-internet era. The NIH, at some unknown level and with some still unclear agenda, is thought to have played some role in squashing local awareness. And the final blow may have been a simple twist of chance: the top health official in the State of Nebraska, the man most responsible for recognizing and reporting worrisome trends in regional pathology, was among the thirty-six stricken.

There were a few tentative entries in local medical newsletters and one unremarkable mention in the Omaha World Herald. But the medical records remained largely private, and as the thirty-six awakened one by one from their comas, regaining their full faculties to a man, the events of the Plague receded from a concern to a puzzlement to an oddity, and then quickly into memory.

PALM TUNNELS

While Henry Cleverby did, over the first few months, find the body art business to be modestly engaging, he himself was tattoo and piercing free. These shortcomings, in addition to his youth and inexperience, gave him a bit of a credibility problem in the parlor. It was a problem to which he paid little mind; he had no interest in inking or piercing himself to better fit in. But having taken one anthropology class in college, he did have at least a vicarious interest in one sub-specialty of the body arts: stretching, large-gauge piercings expanded over time by a series of larger and larger plugs. It wasn't the stretching itself that interested him; he found distended earlobes singularly unattractive. And solid plugs did nothing for him. It was the notion of clean passages through the living body that carried the appeal, the see-through dynamic provided by flesh tunnels, hollow pieces of jewelry also known as spools.

Recent innovations in that area had been the subject of some scattered talk within the industry. It was said that a San Francisco piercing artist had partnered with an Oakland orthopedic surgeon to develop a procedure involving the hands. Henry followed the wispy accounts as best he could from the confines of his midtown studio. He made a few calls, tracked the few leads he did have, and was still in the dark. After some consideration, he flew west.

There he learned that the piercing was made between the third and fourth metacarpal bones – well below the base of the middle and ring fingers – passing from the palm through the back of the hand. The painstaking navigation required to bypass the array of blood vessels, tendons and nerves was far beyond the scope of licensed body piercers; it fell securely into the realm of a specialist hand surgeon, for both the initial piercing and the placement of the successively larger spools. The final spool was more or less permanent, with decorative rims available in a variety of colors and patterns. Surprising himself as much as anyone else, Henry returned to Omaha three weeks later with the city's first metacarpal tunnel. It had already been stretched to twenty millimeters.

PLAGUE

With still so little progress in the dream sciences well into the twenty-first century, Wesley Grassford's case for prior sustained dreamlessness as a relevant common denominator was seen, at best, as anecdotal. And yet his position offered a welcome departure from the hapless theorizing to date; rather than pure guesswork, it was at least an observation based on evidence. His tapes were quickly proven out. The interview subjects cross-checked successfully with the hospital records – all twenty-three had been hospitalized in the period 1968-69 for unexplained coma. And the tapes matched the transcripts – dreamlessness was cited in each interview exactly as Grassford had written.

Grassford's article provided the only viable lead actually gleaned from original sources, and in so doing reconstituted national interest in the Omaha cases. While the medical community's reaction to the concept of dreamlessness ranged between dismissive and reserved, the public lapped it up. The very notion of dreamlessness sounded unattractive and unhealthy enough at face value that, taken to extremes, its being associated with brain fatigue, and ultimately with brain dysfunction, was not a difficult stretch. Extremely prolonged cases could well be imagined to cause, or at least to indicate, a complete shutdown, for a period extending into months. Dreamlessness had imprinted itself in the lexicon of popular medicine. It was science that needed to catch up.

REMEMBRANCES

For reasons unclear to me then or now – perhaps the latent virility coursing through early elementary school boys, perhaps a very reasonable lack of enrollment interest among parents of such boys – male students were ousted from Barat Academy of the Sacred Heart almost as abruptly as we had been admitted. After two short years the experiment was ended, my unblemished string of Tres Biens untimely severed.

To that point I knew Saint Martyrius only as our family church, a dimly lit hall with dark pews and floor tiles the color of dried blood, its dismal effect somewhat tempered by swaths of encouraging stained glass. The Stations of the Cross were primarily modest and wood-carved. But most remarkable to me was a larger carving that constituted the twelfth station, a life-sized crucifix hand-crafted by Monsignor Snurly himself. Snurly was both prelate and artisan, and this work must have stood as the perfect marriage of his vocations, an enduring legacy for the church to which he had committed the last several decades of his solitary life. His gift was tangible, his vision particularly gruesome. The life-sized Jesus was not as I was used to seeing him, splayed in classically elegant lines with his head uplifted in an epiphanic trance. Rather, he was arrayed in a state of unmistakable agony, one arm twisted horribly, his head contorting down and to the side, as if he were trying to pull himself off the cross. The carving was not hung high in the ceiling arches, to be viewed at a distance, but rather right there with the other stations along the outside aisles, to be contemplated up close, with the nailed feet – single spike, no support wedge – right at my third-grader's eye.

I began my term at the parish school, a long steep set of stairs down from the church. If Barat was an ascetic cloister for children of the particularly devout, Saint Martyrius was a rough-and-tumble quarter teeming with the brood of the Catholic city. The families of Saint Martyrius were built to pack pews, to turn elections, to fill battalions. The six kids in our family were a pittance. Families with eight or nine kids were not considered at all remarkable or overlarge. Twelve kids marked the point of distinction – I would soon learn that four of the forty kids in my new class were ones in dozens, and another one of thirteen.

At Saint Martyrius there were no uniforms for boys – we wore our street clothes. And the nuns were of a different and apparently junior order, addressed as "Sister" rather than "Mother" as they had been at Barat. Somehow my Barat background had been put into play; it had become a source of increasing ridicule that first morning among my countless new classmates. At lunch break a boy named Billy O'Malley approached and said, "Choose, Barat boy." I wasn't sure what that meant, but learned soon enough that "Choose" was a code of challenge. I found myself in my first career fistfight. The scrap was just as you might imagine it – the ring of spectators, Billy and I rolling in the playground dust, torn shirts, earth-stained spittle. Billy was a smallish kid to be starting fights, and I worked myself into the universal grade school fight winner's position, sitting on his chest with my knees pinning his arms, the onlookers shouting "Pound him, pound him!" Of course I couldn't actually bring myself to punch another kid's face in that position. The crowd moaned with disappointment as I let him up.

PLAGUE

The story of dream tracking through CTCs – Cogitation Tracking Compounds – is a testament both to man's late but substantial progress in the field of dreamwork and the often-demonstrated impact of pure serendipity in the advances of science. In what is now a well-known tale, a compound with all the essential qualities of modern CTCs first appeared – apparently unknown to its inventors – in foam composites produced in 1965 or just earlier. CTCs would not be identified or understood for another six decades. But there it was, a synthetic compound of substantial complexity and eventual epidemiological significance, formed improbably and inexplicably in a crude facility, the Sandman & Sons factory, nestled quietly in a handsome Renaissance Revival warehouse along Jobbers Canyon.

Albert Sandman was a third-generation Omahan, the most educated of the Sandman line. He'd been a mid-level engineer, employed between the Korean and Vietnam wars in the development of lightweight materials for military aircraft. After his discharge he sprouted a prodigious moustache and became a bundle of entrepreneurial exuberance. He tinkered and tampered with the lightweight materials familiar to him, searching furiously for a niche of practical market applications. In short order he settled on reticulated and closed cell foams, intrigued by the natural fit of their attributes — softness and relative weightlessness — with a wide range of consumer uses, primarily in the area of cushioning.

Through a combination of his own savings, bank debt, and personal loans, Sandman pieced together just enough capital to launch the enterprise. He rented inexpensive space in the Canyon and fitted it to the required specifications, using primarily his own semi-skilled labor. Before long he began to manufacture and distribute a moderate selection of foam-based consumer products. The early business appears to have been active enough that Sandman might well have paid off his debts and maintained a comfortable living on the original model. But the chain-smoking and bespectacled entrepreneur was decidedly far-sighted in his outlook. He doubled down on his debts and charged head-long into the next stage of growth.

Sandman took a feverish and non-delegational approach to his business, even as it multiplied in complexity. He would throw himself pell-mell into product development while ignoring the operating side of his business for weeks and months; and then, as the various stages of the resulting disorder might dictate, he would throw himself just as precipi-tously into the operating side, having not quite applied the appropriate polish to the otherwise well-conceived product.

The cluttered Sandman facility began to churn out a larger line of commercial foam products, a line that might be characterized as entirely unremarkable except for what we now know to have been the baffling presence of CTCs within the foam. His aberrant compound — an indus-trial time warp unexplained to this day — would appear blithely in boat seat cushions and bed pillows for three years, in product lines intro-duced in 1965 and modified, modernized, reintroduced, and remar-keted by the tireless and resourceful senior Sandman through 1968. (The role of his feckless sons appears to have been quite negligible.)

The Sandman warehouse function, stockpiles of pallets and bar-rels of highly flammable material, was quite liberally intermingled with the manufacturing component, including industrial sized heating units that were worn and filthy and maintained in the most desultory fashion. This unpromising combination produced a spirited and robust inferno in September of 1968. The fire was unsparing in its destruction of the Sandman business, despite the stout nature of the brick and sandstone building. (That building stood for another twenty-one years before being razed by dimwitted city administrators in 1989 with virtually all of Jobbers Canyon.) The collapse of Sandman & Sons meant the end of any known CTC production until its "discovery," fifty-six years after the fire, in a much more sophisticated and deliberate fashion.

PALM TUNNELS

Henry Cleverby had been a lifetime nailbiter, a constant fidgeter with his fingers. But his nails now grew unabated as his digital attentions went exclusively to his metacarpal tunnel, or palm tunnel, as he thought to call it. He formed an immediate habit of poking the fingers of his left hand, each in turn, into the tunnel of the right. He ran through the four-finger rotation in a steady rhythm, like a metronome beating a quiet four-four time.

Rather than calling attention to the novelty with a brightly colored spool rim, or even a black spool rim, Henry favored one closely matched to the color of his flesh. He wasn't much of a tanner, so this was a practical solution through all four seasons. The discrete rim made him more comfortable with his second odd propensity, also newly acquired. He would knead his forehead with the fingers of his right hand, his left eye pinched closed, as if expressing fatigue or consternation; but all the while he would peer furtively with his right eye, through his palm tunnel, onto the unsuspecting outside world. It was at these moments that his senses were most keen, that his awareness of his surroundings was most pure and discerning.

PLAGUE

A year before the NIH uproar, Protocol Products of Cambridge had steered a portion of its considerable research and development capacity in search of compounds suited to record brain activity. The aging methodologies still then in practice – the crude manual tracking of neuron-fired electronics (electroencephalogram or EEG), the slightly more advanced magnetic resonance imaging (MRI), and even positron emission tomography (PET) – were awkward and inefficient, and provided no real window into thought.

A brilliant but slightly ungrounded neuroscience researcher at the Massachusetts Institute of Technology, Dr. Anders Hriniak, had been tracking recent advances in the electronics industry built around compound technology. The compounds in use appeared completely inert, but they showed a high sensitivity to a range of proximate wavelength currents. In such conditions they would undergo an imprinting process akin to recording. The imprints were limited to relatively small batches, which ultimately limited compound technology's usefulness in commercial electronics. But the imprints were gained by simple proximity to the source signal and were exceptional in quality, rich and fully layered. Dr. Hriniak hypothesized that such compounds, if applied to brainwaves, would logically provide impactful advancements over the current technologies.

Responding to what was essentially a jumble of sketches, hypotheses and hunches on the part of "an extremely visionary" professor in its own backyard, Protocol boldly opted to back Dr. Hriniak's work. The company placed a substantial initial bet, dedicating large quantities of both elite intellectual resources and state-of-the-art facilities to this arranged marriage of compound technology and brain activity. Protocol's culture was brash and self-promotional; it often traded the benefits of corporate secrecy for those of audacious promise and publicity. Given the compounds' capacity for rich and fully-layered imprinting, Protocol executives were not shy in describing the initiative as "a quest for thought recording – a major leap from the rudimentary plotting of brain activity currently available." It was an arrogant claim, met in the industry and in the greater scientific community with no small measure of ridicule. But after just ten months the Protocol team had produced what they believed to be the world's first Cogitation Tracking Compounds, the first viable agents of recording highly textured activity in the brain.

Cogitation Tracking Compounds, or CTCs, did not initially perform in laboratory conditions as well as the theoretical work had predicted. Human subjects, their heads strapped with packs of liquefied CTCs, or partially submerged directly into basins of liquefied CTCs, imprinted nothing in the way of thought. But Protocol engineers were quick to grasp that baking CTCs into a foam would optimize their usefulness. CTC foam pods placed in close proximity to sleeping subjects were successfully and consistently imprinted by the mental activity of those subjects. No external activation device was required; a certain level of rapid low voltage brain activity, that consistent with REM sleep, seemed sufficient to trigger the response. Engineers quickly fashioned comfortable headgear with pockets for interchangeable foam CTC pods.

With those simple adjustments, the historically cumbersome and invasive procedures associated with tracking brain activity – electrodes, wires, clamps, MRI tubes, the application time of tediously trained technicians – seemed to be near their end. CTCs promised a completely non-invasive approach at a fraction of the cost. Most significantly, a particularly promising compound called Zamaprotocol provided the full multi-dimensional block of signal from the brain that Protocol executives had been hoping for, destined perhaps to provide the first real glimpse into thought.

REMEMBRANCES

The Saint Martyrius school playground was absolutely teeming with big grasshoppers that September. I'm still not sure if we'd hit on a rogue infestation or some fantastical hundred-year natural cycle, but the scale of it was right out of the Old Testament, and I've not seen such a plague of locusts since. We would fill jars with them in a matter of minutes. Kids would hold one in each hand and put them face-to-face until one tore the other's head clean off. I'm not sure why the grasshoppers did that, or why the kids did that, or how the grasshopper heads could have been attached so feebly.

I was now walking to school for the first time, clumping together with other straggling third graders along the way. At that time we toted themed lunchboxes featuring tin sides of superhero or cartoon graphics, with twin buckles and matching thermos. We later progressed to the more dignified brown paper bag. But the actual contents never much changed during my elementary school career – baloney with mayo on Wonder Bread, a bag of fritos, and six oreos. The school had a combination gym and lunchroom, with tables that folded out from the wall. As we sat to our sack lunches, bigger kids would sometimes lift the outside table end, sending our sandwiches, chips, and cookies, if we hadn't quickly secured them, down to the hinged wall end for pilfering by other bigger kids working in tandem.

Sister Mary Theresa, our elderly third grade teacher, was bloated and ruddy, with bright white hair poking out from under her headgear. She had some trouble controlling the classroom. Kids would laugh like hyenas when she said, "Turn to page sixty-nine," although coming out of Barat I had no more idea why than she did. And page sixty-nine seemed to come up more than the mathematical probabilities might suggest. I quickly learned the give and take of punching the elbow engaged in writing, sending the pencil spastically across the page and leaving a large line across the work to be painstakingly erased. Or, less subtly, simply snatching the pencil out of hand and snapping the lead tip in the crack of the desk. Kids were constantly crossing the room in front of Sister Mary Theresa to sharpen their mangled pencils.

In the boys room, as kids lined up at the wall of urinals, the big trick was to sneak up, grab a peeing boy by the shoulders and quickly turn him ninety degrees so he'd pee on the kid at the next urinal. There was no concealing one's victimization; one would simply return to the classroom with the side of one's pants stained wet. This provided no end of hilarity.

PLAGUE

Excitement ran high at Protocol. Several of the company's more experienced and high-ranking engineers transferred onto the CTC project, without in any way infringing upon or dampening the enthusiasm of the younger researchers who had brought it so far. Everyone who had ever dreamed of wearing a lab coat wanted on the case. This was the kind of opportunity that came along only so often, perhaps once in a career, the rare project that might actually hold enduring significance, retain its meaning in casual conversation and on resumes over decades. Troops of lab technicians, pushing their plastic trays along stainless steel cafeteria runners, strategized as to how to become a part of it. Detailed descriptions of the project began to circulate outside the company, a breach, even for Protocol, that warranted threatening internal memos and a heightened security awareness. Reports of its promise were presented at the quarterly board meeting, highly unusual for a speculative product at such an embryonic stage.

If thought itself could be recorded and conveyed, the commercial potential was too big to lay out in the normal course. The military and educational applications were both enormous. And the consumer market was a spectacular prospect; Protocol executives envisioned the ultimate recording technology, supplanting pictures and video to deliver not just mementos, but feelings and sensations in their purest forms. The Protocol strategic marketing team became heavily invested on an accelerated schedule, its plan quite rigorously developed for a product in such an early stage of engineering.

The catch to all this exuberance was that laboratory imprintation was not easily progressing from sleeping to waking test subjects. Sleeping subjects were most easily sheltered from external stimuli; and they produced brain activity in distinctly spaced bursts. On both points they made for the perfect starter sample. Protocol had built a state-of-the-art sleep laboratory on Magazine Street, with more beds than a small hotel. Zamaprotocol performed admirably in that environment, imprinting REM activity with great range and reliability. But it could not make the transition from Magazine Street onto the larger stage; it could not be prodded to record waking thought. This was initially considered a classic early-stage irritation, a hurdle to be cleared in the normal flow of product development. But months went by, a fleet of engineers frustrated time and again, with budgets run amok and marketing people pressing for updates almost hourly.

Protocol CEO Christopher Collins overhauled the project's management and increased its manpower. Still, Zamaprotocol resisted any modifications to its makeup, and any adjustments in its implementation, aimed at imprinting beyond REM. Dream tracking expertise was certainly blossoming at the Magazine Street facility; six milligram pods of foam, strung together like Christmas lights, were recording individual dreams one to a pod, clean as a whistle. But there was no money in dreams. Real progress eluded Protocol Products.

Zamaprotocol was also proving surprisingly resistant to interface techniques. It held impressively layered streams of data generated directly by REM brain activity – scans of imprinted pods showed a depth and quality of recording that far outshone anything that had come before CTCs. But those data streams were unresponsive to the conversion methodologies used in the electronics industry, a step that was, as one internal memo suggests, "quite frankly not something we expected any trouble with." Imprinted pods could be easily scanned to quantify, and to some degree qualify, brain activity. But the imprints could not be converted into the experiential imagery the layered data would suggest, into anything with the narrative tone of real dreaming.

In what was considered a temporary concession, subjects in the sleep laboratory were asked to describe their donated dreams, to the extent they remembered them, and these accounts were recorded, auto-transcribed, and bar-coded to match the corresponding imprinted foam pods. In that way, once the conversion issues had been resolved, pod data could be systematically assessed against the dictated narratives for likeness and divergence. But another string of months went by, and data embedded in Zamaprotocol foam remained like divine poetry set down in unknown runes – inherently fabulous but stubbornly indecipherable. After a year of exertion, the most highly prioritized research project in the whole Protocol enterprise had not taken one substantial step forward. Stress and frustration pooled heavily within the company, then simmered to a sweaty froth.

On June 4, 2026, a brilliant but eccentric young engineer by the name of Zachary Sergeant, an original member of the imprint interface team, working his thirty-eighth consecutive hour, crazed on caffeine and acting on impulse, liquefied an imprinted six milligram Zamaprotocol foam pod, and, in full view of the entire team, injected it into his own thigh. It was sheer insanity, an act of such rashness and desperation that a lab mate placed an immediate call to security. Within a minute Sergeant fell into a deep sleep, but his vital signs remained normal, and he awoke into an exhilarated state just after his first REM cycle. He reported a dream of more power and clarity and wonderful unfamiliarity than any he had experienced before. Staff members retrieved and cross-checked the corresponding donor log. Sergeant's description made an uncanny match.

REMEMBRANCES

Nicholas Street ran up a very steep hill, and Billy O'Malley, now my walk-to-school buddy, lived near the top of it. The O'Malley boys would amaze me with their suicide runs down that hill in red Radio Flyer wagons, barreling down toward 52nd Street and certain death. They would drag their sneakers at the end, but there was no real stopping those wagons, and the runs would generally end in rollovers on the Nicholas Street cement. The O'Malley boys were constantly covered in scabs.

I was wary of the Radio Flyer hellrides and somehow managed to avoid them for several years without losing face. Billy and I found other things to do – playing with plastic army men, for instance. The problem with army men was that they never changed position. One guy stood shooting a rifle; one guy knelt with a bazooka. One guy had his arm outstretched in a hand grenade throw; another crouched to make a radio call. One guy crawled on the ground; another guy with a pistol stood and waved others forward. But all you could do to kill a guy was to knock him over. And they looked stupid knocked over, still in their fighting positions with their stands sticking up in the air. That's where the box of wooden matches came in, as Billy was happy to demonstrate. A small open flame held steadfastly to the knee, and the army man would slowly buckle and crumble to the ground, where he would lie contorted, an obvious and horrible casualty of war.

Billy and his older brother would occasionally duke it out (but never seemed to hold a grudge after), all out physical brawls that were a revelation to me because there was never any fighting in our house. My brother was four years my senior, and although we spent many years sharing bunkbeds in the attic I don't recall any animosity between us, either because he was a good-natured boy, or because I was too little to rate much interest. He would do his own things – working with his rock collection, working on Boy Scout merit badges, or tinkering with my grandfather's forgotten military gear stored in the back attic closet – I remember a nasty triangular shaped bayonet and several cases of bullets that looked like they could drop an elephant – while I would organize my baseball cards or pin pictures clipped from Sports Illustrated to the walls. It would never occur to us to fight. But with no particular malice toward the Klosner family, my brother snuck onto the roof of their garage and chiseled a couple bricks out of the chimney, hoping it would blow over in the next tornado warning. As the chimney survived each passing storm, he would grow increasingly sullen and chisel out another brick or two. Eventually he must have lost interest; the chimney never did fall. I'm not sure why Dundee garages had chimneys in the first place.

PLAGUE

The Sergeant incident created a major stir within Protocol. For shock value and sheer recklessness it was the most noteworthy event in company history. Sergeant had taken an incredible risk to produce a signature moment in the annals of Protocol research, and perhaps in the larger scope of modern science. At the very least he had provided the spark the project so desperately needed. The discovery portended fabulous advance – the dream imprintation as Sergeant reported it was full-featured, multi-dimensional, lifelike. It was the first real manifestation of the power of CTCs.

Injection in itself was, of course, a preposterous notion, both as a research methodology and as an end use procedure. The health risks were completely unknown, and federal regulations would certainly not allow speculative human injection in the laboratory. It went without saying that such a technology was out of the question for the marketplace. An injection-based technology would engender very little beyond a rather suspect recreational application. Only a marginal sort of demographic could be expected to inject each other's dreams.

It seemed manifest that Protocol engineers, buoyed by the Sergeant revelation, would now move the project beyond injection, to convey recorded brain activity in a more useful and accessible manner, by one alternative means or another. It was the next logical step in what was now conceived to be a sequential and inevitable process. But in the next few weeks pods of theorists, inventors, and engineers each looked to the other; and when each was forced beyond his normal tactical reticence to admit that he actually had no such vision, that no one had any such vision, it was a sobering realization. For all the advanced thinkers at Protocol, no one had a clue where to take it next.

Sergeant was both revered and reviled. Some viewed him as a delightfully creative, passionate and fearless innovator, a throwback to an earlier age of science when men took chances, leapt through the narrowest windows of opportunity in search of real time answers. Others branded him an attention-seeking showboat, grossly unprofessional, rash and foolhardy. Many swung from the former position to the latter when it became clear that his contribution had provided no clear path of advancement, a swing in response to the negative drift of the atmosphere in the building, unspoken signals sent from upper management and the top science officers.

Sergeant was called to a number of high-level meetings that began with a collegial, even slightly congratulatory tone, their agendas information-seeking and scientific in nature. But over the following weeks the management personnel shifted slightly; there seemed to be more background information at hand pertaining to Sergeant; the meetings took a more admonitory and disciplinary drift. Sergeant explained how it was that he had graduated in the top third of his class at a prestigious Medical Business School, but instead of following the standard track into biochemical investment banking or pharmaceutical development or health entity management, he had reverted to his real interests in pure science. He had taken a baseline research position at Protocol – the kind of job he could have had without the Medical Business degree. And yes, his parents had died young, and he lived alone, biked to work every day, and played basketball four or five times a week at the toughest playground in the city. Sergeant told and re-told what had happened in the laboratory that day, and in the days leading up to it, what he'd expected, what he'd hoped, what he'd actually experienced after the injection. He readily admitted to having previously swallowed imprinted foam pods, which on each occasion had resisted digestion, failed to metabolize, and passed cleanly, and to having gulped liquefied pods, with similarly uninspiring results. Less readily, he admitted to having smoked CTC crystals.

As Sergeant would later tell it: "Those meetings were a huge bag of mixed messages. It was clear that all the executives were incredibly excited about what the injection showed in terms of the real potential of the project. But they were trying to conceal that – an obvious effort to keep at arm's-length from me and from my deviant methodology. They were obsessed with knowing exactly what had happened in the lab leading up to the injection, as if they needed to convince themselves that I somehow hadn't just pulled some stunt – like I would actually access the dream narrative in advance and just pretend to have redreamed it. I swear at one point the COO was probing as to whether I might be willing to try it again, unofficially of course, in a way that they could somehow monitor without actually sanctioning. He never actually came out and said it. He just danced around it so long that it was definitely out there. But I was already getting such a bad vibe that I took it for a trap. I wasn't going to commit professional suicide, so I didn't take the bait, even though I definitely would have done it again for them if they had asked me straight up.

"I think they got comfortable that what had happened in the lab was legit, but also that they didn't need to go down such a radical and presumably illegal path to solve the problem. Now that they had the power of the product somewhat substantiated, they figured they could take the time they needed to develop it by conventional means, even though things had gone badly to that point. They reckoned they'd figure it out eventually. And once they'd decided that, the next logical step was to send the message that everyone was waiting for – suspending me to discourage unsanctioned lab tactics."

In the end Sergeant was suspended on half pay. Only a strong endorsement from Dr. Hriniak himself may have prevented stronger censure or outright dismissal. Sergeant disappeared for eight weeks while Protocol embarked on another great chase.

PALM TUNNELS

Despite the understated coloration of his spool rim, Henry Cleverby's palm tunnel created an immediate sensation in the shop, with the customers, and in the greater Omaha community of body art. Henry was happy enough to show off his hand, flex his fingers, and describe the multi-step procedure, time and again – the local anesthetic, the ultrasound-guided channeling, the all-important post-surgical dexterity work, the follow-up tunnel stretching appointments. But he found himself oddly reluctant to pass on contact information for the specific Bay Area practitioners.

Since his return from the coast Henry had taken a greater interest in his business, doubling and tripling his face time. He had begun interacting with customers in an easy and disarming manner, characteristics he hardly recognized in himself. He noticed, not without some satisfaction, that customers now held him in distinctly higher esteem. Unaccustomed to his own enthusiasm, he began to actively rebrand the business in pursuit of a more innovative and upscale presentation. He orchestrated interior and exterior facelifts that struck just the right balance – enhancing the suggestions of cleanliness, and of edginess, without feeling overly considered or calculated. Henry's Twilight Tattoo was no longer a parlor; it was a studio. But this was all just a preamble, a preface to what he hoped would be the main story – providing the niche product so many of his customers were looking for.

Henry sought out interviews with a series of Omaha hand surgeons. Most wouldn't even talk with him. Of those he did manage to pitch, only one expressed even a mild interest – he required a first year guarantee, customized surgical space on the premises, and an all-expense trip to the coast – to observe and learn the process. The Oakland-based surgeon was by then embroiled in a dispute with his original piercing artist partner and was doing only sporadic procedures; but he was perfectly willing to be observed, and to consult – in consideration of an exorbitant fee. And the San Francisco deep-spool supplier, the only one Henry could find anywhere – spools tunneling through more than an inch of complex anatomy were clearly a specialty item – required a substantial one-time payment for regional distribution rights. And so, after fees and construction costs amounting to five times what he'd paid for the original business, Henry had added a single product offering. His money fund was largely exhausted, but the golden spike had been hammered home; palm tunnels were on the fast rails to Omaha.

PLAGUE

While part of the Protocol operation continued to probe and poke and prod at Zamaprotocol samples, another part split off onto other CTCs in search of a related but more cooperative compound. They thirsted for one that would imprint beyond REM. And they hungered for one that would "play back," interface less stubbornly with established technology to actually deliver the experiential imagery of recorded thought. Management sloganized an "Escape from Dreamworld" and a "Quest for Commerce." The sleep labs were scaled back. Management lavished the Alternative Compound Development team with high-powered personnel and munificent funding, and it instilled a sense of urgency and work ethic to a level not previously seen at Protocol.

Consumed with the ultimate prize of thought recording, Protocol was caught completely off guard when archrival RoboCorp, Inc. introduced a new technology to replace EEGs, MRIs, and PET in the simple measuring and monitoring of brain activity. The product was not built on a compound platform, but it was slick enough to fill the technology gap in that marketplace. Protocol CEO Christopher Collins and his team, none of whom had any idea that RoboCorp was even pursuing that niche, watched in a state of shared nausea as the RoboCorp rollout took hold, drawing uniformly favorable reviews and seizing market share in great chunks.

This wholly unforeseen development greatly compromised the fallback position for Protocol's CTCs; the highly specialized medical market would not support a redundant introduction. Collins was privately lambasted for prioritizing the blockbuster concept rather than rushing to market with the simpler application. More than ever, Protocol needed a viable breakthrough in recordable, transferable thought and the endless opportunity that would entail.

But the team that remained with Zamaprotocol, including Zachary Sergeant when he resumed active status within the company, sputtered and ground to a standstill. It could not solve either the REM dependence problem or the interface problem. Zamaprotocol, it seemed, could not be harnessed.

And after several months it was equally clear that the Alternative Compound Development team, for all its initial bluster, had also floundered, dismally and spectacularly. Over two years into the project, in the spring of 2027, Zamaprotocol was still the only so-called Cogitation Tracking Compound that had been shown to track thought in any considerable, if not particularly meaningful, way.

Not surprisingly, thought imprinting as a whole began to fall out of favor at Protocol. The upside, while phenomenal, was proving highly elusive, and perhaps fatally so. The CTC project was hemorrhaging cash and debilitating management. It was retarding other initiatives. It had grown malignant, and too unwieldy to tolerate much further. It had become a legitimate threat to bring down the entire company. CTC detractors at the highest levels, including the Board, began to outweigh its wavering advocates, to rout them in conference room skirmishes.

And soon thereafter, Zamaprotocol was headed to the shelves, tens of millions of research dollars to be written off. The public relations department seeded several articles in both the popular press and scientific journals, touting the company's advancements in technology for tracking brain activity, articles that alluded to a spectacularly futuristic and decidedly proprietary approach. This titillated the scientific and investment communities just enough to pad Protocol's reputation as a scientific forerunner and to slightly boost its sagging stock price. But overall it represented sadly insufficient consolation for what was recognized internally as a massive and largely fruitless undertaking. Protocol quietly began the process of redeployment, moving engineers previously dedicated to CTCs and thought imprinting research to other, more promising projects.

REMEMBRANCES

Grandpa Roy and I shared the same birthday, and we preferred our parties to be held jointly, wearing matching conical hats with thin elastic chin-strings and counting candles to the sum of our ages.

It was a source of great pride to me that he and my two uncles, Sam and Chuck Richardson, had all played football for the University of Nebraska. Grandpa Roy had been a track star there, winning the Big Eight 20-yard Dash Championship (back before World War I when they still had the 20-yard dash). He joined the football team as a speed guy, and I still have the old newspaper clippings describing his running down a Notre Dame ballcarrier to save a touchdown in the great 20-19 win for the undefeated Husker team of 1915. Two years later he would be in France with the 42nd Division.

Grandpa Roy's two sons played at Omaha Central High School, which would later produce the great Gale Sayers and Ahman Green. There is a famous high school football story of Chuck, possibly concussed earlier in the game, intercepting a pass, getting spun around, and then running toward the wrong end zone. As he told it, he looked up to see his brother sprinting towards him on the angle and thought, "Oh good, here comes Sam to give me a block." But Sam cleaned him out, saving the wrong way touchdown. Chuck was affectionately known thereafter as Wrong Way Richardson.

Chuck looked like a hero out of one of the old Westerns. He had a pretty wife from Texas – she looked right out of the movies too. He could hold his balance for minutes at a time on our basement Bongo Board, even do jumping 180s without touching down. I idolized him as an uncle, though since he moved to Denver I don't recall a lot of direct interaction with him beyond his slamming my finger in the car door on an outing to the circus; he threw me over his shoulder and carried me inside for ice while I bawled my brains out between stolen looks at my grossly indented digit.

Some fall Saturdays Grandpa Roy would take me to a Nebraska football game. His gold Buick would pull into our driveway just after 8:00. If I happened to be at the sink rinsing out my cereal bowl I could see him out the window striding for the back door in his scarlet sports jacket and the red cap with the little feather. If I weren't standing by the sink — I'd more likely be planted in my seat devouring pancakes — I'd just listen for the slam of the car door, count to ten, and brace for the shout: "Go Big Red!"

After he'd downed a quick cup of coffee with my mother, we would load up with me in the front seat and head right out so as to arrive a good four hours before kickoff. I'd confirm that the gas needle was flush to Full as it always was before a football trip (Grandpa Roy in any event would never let his tank drop beneath half), and we'd drive past Sunks to Dodge Street, heading west past Boys Town and out of the city into a sudden dreamworld of corn, eight-foot stalks swaying in their millions, revealing the subtle contours in the land, the gaps between the rows whirring by my car window like some fantastic deck of cards being forever shuffled.

PLAGUE

Zamaprotocol, even at the beginning, was remarkably inexpensive to produce. The materials were more or less commonplace, the bonding processes shockingly simple. This would prove to be just one more reason corporate heads were so disappointed in its foundering. But in the early stages of excitement it only encouraged them to approve larger pre-production runs than they'd normally authorize in the development phase. Allocation managers budgeted hundreds of headgear units and thousands of pods to be used in the early subject work, with countless blocks of solid Zamaprotocol and dozens of drums of liquid made available for more general research.

These quantities hardly merited a second thought when CTC work was the company darling. And when the Board pulled the plug on CTCs, and on thought imprinting research generally, the inventory assets were just as dismissively abandoned. They were lumped in the writeoff of all the research and development costs associated with the project, a stroke not yet reported to the financial markets but certain to land with a resounding thud.

While they were not long for the Protocol balance sheet, the CTC materials stubbornly persisted on the grounds of the Protocol campus. There was no secondary market for even slightly processed material, and all of it had undergone at least the first stage of the bonding process. CTCs in their various states of development couldn't just be dumped or destroyed with their environmental impact unknown. And so they sat, in pallets and in vats, taking up absurd amounts of warehouse space and serving as a reminder of a very unpleasant chapter in the Protocol story.

Research personnel couldn't distance themselves quickly enough from CTCs. The whole notion was taboo; cogitation was disdainfully referenced as "the C-Word." Those who'd been the most excited to be assigned to the project were now claiming to have pegged it as doomed from the beginning. But Zachary Sergeant was fascinated by Zamaprotocol. He and he alone had experienced the wonder of dream injection, and he couldn't shake the notion that CTCs presented a remarkable opportunity. While recognizing the slow pace of progress, Sergeant's view was that a fantastic initiative was being shut down in an embryonic state. He was helplessly intrigued, both professionally and personally.

At the time when his suspension had become inevitable, Sergeant had tucked a few dozen foam pods into his socks. He'd felt compelled to continue his research in his time at home, and security checked only pockets and bags. But now he began to fill his water bottle, shuttling home half a liter of liquid Zamaprotocol each night, the risk somewhat mitigated by the compound's odorless, tasteless and colorless qualities in its liquefied state. By the anniversary of his suspension, a date he recalled not without some measure of resentment, he was in personal possession of some thirty liters.

REMEMBRANCES

Grandpa Roy would shift into cruise control just outside town. He loved that feature, clicking the control mechanism to seventy-five, then driving with theatrical ease, shifting his legs at his every whim, explaining the process to me every time. There was a particular smell to the gold Buick – newness. The car had to be a couple years old already, but it still smelled just out of the dealership, despite Grandpa Roy's fondness for cigars. The carpet was unstained, the dash immaculate, the seats glossy and full of bounce. The car's engine was apparently as spotless as the interior. Grandpa Roy changed his oil so often that several people had only half-jokingly requested the drainage for their own cars.

Half a dreamy hour sailing past the sporadic farmhouse or silo or stand of hardwoods and suddenly we were over the Platte, a mile-wide river shockingly brown with silt and spread to only a foot or two deep as it loafed through the mudflat. The Platte was the halfway mark to Lincoln. Often a train would join us parallel to the highway as we neared Gretna, hundreds of yellow Union Pacific boxcars and cars for livestock and grain riding right with us.

And then soon enough the State Capitol would come into view, a four hundred foot tower looming over the prairie with its handsome gold dome and "The Sower" on top. (It housed the nation's only unicameral state legislature, as we were told in many a Civics class.) Already traffic was beginning to thicken, Nebraska flags flapping off antennas, drivers and passengers clad in red, assorted red ornaments dangling from rear-view mirrors. Soon we'd pass by the massive concrete stadium with the big red N on its side. We'd drive a mile or more further, make a quick turn or two, and pull into a Texaco station to park, happily noting that kickoff was four hours away, just as planned. As we gathered up our things and set off on our substantial walk back downtown, Grandpa Roy would always hold forth on the merits of that Texaco space, but for the life of me I could never understand it.

In time we would reach the Cornhusker Hotel for the pre-game N-Club buffet. I was generally still so stuffed with pancakes that the spread of cold roast beef, pickles and deviled eggs was not all that appealing. It was a while before we'd sit down to eat anyway, milling about as we did among the arriving lettermen, ghosts of athletes from ancient classes, dressed to a man in scarlet jackets, each with a white N on the breast pocket. Grandpa Roy would introduce me reverently to Husker football legends of yore between servings of potato salad and coldcut and swiss cheese sandwiches. It was hard not to imagine that these men were sizing me up as a potential Cornhusker. Could a lad as skinny as I ever contribute? I redoubled my efforts with the roast beef.

With a couple hours yet to kickoff we'd start the walk to Memorial Stadium, Grandpa Roy sometimes plugging one nostril with his thumb and shooting huge globs that splatted onto the sidewalk. I tried that myself on a few occasions but could never achieve the same clean release.

Grandpa Roy had held his seats for decades – just under the roof overhang, perfect for raincover and shade, just high enough for excellent sightlines – and knew everyone in his section on a first-name basis. The stadium was packed with 70,000 people all dressed in red; the band in its splendid maneuvers, marching now in red-spatted legion behind the majorette and the drum major, she in her sequined swimsuit tossing and twirling the silver baton, he leaning way back like a limbo dancer, kicking his black over-the-knee boots outrageously high in front of him, the strap to his tall furry hat tucked tight under his nose. And finally, kickoff, the ball hanging in the air while the men in red roared down the field, and then the first contact, bodies cracking together as the ball settled into waiting arms. The first Nebraska touchdown triggered a release of thousands of red balloons into the blue autumn sky. The band played "There Is No Place Like Nebraska," and we all sang along. A standout defensive tackle, number sixty-nine, was named Wesley Grassford – Wesley Grassford, my exact name! – and when he made a play I jumped up and announced to our section with my squeaky voice, "That's me in the future." But even then I was beginning to suspect that it was not to be – I would never be good enough to play for Nebraska.

The Memorial Stadium men's room serving our section had a single, long, common urinal trough along the wall. The men would stand in a row, their blended urine gathering to a foamy torrent as it flowed to the middle drain, cigarette butts bobbing like driftwood in the flooding Missouri.

After the games Grandpa Roy was quiet, smoking his cigar and trying not to show too much agitation over the slow moving line of red taillights back to Omaha. But those were about the only times I remember him that way. Usually he was a freakish bundle of energy, the ultimate enthusiast. He would holler and flash his teeth and call me Wesley Boy, and whenever we discussed running theory, which seemed quite often, he would say "Knees high!" and "Bounce off those toes!" and demonstrate by running in place, pumping his knees to his chest and his hands like pistons.

PLAGUE

At the beginning, early in his supension, Zachary Sergeant played with only his own dreams. If he had even a reasonably warm feeling after a night's sleep – a rare enough occurrence for him – he would inject that night's dreams back into his system. On the second and third dreaming he would build clearer recognition of the narrrative sequences, always re-recording, then filtering out the more disagreeable specimens until he'd isolated his least unpleasurable dreams. He grew nocturnal, sleeping late, harvesting and cataloging new material, injecting older dreams, taking notes, building the fledgling science on feel and inclination. But a film of consciousness slipped into replayed dreams. Like a mistier, more subtle variant of watching the same movie on multiple occasions, even the most engaging adventures became stale and subconsciously predictable.

He would jar himself out of his dream world by mid-afternoon, riding to the park for basketball with the unemployed and the nightshifters, games that were substantially more volatile than those he'd always played after work and on weekends. He'd play until his legs were leaden and unresponsive, then stop to eat at Stevie Ray's, where he took a steady stool and found himself waiting for another regular, a bass guitarist named Vanessa Jones.

Women generally found Sergeant to be attractive, but he rarely invested himself to land the women he found interesting, and he quickly grew bored with the women who fell in his lap. But after several deli counter conversations with Vanessa he'd stepped out of character by making the effort to go see her play. She was the rare bass-playing frontwoman, her long-legged presentation an obvious attraction but quickly forgotten in the onslaught of music, her singing a full-throated surprise to Sergeant, who had grown accustomed to her soft-spoken manner at the counter. Her bass-playing seemed almost an afterthought – she never looked at her hands, seemed hardly to realize she was holding an instrument. But her bass lines were far more than a pounding on the beat; they were lyrical and melodic, songs within the songs.

Sergeant spoke to her about the show. She seemed flattered that he'd ventured out.

"I'm sorry I didn't see you. I have a problem recognizing faces in an audience, even if I know the people. Then they think I'm a snob, and that I don't appreciate their bothering to show up. Anyway, it was really nice of you to come."

"I hardly ever see local bands playing originals and come away thinking they were worth listening to. But you were a real exception. I really liked your music." He said it like he meant it, and he did.

He complimented her on her singing, and on her playing, and he correctly identified the two covers she'd played in the first set, admitting he'd left shortly after. Vanessa chided him for not seeking her out during the break.

Sergeant had thought it through on a couple occasions, but was still a bit surprised to hear his own response:

"Look V, I start back to work on Monday and won't be here for weekday lunches any more. Any chance we can get together some time somewhere else? I'm doing some work with dreams that I'd like to run by you."

PALM TUNNELS

Before long, Henry's Twilight Tattoo had more palm tunnel demand than it could service. Novelty appeal was a huge factor – there were still so very few of them in the world. But beyond that there seemed to be something inherently pleasing about the palm tunnel. It was radical body art but not grotesque, disabling, or particularly dysfunctional. (Henry did dissuade one jazz pianist from having the treatment.) As with rings on their fingers or tattoos on their forearms, customers could admire their own palm tunnels directly, without the need for a mirror, or the need to disrobe. And unlike tattoos, the spool rims could be switched up – colors, materials, textures alternated to reflect certain moods, or to fit with certain occasions and outfits.

Henry did not initially publish a price for the procedure – rather he experimented to see what the market could bear, and he was pleasantly surprised at the outcome. Within a few months he was delighted to find he had recovered his entire investment. His hand surgeon, earning far in excess of what he'd expected, came aboard full-time – or, rather, he quit his clinical job, golfing in the mornings and executing a full slate of appointments at the newly renamed Palm Tunnels, Inc., in the afternoons. For all he'd paid his surgeon and the deep-plug supplier, Henry had been within his rights to secure exclusives from both. Having done so proved quite prudent, enabling him to develop the regional market entailing Nebraska, Iowa, and Eastern Missouri through Kansas City, with little risk of competition. By all appearances, Henry was sitting on something rather more than a nice little annuity.

For the first time in his life, Henry was really "applying himself," belatedly fulfilling his parents' longstanding exhortations, though in a field they could never have imagined – except perhaps in their most unsettled dreams. Henry was still by no means in accord with any business prototype. He woke up at his body's whim, refusing to use any alarm, ever. His first waking action was to dive into a video game, to "warm up my brain." He kept a game open all throughout the business day, diving into short frenzies of graphic calisthenics as a transitional tactic between tasks, as a means of dismissing anyone taking up too much of his time, and as a means of revival late in the day when he'd

begun to flag. But who could question the results? Despite his unconventional approach, he was the consummately productive entrepreneur,
churning through to-do lists like a combine churns through crop. He'd
redo his list once or twice during the day, to record new inspirations,
but also to make note of bonus chores he'd already completed, listing
them retroactively for the sheer pleasure of crossing them off.

PLAGUE

Sergeant met Vanessa at the Plough & Stars, a narrow Irish pub that had
occupied its corner on Massachusetts Avenue for a hundred and fifty
years. He arrived a full fifteen minutes before their scheduled time, not
so much to insure that they had stools – it was early enough that that
wasn't a problem – but rather to avoid the risk of her getting there first
and having to sit alone. He ordered Guinness, sat on one stool, commandeered another, and aligned himself to keep an eye on the front
door.

She walked in twenty minutes later, almost exactly on time. He'd
had seven or eight lunches with her by now, none of them explicitly by
appointment. He was very much aware – pleased but a bit edgy – that
this time she was there by design. She held a certain odd fascination for
him; he had the strange sensation that he was always seeing her for the
first time. There was something about her he couldn't quite get his arms
around; she looked different every time he saw her, and sometimes, he
thought, even from glance to glance on the same occasion. Try as he did,
he couldn't quite collect a coherent image of her to carry out with him.
He didn't read this as an intentional effect on her part, or as a particular
assimilation problem on his. Maybe it was the angular aspect of her

face that made her look so different from different perspectives; in part maybe the glasses, the clothes, the hair — but somehow it was hard for him to integrate the whole.

She wasn't particularly dressed up on this occasion. In keeping with the venue, she hadn't pegged it as a big date night, and that was fine with him. But while he couldn't quite pinpoint it, he had the distinct impression that she had gone to some slight effort beyond the level of her many looks at Stevie Ray's. She greeted him with an easy smile and slid gracefully onto the stool he'd saved for her.

They talked about their shared venues, the Plough and Stevie Ray's, for a few minutes. Sergeant was not spewing with chatter, but was comfortable with the conversation that always seemed to come naturally with her, and found himself drawn once again to a spontaneous energy of eyes and movements and intonations. At the same time he felt his own level of distraction on this occasion, felt he'd better introduce the agreed topic on the early side. If he held the dream talk too long he risked her thinking the subject insignificant, a ruse, just another way to have gotten her into a bar; or, worse, thinking that he was queasy or ashamed about it, setting a creepy enough overtone to kill any chance he might just have. Worse yet, he risked her beating him to the punch, steering him to the stated purpose of their meeting and thereby implying a hint of restlessness, or boredom. So at the first break in their conversation he plowed right in.

"V, I told you I'd been suspended from Protocol for practicing unsanctioned research methodology, and I was happy at the time that you didn't ask for more details. I want to tell you what happened, and in a minute I'll get around to why I want to tell you."

"It sounds highly dishonorable," she said with a smile.

"I can't disagree with you," he said, smiling in return. "OK, as you may or may not know, the company is really focused on compound technology as a means of recording brain activity. I'm not giving away any secrets telling you that; there've been articles to that effect, and we're running donors by the dozens in and out of our sleep labs, all of whom are wearing compound pods on their heads. I say sleep labs because, while the goal really is to be able to record conscious thought, so far the most promising compound we have will only record brain activity during sleep, specifically during periods of rapid eye movement."

"So basically what you've got only records dreams."

"That's right. We're building a dream database by having those donors imprint their pods in sleep and then narrate for us afterwards what they remember of the dreams. We use polygraph data to eliminate frivolous entries. It's pretty good work for the donors who survive that screening; they basically get paid to sleep. Scans show that the imprints, or recordings, we're getting are superb in quality, far superior to anything we know that's been done before. But again, they're only dreams, which are held to be of limited commercial value. And, there's another big problem: We've been having trouble converting the data streams into a usable format – the compound conversion techniques that have worked everywhere else in the industry just haven't carried over to our product. So we've been working like madmen for months and months on these same two problems, and there's a lot of money at stake and a lot of pressure, and I'd been up most of two nights, and I had an idea and did something crazy. I liquefied an imprinted pod and injected it into my leg."

"You injected it into your leg?"

"Yes, and just like that I went into a sleep, and I dreamed the dream that was on that pod."

"Whoa. You mean you dreamed somebody else's dream."

"Yes, the weirdest thing ever. Unsettling for sure – I wouldn't want to give that donor a lot of time in my head, or spend a lot of time in his head – however you want to look at it – but it really was a breakout experience."

"You dreamed it just like the donor would have dreamed it – in full detail, and without your perspective, without you in the dream?"

"My perspective was there only in the background, in a faint and delayed observational kind of role, recalled mostly after the fact. I was definitely not in the dream as myself, but I was there as some other first-person lead character, presumably the donor. The dream ran on its own, just as I imagine all dreams to do, and my narration afterwards matched the donor's almost exactly. It had the normal dramatic elements I would associate with dreams – characters, setting, story line. Dreams aren't all that different from movies in that sense, though obviously they're a lot less coherent. But what was really different in this case was the extra layer sitting on top of the action, a whole weird and disturbing second track – the dreamer's ongoing and personal overlay, like an unspoken psycho-response to every frame of the narrative. It played all the way through, like another whole story line I couldn't quite put my finger on."

"I can't imagine what that would be like," she said. "Dreams are so strongly fixed in the first person, at least mine are. Everything is so driven by my point of view – not all that different from consciousness, I suppose, in that sense. But you were processing the donor's point of view."

"Exactly. Which, in his case, was just slightly nauseating. So here's why I'm telling you all this: By suspending me, Protocol management made it perfectly clear that injection work wouldn't be tolerated, and I get that. But it's beyond obvious that the dream injection had opened up a whole new set of possibilities, and no one was even close to finding another way to get anything near the same experience. It was like I'd just started down a path to the place we'd all been looking for, and the whole group was just passing it by. So when I got suspended

I took some of the compound pods home with me, a couple of them donor-imprinted, most of them blank, and I've been experimenting for a couple months now. The donor dreams are outrageous. There's a rush in the weirdness, but they're a little creepy at the core; they linger and leave me feeling kind of wobbly, to the point where I don't really want to go back. So mostly I've been imprinting and reinjecting my own dreams, working through the basic science while trying not to freak myself out."

They both took long swallows of beer.

"But now what's happening is I'm hitting a wall with my own dreams – it's all getting too introverted, too self-referential, a bit stale. Because I'm the source dreamer I can't really recognize that extra layer, the dreamer's personal overlay, which I'm sure will end up being an important part of the work. The bottom line is I need someone else to give me some dreams, not only narrative content, but also a personal overlay track I can live with. For the same reason I don't go to barbers – I don't want some guy with big hairy hands touching my ears and pawing around my head – I don't want some dude with his libido and his man-ego running around in my brain. I'm thinking a woman would be more palatable, more soothing, not some faceless donor or someone from the lab, but somebody outside that I feel sort of kindred with, somebody I feel I can trust, whose dreams I actually would be interested in dreaming and hopefully won't wear me down even after a fair amount of exposure. I don't know you all that well, obviously, and I hope I'm not way out of line, but just from talking to you and hanging out some I think that your dreams would be cool and fun and interesting. I've done just enough of this to know I need a really good fit to go forward with the work – and I can't help but feeling that your dreams would be perfect."

REMEMBRANCES

Grandpa Roy was a madman when we played "Wahoo," a plywood board game with hand-drilled slots for marbles, and all of us became equally drunk with bloodlust whenever we sat to play. He would not sit passively in the face of luck's vagaries. His runaway positive energy would impact the die rolls – he was certain of it – and we saw evidence in virtually every game. Players who exhorted the die as if that one little cube were a whole team of horses, players who themselves chomped at the bit, foamed at the mouth, stomped and snorted, would consistently come up with the big roll to kill the critical opposing marble, or run off the unlikely string of sixes, hooting and hollering and racing their marbles around the board.

(Little is known of the origins of Wahoo. It is somewhat similar to Parchese. The name may have originated in Wahoo, Nebraska; or it may derive from the fact that participants are encouraged to yell "Wahoo!" upon achieving victory; or perhaps both, or neither. While not specifically described in Willa Cather's *My Antonia* or *O Pioneers!*, we felt the game was certain to have taken root in the prairie grassland, serving perhaps to enliven the settler's slow-paced and cooperative existence; taking an opponent's marble is an act of unbridled aggression, providing a childish sense of elation.)

Grandpa Roy's first wife, my grandmother, had died in childbirth. His second wife, Gertrude, or "Gertie," was a Wahoo enthusiast in her own right, and, though childless, she took a similarly headlong approach to her acquired grandmotherly duties. Each year she assumed the ungodly task of hand-making nineteen complete sets of children's flannel pajamas – six for the Grassfords, eight for the Omaha Richardsons, and five for the Denver Richardsons. We would stop by for measurements toward the end of the summer. She would buy reams of patterned fabric – cowboys one year, puppies or zoo animals the next – and mark and cut and stitch at her sewing machine for untold hours, untold days, until she had tops, bottoms, slippers, and nightcaps for the boys; gowns, slippers and nightcaps with lace for the girls; and custom labels sewn in that read: "Hand-made by Grandma Richardson."

The coming out was at Christmas time when she would host a pajama dinner. Grandpa Roy was a salesman for Sandman & Sons, an Omaha-based foam products company, and every year he would stuff his gold Buick with new Sandman bed pillows, one for each of us. Grandma Gertie would fit them with cases sewn of the same patterned pajama material. We would all put on our matching pajamas, pose for pictures with our new pillows, two or three of us hanging from Grandpa Roy's extended arms like they were monkey bars. Then we'd eat Grandma Gertie's chicken & noodles over mashed potatoes – a truly horrible dish – tough to reconcile with the high quality of her pajamas.

Grandma Gertie was notorious for her strange turns of phrase – "Ye Gods," "Honey Child," and "That's the bull that shot father" among them. She was the only person I ever met who said "Santy" rather than "Santa," as in "Honey Child, Santy Claus brought you some nice pajamas this year." She was also the only person I knew who consistently responded to praise with ready agreement. If you said something like "Your pie is delicious, Grandma," she would invariably respond: "Isn't it though!"

PLAGUE

To Sergeant's surprise Vanessa Jones was not overtly disturbed at either his reckless injections, though she hated needles, or his theft of laboratory product; nor was she particularly skeptical as to the concept of dream sharing. She seemed rather intrigued actually. He liked the way she looked at him – fearlessly, right in the eyes, interested.

Vanessa was a person who took her dreams seriously. Just successful enough as a bass player to opt out of any day job, she was almost always at leisure to take her full daily rest. "A lot of my lyrics come from my dreams," she said. She gigged regularly enough to be programmed nocturnally and usually awoke to her first Coke around noon. It was just earlier than that when Sergeant removed her headgear for the first time.

"The pods take on a slight glow when they're imprinted," Sergeant explained as he led her into the pantry and shut the door, enveloping them in darkness. "You can see the string of imprinted pods here. This one is the brightest – I'd say it's the one you imprinted most distinctly. We've observed subjects sleeping in darkroom conditions. We've actually been able to see individual pods taking on a glow corresponding directly to the donor's REM, and we believe that is the imprinting process.

"In our sleep labs we often limit donors to a single pod and wake them up at the end of their first solid REM imprint. That way if the donor remembers the dream – and we've gotten good at timing the intervention to maximize our chances that way – then we have a definitive match between the narrated dream and the imprinted pod – for whatever that's worth, which admittedly is not much right now. If we want to track a wider spectrum, like total dream volume or dream patterns over a full night's sleep, we do it with a string of pods. With you I'd like to isolate specific dreams, but I want to do so in a sustainable and non-invasive fashion, without waking you up all the time. So I gave you a full string of pods that have now been imprinted over a full night. We'll have to wing it a bit to match a specific pod to a dream you can recall, if you can recall any. I almost forgot to ask: Do you remember any dreams from last night?"

"Yes, I think I've managed to reconstruct at least one."

"Good, then we can get started. I'm just starting to play with imprinting and recollection patterns. I'm still not sure whether the dream you're most likely to remember is the strongest imprint from the night or the last imprint from the night. For me it's generally been the last imprint, the one just before I wake up, but you seem to have one very strong imprint here that isn't your last dream of the night. I'm taking that one on a hunch."

Vanessa and Sergeant sat at the kitchen table while Sergeant lit the burner and liquefied the foam. The room was as much a laboratory as it was a kitchen. They ate sliced fruit during the process, and she finger-tapped a noteless bass riff on the table.

Sergeant filled the syringe, then led Vanessa back to the living room, where he flopped onto the couch.

"OK, I'll be asleep very shortly, but I'll sleep just long enough to dream your dream. While I'm out, write down as much of the dream as you can remember. There's a tablet there. Hopefully the one I dream will be at least a partial match with what you write down, and if not then maybe something you'll recall from my telling it." He fitted a headset with a single unprinted pod: "I'll re-imprint the dream in case one of us, presumably me, wants to review it later."

And with that Sergeant plunged the needle into his thigh. "I don't think these quad injections are helping my jumpshot," he said, just before dropping into sleep.

REMEMBRANCES

Grandma Gertie slept nights in an easy chair rather than a bed on account of a quirky back, but that condition didn't seem to hamper her work in the garden. She and Grandpa Roy had grown up on or around farms and made as formidable a gardening duo as could ever be imagined. Their rented house in South Omaha was modest in both structure and size of lot, so they farmed a plot on the western edge of the city, where the land was still open and there was enough of it to grow a real mix of crops. It was as proud an acre as you'd ever see.

We would pile into the Buick loaded up with hoes and rakes, shovels and hoses, buckets and gloves, and head west, Grandpa Roy wearing the most ridiculous old farm clothes and hobo shoes. The little red seeds burst green from the ground, and the cornstalks would be halfway up my thigh by Independence Day. Great melons lay basking on the soil a month later; and the peas and beans were so heavy with crop that keeping up with them was a responsibility akin to milking a cow – it was no once-a-week outing. We would hoe and water – not a weed in the lot – and drink right from the hose. I remember unzipping the pea pods in the early summer, eating three or four peas for every dozen I dropped in the bowl; and harvesting potatoes in the fall, working my fingers into a mound of Nebraska topsoil for five, six, seven potatoes, like digging for buried Easter eggs. Grandpa Roy would eat carrots right out of the ground after brushing off only some of the soil – "Good clean dirt!" he'd say with a grin. We took much better care removing the soil from our tools afterwards, cleaning each one meticulously before putting it back in the trunk of the gold Buick.

PLAGUE

Sergeant awoke on cue, pulled off the headset, gave Vanessa a playful nod, and began immediately to narrate. "OK, so I'm in a curious kind of house, I mean you, you're in a house that feels like it's in a different country. There's a party, or at least a gathering of some sort, and the group moves outside onto a concrete deck — it's not a nice deck, feels very uninviting, with views that are ugly, quasi-industrial. Your younger brother is there — you have a younger brother? — and you feel vaguely uncomfortable about that, and about something else too, like something is missing.

"The party moves again — now it's an urban parking lot, and pretty much everybody there is a middle aged guy. There's something a little unsettling here, but I can't quite put my finger on it. One of the guys — he seems completely unfamiliar — gives you an umbrella and leaves on foot, carrying half an umbrella he's kept for himself. That's all I've got. What do your notes say?"

Vanessa read impassively: "Party in foreign house. Moves to ugly deck. Feeling uncomfortable about Jake and unspecified omission. Party moves again, this time to a parking lot — it's just me and a bunch of older guys — still uncomfortable. One of the guys — I don't think I know any of them — hands me an umbrella and walks away. I notice he still has half an umbrella."

They sat in silence for thirty seconds.

"Was it different having a woman's dream?"

"Yes, I was definitely aware of being in a woman's body." He paused. "Like some part of me wanted to go into a room and take my clothes off." They both laughed. "But of course it wasn't like I could change the dream or impose my point of view at all — nothing like that. It was definitely flowing on its own initiative, like a dream does, except I was you. And you felt like a good person to be. I mean, that's a dream I could definitely go back to."

More silence.

"What do you make of the half umbrella?" she asked.

PALM TUNNELS

Henry Cleverby had never been what was called "a people person," but he tended to remember his customers. There was something about body art, the permanent impression of personal history, the commitment it entailed and the window it provided, that made it easy for Henry to file away a face.

Matthew Leverage was a customer easily remembered in any event. A slender man, on the verge of appearing underfed, with lively, almost manic eyes, he'd had both hands tunneled within the first month. He'd previously been slathered over most of his body with multi-colored tattoos. These were strictly biblical in theme, each depicting a different scene from the Old Testament, pictures like those one might find in an illustrated children's bible – Abraham with butcher's knife in hand, poised at God's command to slay his only son; Absalom caught by his hair in the tree, dangling helplessly before his murderous pursuers; Joshua commanding the sun to stand still so his army could slaughter the heathens before dark. Leverage had worn his hair long and his beard full; this, in combination with his flowing collarless shirts and old-world sandals, greatly reinforced the impression of a Jesus complex. Now, as if fulfilling a prophecy, Leverage was back in the studio, exactly as Henry had remembered him. His pitch was straightforward and unforgettable:

"I'm your first double-tunneled customer, right? Out of all your customers I'm the first one to do that?"

Henry nodded.

"You should honor that. Use it to your benefit. Put me on display. Crucify me."

Henry's four-four beat stopped for a moment, then resumed. Still he said nothing.

"I'm serious," Leverage continued. "Dead serious. Nail me up some afternoon downtown. I won't charge you a cent, and you'll get more publicity for palm tunnels than you could ever dream of."

PLAGUE

The Grassford article changed everything in the world of dreams. Dreams in the mainstream media had previously been considered frivolous to the extent that they were considered at all, sexually charged freakshows of nocturnal insecurity that even psychiatrists had discounted, relegated to the domains of avant-garde music and experimental theatre. But now the long underbudgeted science of dreams was enjoying a sudden boost.

Dreamlessness was not only antecedent to the Omaha cases; it was held to be a quite plausible cause. Along the way it had effectively been legitimized in the public eye, but the paltry science behind it could not even validate the concept, let alone any adverse effects from its presence. Dreamlessness had been cited as an aftereffect of certain brain injuries, but in otherwise normally functioning brains it had not been quantified or even identified.

Dream specialists, or oneirologists, long relegated to the fringes of neurology, were delighted to lend credence to the wave of attention newly assigned to dreaming, or to the lack thereof. "Dreaming is an essential brain function," wrote one oneirologist in a moment of unusual candor. "We may not agree on what exactly dreaming is, or why its function is so important, but we all seem to agree that it is somehow critical. Is it a way to move useful data from short-term to long-term memory? Is it a way to purge unnecessary data from the day?

Are those essentially the same concepts? Is it simply a random processing of images from one part of the brain, neural oscillation if you like, while another part enters its vital shutdown period? Is it therapeutic role-playing, the brain's way of dealing with stress and repression and readying itself emotionally for another day? There is still a lot of discussion on all those points. Meanwhile no one is ruling out the possibility that a prolonged period without dreaming could indicate a damaged brain or could in itself lead to such damage." Almost by popular consensus, dreamlessness had become a condition to be reckoned with.

This was all, of course, quite fascinating to beleaguered CEO Christopher Collins. Collins was dreading the almost certain triple bodyblow the CTC writeoffs would bring with the next quarterly report, massive hits to: 1) Protocol stock, of which he owned several hundred thousand shares; 2) his reputation, which he valued somewhat, though rather less than his stock; and 3) his job security – all because CTCs would imprint only dreams. Never mind that the Board had initially pushed like hell on the project; its failure would collapse on him and him only. First would come the writeoff, with all the internal haranguing that entailed, tens of millions of CTC research and development dollars and the labyrinth of ugly financial forensics, then the disastrous earnings announcements, the ugly investor calls, the public quarterly report, the media. It was not an enticing prospect.

So when the Plague of Comas, and its purported association with dreamlessness, sprang miraculously to the public forefront, Collins did not deliberate for long. Acting not quite as impulsively as Zachary Sergeant had with the syringe, but with a similar sense of innovation and urgency, Collins reversed the internal writeoff and ordered the following press release:

"In answer to the nation's newfound and quite justified concern with dreamlessness, Protocol Products of Cambridge, Massachusetts, announces Cogitation Tracking Compound Technology (CTC). CTC Technology can quantify Public Dream Volume (PDV) with complete accuracy and at very modest cost. With a cross section of local volunteers, volunteers whose lifestyles will be almost entirely unaffected, national health officials can develop and monitor PDV data, by region or in aggregate, without the expense and headache of sleep laboratories or an army of technical administrators. Never again need our country be caught unaware."

REMEMBRANCES

My mother would start every day by juicing enough oranges to produce fresh orange juice for seven – she herself didn't drink it. It's no secret that kids generally take their parents' labors for granted, but I remember thinking very early in life that this was a colossal daily effort. I had tried it myself, standing on a chair, pushing the orange halves down hard on the spinning juicer, and it was no joke, especially in the quantities required. I noticed when making my walk-to-school rounds that none of my friends had freshly squeezed orange juice in the morning.

And she'd do bacon under the broiler every morning; my father would eat it on toast with marmalade, wordlessly, a brooding presence behind his newspaper. For the kids she'd make the hot cereal du jour, a weekday rotation of Oatmeal, Cream of Wheat, Coco Wheats, Maypo, and Malt-o-Meal; while she cranked out five sack lunches we would pour on the half cream and heap on the sugar, slurp it in and jump up for more. Sometimes we'd empty the pot; sometimes we'd leave an inch or so going cold and rubbery, sure to retain its pot-shape when dumped in the sink.

When my father had left for work she would turn on the radio, tuned to AM KFAB, with some talk and some soft music. As we filed out for school she would begin the transition to laundry. Our house had a clothes chute, air conditioning ductwork that ran vertically from my brother's and my shared room in the attic, through the second floor where four bedrooms housed my parents and my four sisters, and down to the kitchen. Access to the clothes chute was through tiny doors in the wall, both in the attic and on the second floor; and in the kitchen the laundry would pile up invisibly behind what looked like any common kitchen cabinet. All in all we thought it a very clever system. But behind that cabinet door was a nightmare of stench and crumple, the clothes packed musty and tight, and when you pulled out the bottom section the backed-up loads would dump down from high in the chute. You knew my mother was behind in her labors when the backup reached the second floor access door. The washer and dryer were just off the kitchen, in the passage to the TV room, so the laundry work was very much integrated with the household. My mother was forever at the ironing board, always dressed smartly in a blouse and skirt, never in pants.

Staying home sick was the next best thing to Christmas. It was breakfast in bed and 7-Up all day. My mother would lather my chest with Vick's Vap-O-Rub, crank up the steam machine, and rig up a tent for me on her bed with broomsticks and sheets. The steam machine would pour a Vap-O-Rub fog into the tent, and I would breathe deeply as instructed. I only remember abusing this privilege once, parlaying a slight cold into a stay-at-home day so I could watch Mickey Mantle and other New York Yankees make a celebrity appearance on The Match Game, one of the weekday morning television game shows. I think she was on to me but let it go.

After school I'd open the cereal cupboard to a huge selection — Frosted Flakes, Life, Trix, Fruit Loops, Alpha Bits, Honey Comb — and gorge, going through half pints of half cream like hotcakes. Then it was half a stick of Juicy Fruit — my mother's strict gum limit — and some cartoons (Yogi Bear, Tennessee Tuxedo, Snagglepuss) before heading out to Sunks. My mother would sometimes be wrapping up her Barat Boutique gatherings. Our basement was finished with red wall-to-wall carpet, ceiling tiles and wood paneling – this is where we'd huddle in the south-west corner when the tornado sirens wailed once or twice a summer. She and her friends would spend Wednesday afternoons down there, smothering the ping pong table with a frenzy of handcrafts, designing and assembling items for sale to benefit Barat. Some of the ladies were very talented, more were not, but as a group they were prolific – they cranked out product, and a lot of it. My mother would conscript us to pin sequins and patterned velvet into Styrofoam balls (courtesy of Sandman & Sons and Grandpa Roy) for Christmas tree ornaments. Or to shove cloves into oranges – I still have no idea what those were for. Mostly they just laughed and carried on and laughed some more. I had no idea what was so funny for them, but sometimes it made me laugh too.

In the summer my mother would pile us in her station wagon for the sprint to afternoon swimming practice. We were generally running tight, or just plain late, but she was a skilled, fast driver, and once we got out on the open road she would put the pedal to the floor. Her station wagon had a speedometer that gave readings by stretching a color stripe like thermometer mercury across a horizontal grid on the dashboard. Except instead of mercury gray, this one would run from green at low speeds, to orange, to a bright red at the very highest speeds; and we would shriek with delight as she careened over the hills and we lifted out of our seats and watched the stripe turn its reddest red.

PLAGUE

Collins' maneuver was nothing short of brilliant. Not only did he forestall writing off the CTC investment and triggering the inevitable stock slide to follow, he produced the exact public sector response he was looking for. The press reacted to Collins' announcement as if the government's monitoring of dreamlessness at some level was a foregone conclusion, though no federal agency had even entertained the notion to that point. Protocol was regarded as the first of many scientific corporations certain to throw their hats in the ring, to join in the rush for contracts, though in reality no other company anywhere in the world was even sniffing at CTC technology. Protocol's stock actually rose on this largely manufactured impetus; clearly the public had taken an interest.

The quicker polls are processed and disseminated, and the more reliably elected officials pander to them, the more perfectly representative democracy becomes. Protocol's home state Massachusetts Congressmen followed the Collins press release with an immediate push, both publicly and in private consultation, for governmental oversight of stability in public dreaming. The logical agency to administer such a program was the NIH, overseen by the Senate Committee of Health and Education, which was chaired by Jeremy Cleverby, the veteran Democrat from Nebraska. Cleverby, who shared very few interests with his colleagues from Massachusetts, was nevertheless an early advocate on purely scientific grounds. Within four months Protocol had its first federally contracted assignment.

The engagement charged Protocol with monitoring dream activity through a network of volunteers in conjunction with the NIH. The initiative was branded around the name Dreamtracking, and the first chosen test market was Washington itself. On the heels of an award-winning marketing campaign by the Protocol in-house agency, Dreamtracking demonstrated immediate public appeal, especially among young people. Nearly fifteen thousand volunteers registered to track their dreaming.

This represented a substantial oversubscription of the projected regional dream network, a good problem to have, surely, except that the NIH politely declined to expand the scope of its contract. Christopher Collins insisted on making some use of this consumer surge; why exclude thousands of eager donors simply by the sequence of their registrations? After weeks of heavy brainstorming, Protocol made the surprising announcement that it preferred higher IQ subjects and would select from its volunteer pool on that basis. This position was both sophomoric and scientifically dubious, as some were quick to point out, but it was also just arrogant enough to tantalize both the media and the aspiring public. Moving with surprising agility for a company its size, Protocol quickly installed a cyber-test of mental acuity for all its dream donor volunteers. The great majority of them actually took it.

The cyber-test was a tactical success on many levels. On its most practical level, it successfully thinned the Dreamtracking herd. Somewhat counter-intuitively, it also boosted public awareness. The test was cleverly designed by an ad hoc committee of Mensa enthusiasts within Protocol. It garnered so much interest that thousands who had not signed up for Dreamtracking took the test anyway, comparing their scores and debating the questions in their offices, bars and chatrooms. But the delaying effect may have been the test's most significant contribution. Protocol needed time and needed it desperately. The headgear and the removable foam pods were production ready, but Protocol still had no means of uploading the dream data.

At its best a company, even a large company, is just one step up in complexity from a team of athletes or a band of musicians, which are in turn just one step up from an individual performer. For all of them there are crucial tests, sometimes just one absolutely pivotal moment, neatly scheduled or completely unexpected, that either sink the operation or propel it to prolonged success. The upload gap was just such a moment for Protocol Products.

Under absurd time pressure, and with the sizable federal contract, the reputation, and perhaps even the survival of the company hanging in the balance, Christopher Collins stopped virtually everything and put his best teams to work. His thought was to deploy them independently at first, and then to narrow the field to back the best concepts. A brilliant scientific mind in his own right, but not as specialized as his best inventors and designers, Collins was forced to make the early determinations largely on instinct, to read beyond complex engineering presentations for more fundamental underlying human indicators. He considered flow-charts to be no more important than conviction, individual demeanor, and telltale mannerisms – all of a parlance he readily understood. The more complex and confusing the presentation, the more Collins read muddled thinking on the part of the presenters. The simpler the idea, the more open and disarming the approach, the more he liked it.

Dr. Anders Hriniak had initially drifted between several high-powered groups, but soon found himself working more prevalently with Zachary Sergeant, with whom he had enjoyed an easy working relationship in the past. Collins, whose professional survival had depended for some years largely on his ability to read and understand Dr. Hriniak, was quick to see this. He sensed early in the process that Sergeant, of all people, was emerging as a possible fulcrum in the effort; Sergeant was just enough outside the box to engage Dr. Hriniak, with a resulting likelihood to hit on something that just might work. Sergeant was one to cut to the heart of the matter; his profile was favorably inclined to deliver simply and decisively within the time frame if he were to deliver at all. Collins met personally with Sergeant, well before Sergeant's upload vision was particularly in focus, to ensure that he carried only a tolerable level of hard feelings from the suspension, that he was motivated, sufficiently coddled, and empowered.

Sergeant's ideas began to take a more tangible form over the next several weeks. Believing that his bet on Sergeant had begun to pan out, Collins raised the stakes, funneling resources at critical early moments toward this most unlikely of project leaders. He coolly shuffled senior engineering personnel in support of the relatively low-ranking Sergeant, grappling with egos, browbeating and cooing as each personality required, strengthening the team with each step. The hum of steady progress – the fruit of Sergeant's vision and the strong mix of talent at his disposal – just bridged the inherent turbulence in the team dynamic.

The timely result, of course, was the Podreader, a triumph of elegant design and simple user interface, sleek and sturdy, a handsome handheld device allowing the donors to easily upload their dream data while avoiding any errors of duplication or mistaken dating. Protocol took the Podreader from concept into production, and secured its contract with the NIH, all within a remarkable five months.

The donor volunteers who had survived the controversial screening were at last rewarded with the arrival of their personal Dreamtracking kits: headgear, multiple sets of removable foam CTC pods, and a Podreader. The system went live on July 14, 2028. There was hardly a hitch. Almost immediately the small army of Washington volunteers was tracking its collective dreams, showing good faith every Sunday by forwarding its week's worth of REM imprints to the NIH website. And every Tuesday the newly image-conscious NIH would issue its report.

PALM TUNNELS

Born completely by chance into a geographical stronghold of Christianity, Henry Cleverby was a straightforward and unabashed non-believer. He revered pre-modern church architecture – was actually a student and awe-struck admirer of the great Gothic cathedrals and Renaissance basilicas. But he considered it self-evident that religion itself was bald-faced mythology, delusion run amok – sprung from pre-hygienic, barely literate men; grown into violent hordes bearing Easter Bunny banners through the centuries; and carried now even into educated generations, against all modern logic. Critical religious tenets – the origin of man, the origin of Earth, the prominence of Earth within the cosmos – had been systematically disproven with the development of science. And science was hardly the only antagonist; the world's religions also contradicted each other, flatly and unequivocally, none more feasible than the other. Where was the sense in any of it?

This was all quite clear to Henry, but still, he didn't rule out Matthew Leverage and his deranged proposal. Something about it had a certain beautiful business logic. The staging would be compelling, controversial, unignorable. But the underlying agenda would be intriguingly opaque, a point of wonderment, free of any branding and completely neutral in tone, expressing neither sanction nor rejection, neither ridicule nor reverence. It could be interpreted – applauded or lambasted – in perfectly equal measure, on either side of the belief spectrum. The relatively silent disbelievers might have something to rally around, or to deride. The righteous faithful might have a cause to embrace, or to defend.

One thing was certain: People on both sides couldn't help but be curious about the crucifixion logistics, and, in the end, have the palm tunnel concept forever embedded in their brains.

It might just be a perfectly galvanizing event, suitably edgy – provocative publicity at a manageable cost.

PLAGUE

Sergeant was the one taking the injections, but it was Vanessa who was drifting toward addiction. She had a rush of singular connection when Sergeant injected her dreams, not manifest as a flood of feelings toward Sergeant, but as a more diffuse sensation, an elevation wrought of dreams – even the unpleasant ones – brought boldly to light, and a mysterious sense of heightened possibilities. The one-man audience seemed to stimulate her dreamflow; it blossomed madly, leaving her lingering as if in a netherworld for the first hour after waking, and yet refreshed and invigorated for the new day as never before.

She found herself becoming less nocturnal, syncing her hours more closely to Sergeant's, as he did to hers. She had more composition ideas, both lyrical and melodic, than she could set down, and often left Sergeant's apartment in an inspired dash to the studio, having begun to dream in specific keys and progressions.

She understood that Sergeant was not hearing her scores with the trained ear of a musician, but she also knew that on a narrative and emotional level he was living her dreams freshly minted, raw, and completely unfiltered. She was wholly exposed, unable to couch the presentation in any way, to edit out potential humiliations, to downplay her fears or her darkest desires. In a way, that was the thrill of it. Often she had very little idea what might have been included in a particular dream, only to remember all too well upon Sergeant's narration. These discoveries – the revelations of the dreams, or of certain elements within them, that she hadn't even at first recalled – astounded her time and again. More often than not, this process of unveiling entailed a strong dose of mortification, but she swallowed it down in the new spirit of things.

Sergeant was suitably professional when he had to be, not probing too deeply or personally but steering his commentary to a researcher's bent as needed to keep her at ease and on pace. And in truth, for all the intrigue and the personal bond Sergeant felt with Vanessa's dreaming, his scientific training was never far from the surface. Clearly, he had abandoned any pretext of holding his private work to lab-quality precision; on many levels he was playing to instinct, working to gratification. But as gentle and as low-key as he was with her in assembling and breaking down her dreams, he was unbending, meticulous and clinical in his follow-up work. He took pains to write up each narration, day after day, week after week, in the terse impersonal style of the Protocol laboratories, making as many clinical notes as he imagined might be relevant – diet, exercise, REM count, point in the reproductive cycle, sources of waking hour stress – and cross-referencing each file with the corresponding imprinted pod.

As the collection of her dreams grew larger, certain characteristics of her sleep world began to resonate for him, not as something he could at first intellectualize beyond the notion of the personal overlay he'd encountered in all donor dreams, but as something he had begun to sense more deeply in the fabric of her dreaming. He couldn't quite put his finger on it; they were not so much narrative patterns, nor particular fears or obsessions – although those definitely existed – but rather a palette of distinct emotional overtones, repeated throughout her catalogue, recognizable to Sergeant with his critical mass of exposure to her, but not at all patterned or predictable.

Sergeant began to go back through the narrations, creating simple taglines to indicate emotional context and re-sorting the files accordingly. He found that emotional tones were not exclusive within a particular dream; most of her dreams jumped between two or three of them. But each tone rang clearly.

VANESSA JONES – March 19, 2028

I am walking briskly on unknown streets, trying to escape a primitive urban landscape. Everything is dry and bare, the street cracked and uneven. Jagged masonry half-walls front dirty one-story plaster homes. They are packed closely together, with flat roofs, and open gaps for windows, and dusty blankets hanging in the doorways. There are clotheslines but no clothes, homes but no people. I duck into one of the houses, which has only one room and one piece of furniture, a crude table of dried gray wood. The table holds two babies lying on their backs.

They are soundless dolls with fixed glass eyes; but they are real babies by feel and weight. I dust them liberally with flour, coating them all over before realizing I have mistakenly added sugar to the mix. I begin picking off the sugar granules, but the babies are squirming; the work is tedious and difficult. I flounder at this for some time, and the babies fly away down the street.

I escape the urban enclave and contemplate it from a distant hill. I resume my walking, come to a river, and wade right into it. The current is heavy and strong, and I am swept along amongst miniature (six-foot) killer whales. This is exhilarating, though I fear that the smallish whales will bite mulitple chunks out of me, just from curiosity.

The river ends abruptly and spits me out onto the avenue.

(Failing, Entrapment, Disquiet)

VANESSA JONES – March 20, 2028

I'm with Anthony near a tall bell tower that stands alone in a deserted stone plaza. Anthony is an unpleasant and unattractive bar manager whose behavior suggests that he has somehow, in spite of himself, attained a position of power. As he prattles on I rue the fact that he does actually wield some power over musicians like me. He and I enter the tower and start up a long flight of wooden stairs. On the third or fourth landing he leans in, kisses me, and tells me he loves me. This is absurd to me. I say, "No, you don't," and laugh uncomfortably. We wind further up the stairs, get to the top, and go out a door onto an open-air platform that feels so incredibly unstable that I have to lie down. Anthony leaves and locks me out. I am distressed for a time, but discover an alternate exit at ground level through a garden fence draped in a flowering creeper. I'm surprised I haven't noticed this before, but perhaps I have been distracted because my teeth are all falling out. Some are already gone. Others hang by only a remnant, or wiggle freely at the prod of my tongue.

(Entrapment, Dismemberment)

VANESSA JONES — March 22, 2028

I am walking a childlike person, perhaps little Jake, down unnamed streets. The day is overcast and threatening; clouds as dark as slate are moving with intent, as if rushing into battle positions. The child is relatively new to walking but can manage on his own; he takes my hand as he chooses, not because he must.

I am talking to the childlike person, trying to take an interest in small things. We come upon an implement or ornament of some kind, in pieces, broken, incomplete. The child is curious about this and would like an explanation. I cannot identify the item and therefore cannot provide an answer.

A woman with a baby stroller happens by, and I ask her about the ornament. The woman's answer is surprising and oddly satisfying: "It is for horses to come through."

(Failing, Disquiet)

Unraveling the chaos of her dreamworld was endlessly intriguing for Sergeant, the perfect puzzle. The quest for layers of order, meticulously unearthed, moved quickly from pastime to ardor to obsession. His real work was no longer at the laboratory, but in the time before and after, time he prized and protected. And the process of harvesting, discussing and categorizing her dreams seemed to have a rollforward effect for her, bringing the world of reverie into more prominence within her waking life, elevating her dreams to a larger frame on the wall of her consciousness. She felt this begin to slip whenever she missed a session with Sergeant, and to slip quite markedly if she missed a string of sessions. And so Vanessa, customarily the one applying the brakes to this type of alliance, found herself lobbying tactfully for more mornings with Sergeant. The weekends were a given, but even Sergeant, the

"Prince of the Podreader," as he was now called at Protocol, couldn't arrive at the labs later than 9:30.

REMEMBRANCES

Answering the dinner bell from Sunks would bring me by the McGroarty house, just downhill from us on Cuming Street. The McGroartys were an elderly couple, their house a small single-story home, an anomaly in Dundee, the brick painted fairy-tale white. Whereas all the other home-owners watered their lawns with sprinklers, Mr. McGroarty watered his lawn by hand, standing out there holding the hose, gnome-like and motionless under a big straw hat, his chin on his chest and his pants pulled high over his jutted belly, for an hour or two every day. I never said a word to him in all those years, but his presence every fair weather dusk was somehow reassuring. His lawn was thick and soft under his care.

It was my job to feed the dog, a big old shorthair, before our own dinner. I would open a big can of Ken-L-Ration with the modern new electric can opener, run a kitchen knife down the sides of the can to loosen it up, then go outside and shake the food into the bowl. If I executed correctly it would come out with a gross sucking noise and plop into the bowl shaped exactly like the can. The dog would wolf it down appreciatively. Then he'd go back inside and lie down on his floor pillow to lick himself. That pillow was the same Sandman model we all had in our beds, which grossed my sisters out to no end.

Weeknights were sitdown dinners that I don't recall being a lot of fun – lots of tension around finishing one's Bird's Eye frozen vege-tables. For all my mother's morning efforts with the freshly squeezed orange juice, she seemed dispirited by the evening, especially in winter; those frozen vegetables, ripped from their packing materials and then boiled to a pulpy mass, were woeful. We had long standoffs, the table fully cleared but for one or two kids sitting there with cold lima beans. My sister Mary Margaret was known to squish them in her hand when no one was looking and dump them behind the kitchen radiator.

After dinner it was newspapers and television in the tiny TV room with his and her easy chairs, kids on the floor in front of my father's most notable extravagance, an ornate wood-finished console, large enough to swallow the entire space, complete with radio, record player, and color television. The radiator in that room had a wooden cover that held an array of magazines – Life, Look, Time, Sports Illustrated – neatly fanned out and sorted by title and date – three or four weeks worth per title. It was in this room where I had my first television memory – of our family watching President Kennedy's funeral. And it was here where I humiliated myself by running out of the room during the annual telecasts of The Wizard of Oz, when the cackling Wicked Witch of the West rudely supplanted Auntie Em in the glass ball, or the flying monkeys lit the noble Scarecrow on fire; or of The Robe, when the centurions hammered the spikes through the hands and feet of the all-powerful but oddly compliant and long-suffering Jesus.

On hot summer Nebraska nights we'd peel Grandma Gertie's sweltering flannel cases from our pillows, then line up in front of the window-mounted air conditioner, waiting our turn to push the naked foam tight to the grill. We'd hold it for an out-loud count to fifty while it soaked up the cold air; then we'd run back to bed and press our faces to the freshly chilled foam, hoping to get to sleep before the coolness wore off. If I woke up to pee on those nights I'd sometimes see a pillow take on a glow. It helped me find my way through the dark, to the bathroom and back to bed.

PLAGUE

The NIH mandate was simply to establish a baseline, a norm of Public Dream Volume (PDV) so that any significant decline could be recognized early. No such research had ever been undertaken on anywhere near this scale. But to the credit of both the NIH and Protocol, even the pilot program tracked dreaming not just in aggregate volumes, but by gender, by age, and by day of week. These simple metrics greatly enhanced what would otherwise have been a rather dry presentation to the media and web-browsing public. As the early results were released, certain fundamental dreaming trends began to emerge for the first time. The public seemed intrigued with early indications that women did dream differently than men, that the old dreamed differently than the young, and that weekend dream patterns varied slightly from those midweek.

Dream donors were thrilled to be part of such pioneering and entertaining work. The program took on the feel of a giant community science project, with broad-based participation and real time results. What would once have been considered substantial advances in understanding were now regular weekly events. Knowledge in the field seemed to double or triple every month. With such a compelling string of emerging trends, news sites and news programs couldn't help but maintain regular coverage. And the NIH website, enhanced by Protocol creative personnel, emerged as something unlike any government site to date, dorky and bureaucratic, but offbeat and oddly lovable. Posting data from Protocol dream kits and enhancing the presentation with Protocol-provided analytical content, the NIH found itself operating one of the top sites in the Washington market, with traffic surging nationally as well.

For a fledgling project still regional in scope, the Dreamtracking initiative quickly became something approaching a national rage. The dorkiness of Protocol headgear became a point of campy pride, like propeller beanies in the late 1940s and potted plant Devo hats at the dawn of the 1980s. Dr. Hriniak and Christopher Collins made the talk show rounds. People began to consider their dreams, to remember them, to speak about them. Schoolchildren began to keep dream journals. The wait list for the Washington corps of volunteers grew six-fold, and Congress was flooded with constituent demands for Dreamtracking in other metropolitan areas. Protocol took the perfectly astute course of beginning volunteer lists in those potential markets. This furthered the general assumption that the program was going national and fanned the momentum on Capitol Hill to make that happen. Protocol stock was through the roof.

But Collins was not one to sit and admire his work. In the midst of this great flurry he ordered another shrewd tack. Again smacking of brilliant arrogance, Protocol began a campaign of rebranding a term it hadn't and couldn't trademark, a term well within the public domain. Protocol, after all, was not in the coma business; the coma prevention business was perhaps more accurate. But what Protocol really owned, with not a competitor in sight, was the Dreamtracking business. And so in all internal communications, in all dealings with the press, in all website citations, the "Plague of Comas" was no longer to be found. The term was expunged from the lexicon of history. It was, and had always been, the "Plague of Dreamlessness." And with discipline and doggedness, over time, just as Collins had foreseen it, the Plague of Dreamlessness began to stick.

REMEMBRANCES

Grandpa Roy tended a second garden much closer to his house – my Grandpa Andrew's rose beds. Grandpa Andrew lived in a stately red brick house on 38th Street, directly across from the grounds of Barat Academy of the Sacred Heart, with dark wood finishes and heavy velvet curtains. He was a good deal older than Grandpa Roy; he'd been an army captain in the Spanish American War. Grandpa Roy was decorated in the Great War twenty years later, serving as a lieutenant in the 42nd or "Rainbow" Division. He'd shipped to France in 1917 and spent most of the following year at the front – Champagne-Marne, Aisne-Marne, St. Mihiel, and Meuse-Argonne – winning a Purple Heart for "bringing back Sgt. Fuller from behind enemy wire which was being swept by machine gun fire."

The rose bed soil would be baked like cement, and Grandpa Roy and I would attack it with our hoes, felling weeds and breaking up hard chunks, all the while forming soft mounds around each bush. Progressively a sort of riverbed system took shape, each tributary cir-cling a bush and running back to join the main. When the trenching was completed, we'd mix the rose-feeder solution and pour it at the top of the channel. The solution would stream cleverly from bush to bush, all on its own, turning the tan-gray powder in its path to a dark brown mud, and I watched it to the very end, like an irrigation engi-neer viewing his work from a cropduster. At that point our labors were complete – save of course for cleaning the tools. The roses were spec-tacular, an array of reds and oranges and whites and yellows – Omaha's finest rose patch east of Memorial Park.

We'd wash up and head upstairs to pay our respects, freshly clipped roses in hand to be distributed among the women of the family as per Grandpa Andrew's instructions. Grandpa Andrew, already in his nineties and thirty years a widower, would typically be reading in his study upstairs, surrounded by hundreds of volumes. The respect between the two men was tangible – one in his bowtie and sleeveless cashmere sweater offering sherry, and the other in his gardening togs with shoes so old they might have been worn at Gettysburg, dirt still under his fingernails – one with only the slightest wisps of snow-white hair, the other with a square jaw and black horn-rimmed glasses. The conversation was long and fond, the older man incredibly well-read and dry-witted, the other with a laugh so high-spirited it was downright fierce, with his head thrown back and his mouth wide open and his teeth all bared.

Born on Halloween of 1875, Grandpa Andrew was the ultimate self-made man. Raised in poverty and more or less self-educated before entering Creighton Law School, he had become senior partner in a law firm that bore his name – Grassford, Congdon, Laughlin & Higgins. Their distinguished list of clients included two pillars of corporate Omaha, the Union Pacific Railroad and Mutual of Omaha. His father was an Irish immigrant who had served as a teenage laborer in the Civil War with the famed Iron Brigade. The elder Grassford survived the war, but did not do so in good health, and died while Grandpa Andrew was still a child. Grandpa Andrew liked to tell the story of his lining up at the cracker factory as a young boy, collecting the complimentary brokens in a basket to help his mother feed the family. But he was happy enough to spoil us, rewarding me richly from a stack of freshly-minted one-dollar bills he kept in his desk drawer for my first literary efforts – five or six pages of extra-wide lined paper with narratives of high adventure printed in number two pencil ("Fortunately I had some kite string in my back pocket and just managed to tie the monster's hands.")

Forever rankled by his limited formal education, Grandpa Andrew was an education and reading fanatic. He gave each of us an open account at the local bookstore, and ordered us special stickers to paste on the inside front covers of each book. My stickers said, "My Book," followed by a space to print my name, and were bordered with little baseball players, cowboys and astronauts. He read a book every couple days for as long as I knew him, noting certain passages with checkmarks in the margins. His checking pencils were red or black, the leads thick and waxy, almost crayon-like, never sharpened but rather peeled back, the paper spiraling in your hands. His checkmarks were uneven and squiggly, as you might expect of a man in his nineties. And yet he still walked to work every day, nearly two hilly miles in all kinds of weather. Who knows what kind of work he was doing at that age, or how this went over with the younger attorneys, but we never had any reason to believe it wasn't still top notch.

When not doing calisthenics – he did deep knee bends, toe-touches and arm rotations in his boxer shorts every day – he was meticulously dressed at all times. A soft droopy bowtie from a bygone age and a light cashmere sweater-vest were the norm. When we'd arrive for a visit his longtime housekeeper, a squat Norwegian woman named Thora, would present us with a wicker basket of tootsie pops. We'd each choose one, reveling in reds and purples, ever eschewing oranges and browns. Then when we went upstairs to sit with Grandpa Andrew in his study he would offer us sherry, even though we were only kids. Somewhere in his second-floor rooms he kept an enormous jet-black Smith & Wesson revolver. He would tell the story of practicing railroad law against the unions and having his house bombed. One night in those years he'd been so spooked that he'd taken the revolver downstairs and shot himself in the living room mirror.

PLAGUE

Zachary Sergeant was now cleared for personal possession of as much Zamaprotocol as he liked; his pilfering days were long over. As Protocol and its pilot project became a point of pride for Cambridge – Greater Boston was also said to be the next Dreamtracking market – Sergeant's local reputation began to grow, not from any particular press coverage, but rather from an undercurrent of insider talk, at parties, in bars, over lunch. It was not Sergeant's style to try to reshape his social base on the heels of his success. When he left his apartment he was almost always headed to Protocol, or to the city courts, where no one knew, or cared to know, anything about him beyond his basketball attributes. He was engrossed in his dream sharing with Vanessa, and, expanding his waking hours, filling the space between her dreams, he had also begun to paint. His apartment, sprawling and sparsely furnished, had become a maze of unwieldy canvases on tippy easels, of shoddily placed dropcloths and colored glops in various states of drying on the hardwood floors. It was apparent even to him that his stock was up in the world, that his opportunity for dream sharing had taken a big leap, that others would take the risk with him now if he would only ask. But he had no interest in expanding his inner circle, his circle of two.

Her dreams were enlivening for him, unsettling, but in a vaguely appealing way. It was the closest he'd ever come to understanding what it was to be a woman, or to understanding what it was to be someone else, period. While his filed narratives remained more or less clinical, he had now grown adept at verbal recantation, able to recite not only the face-value content of her dreams, but also their textures and colorations, slicing through the narrative tangles and absurdities to touch softly on her fears and her warm places, her revulsions and her loyalties, her regrets and her aspirations.

It was gratifying work watching her bloom and blossom within her dreamworld; he bloomed right with her. This space of theirs carried no rules of comportment or speech, but for him it also precluded doubt and hesitation and uncertainty. He was made for the role, and she for hers, and the sense of that was flush in both of them. And so while his science called out for a more diverse body of dream experience, he made no move to bring others in, not for fear of exposure, but from some slightly blurred sense of equanimity – with a hint, oddly enough, of resolution.

VANESSA JONES – April 7, 2028

I make an unpopular remark, then struggle to justify it. The group is persistently unsympathetic, and it is time for me to leave. But my shoulder bag is heavy, and I also have to carry two other bags and a heavy woolen coat. I stop at a service counter to buy a second overcoat, this one red and quite attractively priced at $10.

I eventually arrive at my drab and dubious residential complex. I pass through the halls and open my door to find people in my room, including a man cutting baking paper on the floor. I realize my bed is missing. After a while, I work up the courage to ask them to leave and not come uninvited into my room any more.

Later I find myself in a communal area within the residence, singing along with the ambient music. My singing is bad, and I feel alone.

(Isolation, Slogging, Failing)

VANESSA JONES — April 8, 2028

I'm with a man I hardly know, pulling up in a car at a shopping center. We get out of the car, and I have trouble closing the door. Recognizing that the door hasn't latched correctly the first time, I close it again, but it remains ajar. The man responds with a story about his car problems — his friend felt responsible but it wasn't really his fault.

Instead of entering the shopping center, we head off on foot, beginning on a suburban street where I had lived before. We come upon a steep topographical decline and after a moment of hesitation we begin to float and fly above the landscape. We are connected physically in flight, and are possibly mutually dependent. This is a disturbing and disappointing arrangement for me. As we fly he makes inappropriate comments about some little girls below. After a time I take more control of our flight and we land.

I am on my own again, considering breakfast options at the hotel. I place my order, but am soon disappointed with my choice as I watch a male patron eat his substantial and delicious breakfast.

(Flying, Entrapment, Disquiet)

VANESSA JONES — April 9, 2028

A ballerina sits on a park bench, possibly waiting for a bus. It is apparent that she has foot problems. She has removed her pointe shoes — they sit next to her on the bench with the pink ribbons arranged in the picturesque manner of a still life — and is rubbing her feet as I walk by. I observe that she has no bruising or redness, bleeding or cracking, but has seven toes on each foot. My mouth begins to open in a gasp, but I snap it shut, suddenly aware that my teeth are falling out in twos and threes.

(Disquiet, Dismemberment)

One morning after Sergeant had biked to work, Vanessa wandered through the paintings, slinking sideways through the narrow passages between them, careful not to kick or topple the stands. She saw many of them as if for the first time, drinking them in and understanding clearly what she knew she had already known, that her small circle with him was not complete. She sat at the table to write. The note was in large format, inked on a two-by-three foot sketching pad and set on an easel:

"Zack: For all the time I've spent in bars and around the people in them, the bartenders, the musicians, the drinkers, the one thing I've never been able to stomach is junkies, specifically needles. The first time I sat here and watched you inject yourself I had a sense that after all the years of staying clean I was suddenly on the brink of becoming the worst form of lowlife, even though I actually admired what you were doing. I think it's just how I react to needles. But I'm ready to get over it. This thing with you has been good. It's time I took you in. Tonight we both wear headgear. V."

PALM TUNNELS

The first palm tunnel crucifixion took place on a Friday afternoon in spring. It was a well-orchestrated event; while it carried no branding, it spoke of a sophisticated organization. And in fact, Palm Tunnels, Inc., was becoming just that, having by then opened a posh off-site office and two more studios, in Lincoln and in Des Moines, with another slated for Iowa City.

Matthew Leverage, barefoot and wearing only a loincloth, picked up his cross in Council Bluffs, Iowa, at the base of the pedestrian footbridge over the massive, seasonally swollen Missouri River. A coarse assemblage of oversized, unfinished timber, the cross weighed over two hundred pounds. A small troop of bodybuilders theatrically dressed as centurions hoisted it roughly onto his shoulder. The cross would have been completely unmanageable for Leverage to haul if not for the cleverly concealed rollers on one corner of the bottom. Still, it was an incredible undertaking for such a slender man, lugging that load over the long and wind-whipped walking bridge, followed by the troop of callous centurions. He fell once, and then for a second time, onlookers lining both banks of the river gasping with each tumble. Some spectators were in various states of drunkenness, in attendance primarily to heckle. Others were taking it in with bit of a picnic air, a lark of an outing. And others carried more intent and silent demeanors, something akin to respect, or even reverence. They all seemed to follow on foot, some enthusiastically, some with hesitation, as he worked his way from the river into the city.

Leverage took a particularly nasty third fall on Sixth Street, bloodying a knee and crushing the fingers on one hand. He struggled for several more blocks, staggering into the heart of downtown, where Henry Cleverby had paid the city a handsome sum in police details and event fees to hold the culminating sequence in a small but centrally-located park. Just as the office workers' lunch break was coming to an end, the theatrically dressed bodybuilders stretched Leverage roughly onto the cross and, with one crew on each hand, swung barbaric-looking hammers, driving heavy iron spikes with loud ringing whacks through both palm tunnels and into the timber. They strapped his feet to the support wedge, then gathered at the head to lift the cross slowly upright. Leverage groaned as he settled into place, his head at thirteen feet. The crowd was stunned, silent for a moment. And then someone jeered, and half a flatbread sandwich struck Leverage on the cheek, leaving a smear of mustard. He was powerless to remove it. His fingers were throbbing, his shoulders aching, but it was the mustard that would most distress him over the next several hours.

PLAGUE

Zachary Sergeant loved the idea of sharing his dreams; he had actually hungered for it. But when the moment arrived, he was surprisingly apprehensive. The mutual expectation was that Vanessa would be nervous taking her first injection, but it was he who could actually hear his pulse, feel it throbbing through his body, as she plunged the needle. As she slept he fidgeted about, trying to calm his heart rate with music and mindless housework. And then she was up, awake and immediately narrating – aloud! – scenes from his deepest and darkest places. He was mortified. "It's over," he thought.

ZACHARY SERGEANT – June 7, 2028

I'm in an urban public women's room having stand-up practice sex with a face-less dreadlocked woman near the sinks. The room is large, housing several stalls. Its walls and floor are of unpainted cement or maybe ancient stone; it is poorly lit and unpleasantly damp with vaguely oppressive low ceilings and poorly placed fire safety sprinkler heads. I am worried about people coming in while I am having this practice sex. A couple does come in, including one person I know, a woman from work, along with another man. I scurry to conceal myself near the stalls, but do not shy from eye contact with the man. Our exchange is unspoken but speaks clearly of mutual reproach.

The woman I know from work somehow has not seen me. She goes into a stall and shuts the door behind her, though the door doesn't affix itself properly to the jamb. I watch her pee through the opening. She still doesn't see me.

The man goes into a different stall and leaves his shoes on a bench outside the stalls. I notice that they are my size. Suddenly I am wearing one of them while climbing a long set of steep and winding outdoor stairs carved of stone. I compare the relative features of the man's shoe and my own. One is a low-cut basketball shoe from a few decades ago. The other is a leather shoe or boot, utilitarian and vaguely military, from a few centuries ago. To my surprise, I am quite favorably impressed with the older shoe.

(Eroticism, Debasement, Disquiet)

And so their dream sharing began in earnest.

VANESSA JONES — June 7, 2028

I am wandering among squat monolithic buildings suggesting an ugly university or tech school. I am expecting to shower in this complex, but can't find anywhere to do it. I am rerouted down a gray corridor into the basement bathroom on Cambridge Street, where I shower but see no towels. I move something out of the way to reveal a hidden shelf loaded with fresh and fluffy folded towels. A man and a teenage girl, possibly his daughter, come in, also looking to shower. I give them some travel soap and travel shampoo and point out the towels.

I go by a tennis court where a large crowd is gathered to watch famous people dance. Jake falls down, dragging me with him. Someone points out that I have fallen into dogshit and have it all over myself. This is unfortunate, as I have a pending lunch date — sushi with a bad friend and some of her bad friends. I am running late, and spot my bad friend, but slip unseen into my apartment to clean off the dogshit, leaving the apartment door open but the lights off, closing

the bathroom door and locking a half-door further in. I hear my bad friend
downstairs grumbling about my tardiness. I shower, then slip out of the apartment and board a bus.

I speak to a nice young couple on the bus to get walking directions for my
arrival. But when I do set out on foot I become almost immediately lost. I feel
alone and want to go back.

In the sushi restaurant one woman eats a selection called "The Performer." It
begins to move in her mouth and she becomes alarmed. I see this clearly but am
still amenable to eating my own "Performer." A girl walks by with a zip-lock bag
taped to her arm and filled with salmon. I notice that she is holding her fingers
strangely and determine that she is mimicking her sister, who wears multiple
rings. Now an older woman has come to meet me outside the apartment to discuss
some serious matter, but we mostly just watch the ocean.

(Debasement, Disquiet, Isolation)

ZACHARY SERGEANT — June 9, 2028

I'm flying with my two sisters. But there is no plane; we are seated in a line, as
if on a toboggan, with me in front, captaining, though there is nothing to sit on,
no floor, no wings, windows or walls. We're at thirty thousand feet, but the sheer
face of a mountain looms ahead, and I can't seem to steer decisively away from
or over it. My steering mechanism, the only mechanism in play at all, is a toy
balsa wood airplane, which I hold and tilt at various angles ahead of me in an
increasingly futile attempt to change our course. The balsa wood plane slips out
of my hand and I look over my shoulder to see it shooting away behind us. I now
acknowledge to my sisters that we are going to die. Some relatively untroubled
conversation follows.

I grab a blue rope (hanging from the sky?) and climb to safety, but find
myself lying on a truck trailer, with another trailer braced maybe a meter above
it. The supports begin to fail and the top trailer seems certain to collapse onto

my trailer, entrapping or crushing me. But, pushing up, I find the trailer to be surprisingly light and manageable; I am able to lift it on one edge and climb to safety. The trailer is filled with aluminum cans headed for recycling.

(Flying, Failing, Entrapment)

REMEMBRANCES

My father had served as a lieutenant commander aboard the destroyer Rosebud, running convoys in WWII and, as he told it, vomiting over the side into the foamy North Atlantic. He was then drafted back into service for Korea, which greatly soured him on his military experience and may have tilted his general life outlook down a notch or two. At the very least it caused him to have a late start with his family. I remember him exclusively as a bald man – he had hair only in old pictures. By the time I was five he was already into his fifties.

Andrew Jr. was a guy who never seemed quite happy in his station. As the son of Grandpa Andrew it followed that he'd been east to the finest schools. But somehow he'd ended up back in Omaha, perhaps feeling that he needed a professional jump-start after so much lost time. I imagine he might rather not have been in his father's law firm, waiting forever to take a more senior role, might rather not have been practicing law or living in Omaha at all.

He would sprinkle his language with nautical terms – a real anomaly in Omaha. (I never got much past port and starboard, fore and aft.) He could gauge time out of the blue, accurate within five or ten minutes, by simple dead reckoning – never wore a watch except in the courtroom. He was a charming guy in adult company. But he was not by nature a family man, or a Midwesterner, not a guy who took a lot of pleasure in clowning around with his kids, in sitting on the porch, or in do-it-yourself projects, gardening, or lawn work. He was more of a sportsman, and his tastes were more patrician, or at least Eastern – living somewhere else he would have done a lot of skiing and sailing. The pleasure he took from the sports he did play seemed somewhat elusive. He would throw tennis racquets over the fence in family doubles with his kids, and while this was never surprising to us, it did strike us, even at our early ages, as unusual. He would take his solace in more faraway places, listening to opera on his record player, for example, when he wasn't on the golf course.

He was a scratch golfer with six kids, a guy who after his Saturday round would come home to drink a beer at the kitchen table when I'm sure he would rather have had several in the men's locker room. His time with the children was consistently orchestrated to accommodate all six kids at once.

He had some hopes for me as a golfer, although I didn't have much interest in the sport. He took me out on the course one day, just the two of us, the only one-on-one outing of any type I ever recall having with him. I hit a few decent balls, in the air and relatively straight. Then he ventured a piece of advice. I was so determined to make the tip stick, so nervous really, that I flubbed the next several shots in succession, hitting a series of plow-up-the-fairway chunkers, grounders, and shanks. He hit a few shots himself, then reared back and threw his club forty yards down the fairway. I remember its whirring end over end like a springtime maple seed, twirling down to settle softly in the turf.

PLAGUE

With the huge success of the Podreader and the Washington pilot program, Christopher Collins began to spur his company to expand its scope. With Boston now officially approved as the second Dreamtracking site, the NIH contracts were, in total, the largest in Protocol's history. And a path had been paved for colossal growth beyond them. Data providing dream volume by age and gender and day of week had proven to be of interest to a wide range of the public, scientifically germane, and fully fundable by the government. The simple prospect of expanding the program into other population centers would add a compelling regional comparison, extend the national safety net against the Plague of Dreamlessness, and entail more sales growth than most companies could even dream of. But Collins was after something even more riveting, something more personal and sustainably fascinating to the individual consumer. He wanted content, the mist and scent of real dreams.

Sergeant, of course, had been completely immersed in that domain. Working without direct funding, without dedicated support staff, and completely without authorization, his progress had been significant nonetheless. He had begun to refine his ideas on the nature of dreams, moving swiftly toward something of substance.

He and Vanessa had classified ten emotional tones in their dreaming, several of them common to both, some found only in the dreams of one or the other. These narrative "Dream Tones" seemed so distinct that he began to wonder in earnest if they might have exclusive numerical bases within the resonance range of the imprints. With his Podreader work essentially complete, he was able to throw all his energy into that thought.

He began to scan each of his and Vanessa's imprinted pods, compiling data on the slight resonance variations within them. Before long he found that within their dream samplings each tone was associated with a particular segment of the resonance range. Dreams with multiple tones alternated their resonance accordingly. Sergeant was quietly exhilarated by those findings.

He dove headlong into expanding his database. He pored through the Protocol dream libraries, pre-selecting those dreams that had been harvested individually, ensuring that they corresponded to a given imprinted pod, rather than those dreams harvested in clusters. He read the donor narrative log for each dream and assigned tones to each. He then scanned the corresponding pods to cross-match their resonance levels.

This was time-consuming labor, and his prolonged engagement with the dream libraries raised some eyebrows in the workplace. But the "Prince of the Podreader" had become a protected species at Protocol. He now enjoyed a freedom in the workplace that only Dr. Hriniak had enjoyed before him.

Sergeant understood the control problems inherent in data drawn from the accounts of hundreds of donors with a span of recollective abilities and narrative styles. But on balance his ideas seemed to foot with the dream library data. In ninety-six percent of the cases, his subjective classification of the donor's narration aligned with at least one resonance level on the corresponding pod. In seventy-eight percent of the cases he was able to predict two or more resonance levels. And one hundred percent of his narrative assessments from the more controlled sample – those dreams he had dreamt personally, either organically or through injection – were predictive of resonance levels, and vice versa. It seemed clear that his hunch had panned out.

On a more macro level he found no imprints of resonance outside the range he had observed at home. He did identify two narrative tones, which he labeled Fleeing and Falling, that had not appeared in his or Vanessa's dreams; these slotted nicely into gaps in the resonance scale. After discussions with Vanessa, he accepted them as valid tones, taking the total to twelve. The aggregated tones now spanned the range rather evenly.

As Dr. Hriniak faced ever more management pressure to produce content metrics, Sergeant considered his options. Disclosing his findings would greatly increase the risk of exposing his injection-based and unauthorized dream sharing activity, a substantial hazard considering what scrutiny his methodology would certainly face. And his scientific position was neither optimally documented nor optimally conclusive. But he admired Dr. Hriniak, and he understood that the vise was turning. In his heart, he believed the science to be inherently sound. On balance, the imperative was to come forward.

On November 3, 2028, Sergeant presented the dream tone model to a small committee headed by Dr. Hriniak. In order from highest to lowest range and compression, and with backing charts representing data from 1,300 Protocol file dreams, he proposed these tones:

Striving
Slogging
Falling
Failing
Fleeing
Flying
Isolation
Debasement
Disquiet
Dismemberment
Entrapment
Eroticism

Dr. Hriniak and the committee were astounded. Two days later Sergeant presented to Christopher Collins and the entire executive team.

PALM TUNNELS

The public response to the Matthew Leverage crucifixion was resoundingly, overwhelmingly negative. Those leaning toward humanism objected to what they considered a wanton display of sadism; children, at the very least, should be shielded from such a spectacle. Those leaning more to devout and fundamental Christianity objected not so much to the sadism – how could they, with the crucifix as their brand icon? – but to its having been put on display without official sanction; they charged sacrilege on several counts. But privately Henry Cleverby saw the demand for palm tunnels rise threefold in the following two weeks – exactly as he had foreseen it. What he hadn't forseen was fielding a dozen calls inquiring into the possibility of more crucifixions, zealots from all walks of life looking to make the ultimate pilgrimage, the ultimate show of faith, with little or no regard for cost.

Henry had laughed off the first call, and then the second. It was a one-time PR play, plain and simple, he'd said. But as more calls came in he began to listen, and to consider. These people were serious, he thought, beating a steady four-four time. They would pay handsomely to star in what amounted to simple reruns, matinee reprises of the original theatrical production. Henry found himself beginning to engage with these callers – why, he couldn't say. It was no longer public relations; it was driven more by curiosity than by profit. Acting with a willfulness unusual for him in business, he pieced together a couple of staging dates, accommodating a few of the more lucrative proposals.

Within the month, he pulled off his first privately contracted crucifixion, and then another, moving deliberately, assimilating the requirements of this offbeat brand of events planning. He wondered why people would pay to be displayed in such a humiliating and hideously uncomfortable manner. But several of them did exactly that, without a second thought. The early crucifixions proved as practicable as they were profitable. And a crowd was never lacking; for all the initial criticism, the public seemed quite intrigued.

Perhaps the spectator reception was what drove him to it, perhaps not, but Henry made the decision then and there to stake a claim on this strange ripple in the marketplace. He formed a second corporate veil under the brand "Calvary Enterprises." He established operational protocol and handpicked a small staff to execute it. He bought a vacant lot downtown, brought in fill and loam to form a modest hill, and seeded it with simple prairie grass. At the crest of the hill he had a custom inground stand installed with a concealed hydraulic lift. And with that he was in the event business.

PLAGUE

After Washington and Boston, Protocol, with its customary sense of theatre, had pushed the NIH to name Omaha as its third Dreamtracking market. The promotional people considered it a sure-fire home run, correctly anticipating that the media would react to an Omaha announcement by rekindling all the intrigue of the Plague of Dreamlessness. This would keep Dreamtracking, and Protocol Products, securely in the limelight. The NIH was more than happy to oblige.

NIH Director Nate Howard had a healthy appetite for any attention that wasn't overtly negative. From the standpoint of public health, Omaha, as the site of the original outbreak, was the most logical choice; and Omaha would counter some of the usual charges of regional bias that had surfaced in response to the first two spots going to East Coast cities. It was also fitting that Nebraska had been the home state of the recently deceased Jeremy Cleverby, who, from the start, had been the pivotal congressional advocate of government-sponsored Dreamtracking.

The Omaha rollout exceeded expectations. Retrospective coverage of the Plague was far more endemic than the Plague had ever been, a staple of every talk show and news show for the better part of two weeks. Just as that coverage was beginning to trail off, Protocol played its trump card, announcing its Dream Tone Classifications and its plan to track those twelve tones by gender, by age, and by region. The introduction was masterful in its timing and produced exactly the content buzz Christopher Collins had envisioned. Protocol delivered its product upgrades before the month was out. And shortly thereafter the standard demographic groups and individual donors in all three active metropolitan markets were developing dream personality profiles through objective and quantifiable calculations.

Public interest spiked to record levels. The press began a weekly frolic with the results, headlines barking, "Omaha Tops Erotic Dream Scale," or "Boston Big on Dismemberment."

"I'm primarily a Slogger," one donor posted on a dating website, "with traces of Falling, Flying and Fleeing. I'm coming off a disastrous relationship with a Debaser and Dismemberer – D Dreamers need not apply."

Constituents in active markets demanded additional capacity to accommodate more users in their cities. Constituents in untouched markets demanded that their cities be included in the project. By the sheer force of public will the wheels of government were turned; the NIH was granted budget increases to fund a greatly accelerated expansion. While the NIH hadn't quite endorsed the science of Dream Tone Classifications, it had continued to push expansion, and hadn't objected to Protocol's Dream Tone reports as long as they were housed on Protocol's own website. Bureaucracies love growth. And even bureaucrats enjoy popularity.

Dreamtracking grew geometrically from Omaha, spreading in all directions like some genetically mutated wildflower, highly invasive and yet irresistibly attractive. Protocol and the NIH had learned each other's workings, carved out their respective roles in the undertaking. They had perfected the rollout model and staffed accordingly. Now, as they said, it was like cutting cookies, stamping one large metropolitan area after another out of a huge national map made of dough. San Francisco, Chicago and LA were the next to fall in. Austin, Minneapolis, Denver, Seattle. By the fall of 2029, Dreamtracking was underway in the forty largest cities in the United States. Protocol had provided a quarter million Dreamtracking kits and continued its partnership with the NIH in tracking the weekly dreaming activity of every donor. Protocol capitalization had quintupled, and there was still plenty of upside, both domestic and international.

The public was having so much fun with the findings that it was almost impossible for the project's detractors to rein it in, to recall that the mission was really to establish dream volume baselines and monitor for any regional decline, and that virtually no progress had been made to handle such a decline if it were identified. As it stood, the only response would be to establish regional capacity in preparation for a large-scale coma outbreak – more beds, dedicated holding centers, and specialized staff. It all seemed quite remote.

REMEMBRANCES

Saturday was golf day for my father, so Grandpa Andrew would take the slot, visiting us on Saturday afternoons in a white dress shirt – short sleeve linen in the summer – and his signature bowtie. Grandpa Andrew had given up driving long before; if you ran to the window when he came over you could just catch a big yellow taxi pulling out of the driveway. On summer Saturdays he'd arrive about noon, and we'd all pile into my mother's paneled wagon, heading directly to Hinky Dinky. While my mother would load multiple grocery carts with cold cereal, fresh meats, dog food and the like, he'd take us kids into the produce section, where we'd pick out the most pear-shaped pears and, at his direction, chomp right into them.

Afterwards he'd take us out into the yard, each of us armed with our own weeding tool, to dig dandelions. We'd always take special care to get the root, comparing to see who'd pulled the longest. Then perhaps he'd have a hand of casino with my younger sister Mary Elizabeth and me. He was a gentle grandfather, always letting us win, drawing little animal pictures or human stick figures with bellies and buttons and hats. If there was Wahoo it was not the raucous sort we had with Grandpa Roy.

During baseball season he'd sit at the television to watch the national Game of the Week broadcast with me. My mother would supply us with a huge bowl of grapes to get us through the game, and I would eat them inning after inning until I could do nothing but flop around on the carpet, stuffed like a fat little hamster.

PLAGUE

Zachary Sergeant and Vanessa Jones had been dream sharing for just under two years. Vanessa was completely consumed in composition and recording, playing out only in the most financially favorable gigs, or those that offered the most exposure. She had circulated a demo tape that was bursting with originality and songwriting prowess from the first track to the last. She was in a position to believe that her first recording deal was not to be with a regional or niche brand, but with a major label carrying industry clout and both studio and marketing expertise. And it would happen soon.

Sergeant, again allocated a staff of his own, was shoring up the science behind his Dream Tone Classifications. Protocol was prioritizing a formal documentation of the tones, a thorough study of the link between pod resonance levels and written donor narratives. This work was considerably overdue given the legitimacy the national dream community had so readily assigned to the Tones. The sleep labs were again operating at full capacity, generating waves of new test samples to supplement the older files.

Fortunately, most of Sergeant's early conclusions were holding up, so little backtracking was required. Sergeant himself found the backup science tedious, though his own role was purely administrative. He had reached his conclusions and proven them to his own satisfaction. The rest was simple monotony, driving the test pool up to generally accepted levels of scientific rigor.

From a laboratory standpoint, Sergeant was far more interested in finding a technology that would unleash the same narrative punch from a CTC pod as injection. But this was a tired pursuit, a sore spot for Protocol management, which had already spent millions in the abandoned search. In discussing this with Dr. Hriniak, Sergeant had to admit that he didn't have a particular idea worth rallying behind or staffing. Dr. Hriniak gave him free time to explore, but Sergeant knew he was essentially idling.

The other laboratory pastime that had originally appealed to Sergeant – sampling selected public dream content, romping through fantastic worlds completely unknown to him – he had largely abandoned as far too unsettling. While he still carried a proclivity for the occasional crazy outlier from the Protocol files, he couldn't inject in the labs anyway; it was far too risky, even in the confines of his office. And beyond that, he knew he needed to cut back.

Sergeant had by now injected something in the neighborhood of a thousand dreams. The lion's share were Vanessa's, and he was quivering with creativity just in the wake of that work. He could hardly build easels and frames fast enough to accommodate his painting, and he'd taken an increasing interest in the associated woodwork; the handheld tools and rough stock he used in the easel and frame assembly were rapidly succeeded by a table saw, a drill press, a lathe, and fine pieces of finish stock for cutting boards, game boards and simple furniture. Soon he'd migrated completely to woodworking, the paintings stacked against one wall to make room for his urban woodshop. Sawdust footprints lay thick on the floor, and sawdust coats clung to the windows, mottling the low-lying Cambridge sun.

Early on he had encouraged Vanessa to sample some of his favorites from Protocol's dreambank. She'd relented half a dozen times, taking a few of the anonymous dreams. But she'd found them exhausting, often alarming, and ultimately distracting. She had her hands full with Sergeant's subconscious and her own burgeoning dream world. She was still averse to needles and didn't want more injections than were necessary. And she, more than Sergeant, fretted about the long-term health implications. No one had ever been down this path. There was no blueprint as to safe levels of Zamaprotocol, or as to how effectively it flushed from the body, and at what, if any, long-term cost.

One morning on a hot Tuesday in July, Sergeant removed his headgear to find that none of the pods were glowing; they lay inert and laboratory white. "No use injecting any of this," he said to Vanessa.

That night he changed out his headgear and all the pods. He awoke to another barren morning. "We don't have any records at Protocol of any empty imprints, so this is definitely weird," he said. "And I definitely don't have any conventional memory of a single dream from the last two nights."

Vanessa insisted on injecting one of Sergeant's blank pods and confirmed that it held no content. It didn't even put her to sleep. That night she imprinted several pods Sergeant had previously failed to imprint; they did not seem defective. Sergeant, meanwhile, tried a third set of pods and came up empty once again. He took that set to the labs and had them scanned for even the slightest trace of resonance. All negative. He brought a scanner home and personally reran the tests. They confirmed what he and Vanessa feared. He was dreamless.

PART TWO

REMEMBRANCES

My brother and all the other older neighborhood kids shortcut the one-mile walk to Saint Martyrius, slicing diagonally through Memorial Park. This was obviously the quickest route, but one which required crossing a small but steeply cut ravine carrying a rocky creek at the far edge of the park. A large municipal pipe ran over the creek; walking on it saved the time and trouble of working the downgrade, maneuvering from rock to rock across the water, and then laboring back up the far grade. By today's parenting standards the pipe was an incredibly dangerous crossing, teetering twelve or fifteen feet over the rocks, but it was a twice-daily routine to most kids, hardly meriting a second thought.

I, on the other hand, was still a bit shy of the pipe as I entered fourth grade, an age when crossing under was as dishonorable as taking the long wimpy way on sidewalks. So it came as a relief when I found myself in a Stingray gang, riding to school every day that weather permitted. Stingrays had turned up in Omaha at about the same time as color televisions. They were one-speed Schwinns with banana seats and chopper style handlebars, dramatically different than any bike that had come before. With their short spokes they weren't good distance bikes, but were very maneuverable and conducive to quick acceleration. They were great for slamming on the footbrakes and laying scratch. Whereas color televisions spread slowly through the neighborhood – I had gone to Billy O'Malley's house to first see orange flame spewing from the Batmobile's exhaust – Stingrays spread like wildfire. Every kid I knew had one. Before too long some of us had extra thick rear tires in colors. Green, red and blue tires would leave corresponding color patches on the street.

Nicholas Street was the furthest from school, so Billy O'Malley would pick me up. I'd be waiting on my bike at the edge of the driveway, and he wouldn't even have to slow down on the Cuming Street hill. We'd mark the morning progression by crossing Happy Hollow and picking up Jeremy Cleverby, Chris Carmen, and Mikey Langston along the way. 57th Street marked the top of the best hill in the neighborhood – long, steep, and stop sign free. We would gather at its crest like Indian warriors staring down at Custer, then roar down the three-block drop, pedaling furiously until our legs couldn't keep up, speed peeling the hair back off our foreheads. The bottom came to an abrupt T, funneling us into a hard left turn. At least weekly one of us would swing too wide, hit the high curb and cartwheel boy-over-bike into the grass, while the others kept pedaling with the whipsaw momentum of the hill, our eyes watering with laughter and the wind.

PLAGUE

After nearly a week of dreamless sleeps, a week of testing, eliminating variables, and generally confirming his troublesome state, Zachary Sergeant knocked on the door of Dr. Hriniak's office.

"Dr. Hriniak, do you have a few minutes?"

This was going to be awkward, to say the least. Dr. Hriniak had backed Sergeant after his one-off injection in the lab, but could Sergeant expect that kind of support after this long run of subsequent violations? He expected that he probably could, if only on the basis that Dr. Hriniak valued scientific curiosity above almost all else. Still, he dreaded the conversation. It was not that he feared Dr. Hriniak's wrath or vengeance – Dr. Hriniak was far more likely to interpret negative developments as data points rather than as personal affronts – but because Sergeant knew there was a hint in his work of upstaging Dr. Hriniak. That had not been his intent, but it was also not something he had ever quite reconciled with himself.

"Dr. Hriniak, I'm afraid I have a bit of a confession to make. You remember of course when I injected myself in the labs. When I got suspended I couldn't see letting the work just stop. It was all just beginning. So I took some Zamaprotocol home with me and started tinkering. At first I injected mostly my own dreams, learning the process, exploring. One thing led to another, and, well, I've been at it for two years now, working mostly with my partner's dreams."

Dr. Hriniak was silent for a moment.

"Well, Zack, there's no doubt that your initial injection set up a very interesting platform for research. I've been tempted to try it myself. But there's a line we can't cross here, which is, of course, why we didn't pursue it – and, of course, why you've been so guarded on the matter. The facts are that you've been reckless with your health, and that of your partner, and you've taken serious risks and ethical liberties on a number of other fronts. Is your partner someone outside Protocol?"

"Yes. She started injecting my dreams about six months after I was doing hers. Our work together was really the key to discovering the Dream Tones. You might have guessed that. I would have been much more unlikely to work them up just from the written donor narratives."

"Your work on the Podreader and the Dream Tones has been instrumental in a lot of progress. No one questions that. I suppose the obvious question is, why have you come forward now?"

"I haven't had a single dream in just over a week. I'm waking to pristine, unprinted pods, as confirmed by both injection and resonance testing."

"Absolute Dreamlessness?!"

There was a moment of awkward silence before Sergeant spoke again.

"In the week that I've been dreamless, I've also had diminishing returns injecting my partner's dreams. Her dreams are getting foggier to me with every injection. They're also leaving me with headaches now, which they never did before, and the headaches seem to be getting worse."

"Any other symptoms?"

"Grogginess over the past few days. Otherwise no symptoms over a period of almost two years, although we've made a number of positive observations during the dream injection period. We've noticed enhancements in mood, energy, and creativity, for starters, perhaps a reduced reliance on sleep quantity. My partner has no negative symptoms whatsoever – she's still having normal dream flow. I suppose that's consistent with the Omaha model in which no women were affected."

"Her normalcy may also be consistent with the fact that she's been injecting Zamaprotocol for a shorter period of time than you have. If you're thinking about Omaha I imagine you're also contemplating coma."

"Well, who knows what to believe there – the dreamlessness precondition was strictly anecdotal, as you and I have discussed on many occasions."

"Anecdotal, but apparently universal."

"As we've also discussed. Your guess is as good as mine, but the answer is yes, I do believe that barring some rejuvenation of my REM imprints I'm a legitimate candidate for coma. If so, I can only hope to come out of it as well as the Omaha victims."

"Agreed."

"Dr. Hriniak, I'm under the impression that we have no record of dreamlessness anywhere in our sleep lab files. Anyone who showed REM sleep imprinted a pod. Is that your understanding?"

"Yes, even the faint early sleep REM signals have left some small trace of themselves. Are you sure you're even having REM sleep?"

"No."

"We'll check on that, obviously. But for now, if we assume that your dreamless state is a symptom unique to you and then look for exposures that are similarly unique to you, it doesn't take a genius to suspect that the most likely cause would be the injections. The obvious step would be to suspend them immediately and wait for the dreams to return."

"The Omahans weren't injecting Zamaprotocol. CTCs didn't even exist. So if injection has caused dreamlessness in me, what caused it for them?"

"A question many of us have pondered since the NIH first brought this public."

"Anyway, as of this morning I have stopped the injections."

"And your partner?"

"She stopped injecting once I stopped producing."

"Good. Going forward we need to concentrate our full energies on solving this matter and getting you back to REM normalcy. We can't tolerate the disruption of a corporate review on this right now. We can't tolerate the risk of your being banned from the workplace and from all the resources we have here. Consequently I'd be willing to keep this between us for now and to work with you to try to understand what's happening and hopefully see you back to normalcy."

As Sergeant shut the door behind him he felt a wave of relief. It was good to have it off his chest, and if anyone could pull him out of dreamlessness, it was Dr. Hriniak.

PALM TUNNELS

Much to his own surprise, Henry Cleverby had hit upon a hidden well-spring of spiritual exuberance. With no more marketing than word of mouth he was running six crucifixion events a week, then ten, then twelve. What had once been a fanatical rarity on the fringes of the third world was making a sudden splash in Middle America. Customers from multiple states were paying exorbitant fees to follow this simple path to redemption. Some paid more exorbitantly than others. Simple cru-cifixions ran at one rate; more extensive productions, running at prime times and including full cadres of centurions and cordoned cross-car-rying marches through the streets, ran at rates far higher. The onset of wintry weather had only a slightly deleterious effect on traffic – some crucifees actually preferred it.

Reactions in the city were fervent and mixed. Municipal officials had been caught off their guards. While many of them suffered some degree of unease with what was emerging as a new face of their city, the proverbial horse was out of the barn, and shutting it all down now entailed some daunting freedom of speech issues. One legal challenge was summarily dismissed in preliminary hearings, and years would pass before any others would follow.

Among the established faiths, the more longstanding, well-endowed and staid denominations rejected these quasi-public crucifix-ions out of hand, both publicly and at the pulpit. The result was a steady trickle of defecting parishioners who were ineluctably drawn to this novel spectacle, perhaps in spite of themselves. But the more agile and autonomous churches embraced this new visceral wonder, some actu-ally sponsoring periodic crucifixions of their own more robust believ-ers. These groups saw their ranks thickened and greatly energized as a result. Several completely independent organizations also popped up, the New Stigmatics among them. These groups shared a novel outlook, de-emphasizing brick-and-mortar churches and traditional liturgy, trading pews and hymns for the simple, stark reality of the rough-hewn wooden cross.

Calvary's business grew extremely brisk. Customers were flooding in regularly from all over the Midwest, Texas and the Deep South. Some sought repeated crucifixions as a form of periodic cleansing. Others saw crucifixion as a singular rite of passage, the Christian Bar Mitzvah, the sacrifice of Confirmation reinvented and greatly escalated. One new sect contracted for a slew of future events, scheduling crucifixions for each of its young males on their thirty-third birthdays. Another sect, this one comprised entirely of women, pioneered the first female crucifixions, wildly popular as spectator events, though the city drew the line on frontal nudity. Yet another sect organized and financed a series of crucifixion vigils, eight three-hour crucifixions providing round-the-clock coverage on particularly significant theological dates. The dramatic uplighting installed for these events became a permanent feature, accommodating a healthy volume of ongoing evening crucifixions. Friday and Saturday nights became singular happenings, with crowds of bar-goers reliably jeering the crucifees, setting a campy atmosphere that seemed oddly satisfying to both parties. Rancid fruit and witty taunts were trademarks of these crowds, who referred to themselves, quite fondly, as "the Rabble." In certain circles of this new environment, palm tunnels were now carried as badges of honor, suggesting the mark of an ancient and venerated order of stigmatics rather than that of an angry and isolated self-mutilator.

Some who had bought the earliest palm tunnels were appalled at this new marriage of their particular body art and religious zealotry. Certain individuals covered head to toe in tattoos and piercings complained bitterly at being associated with "those freaks." But by the same token, some of the crucifees were not the least bit religious; they underwent the ordeal, as one customer put it, "just for the head rush." A few customers did it on a whim, grinning down at their drinking buddies who reciprocated, predictably, with hurled vegetable matter and clever insults.

In any event, Henry had tapped into a massive and wholly unanticipated public vein. He found himself riding a sensational cultural wave, ending his video sessions by nine each morning and heading off to work as he'd never done before, leading a swelling number of associates and swimming bemusedly in the associated cash flow. He began discussions with the San Francisco based deep-spool supplier to extend its product offerings, and to extend Calvary's exclusive over several more states. Bankers vied to finance his expansion; he could not open outlets fast enough. Palm Tunnels and Calvary Enterprises had begun to open markets in tandem, building studios and crucifixion sites in a handful of mid-sized cities through the Midwest. The two businesses were in perfect harmony – Calvary would not provide crucifixion services to those without certified dual twenty-millimeter palm tunnel installations, and the spectacle of each crucifixion sent dozens of new prospects into the Palm Tunnel studios.

PLAGUE

Sergeant was touched by the single-minded assault Dr. Hriniak launched on his dreamlessness. Dr. Hriniak had begun the very next morning, dedicating himself on a full-time and fervent basis, mumbling to himself, filling his office whiteboard with calculations and flowcharts, running tests, making calls. This continued for days and then into weeks.

Sergeant was well aware that Dr. Hriniak, even with the creative license he enjoyed, couldn't possibly justify that time with Christopher Collins and the other Protocol chiefs, that he was turning in one empty work week after another from their point of view, necessarily dissembling about it and steadily undoing his reputation for both productivity and integrity one day at a time.

Dr. Hriniak cashed in chits with several of his many external colleagues, both at MIT and at Massachusetts General Hospital. Through them he was able to track Sergeant's blood as it returned to normal. Any detectable trace of CTCs had flushed within a month. And yet the flat-line sleep continued.

Research indicated with near certainty that no overnight sleeper in the Protocol labs had ever recorded a blank. REM sleep had always occurred eventually, and had uniformly triggered imprintation upon its arrival. But Sergeant's sleep was completely devoid of REM. It lacked the atonia normally associated with REM, and it lacked the rapid low voltage brain activity easily seen on the EEGs of REM sleepers. It was no mystery that his divested brand of sleep would not imprint CTC pods.

Dr. Hriniak was in steady contact with the data people at NIH, secretly fishing for any indication that Sergeant was not alone, that dreamlessness was not uniquely his. "Listen," said one top-ranking analyst, "it's Protocol that's always pushing for patterns within normal dreaming, narrative detail, and so on. It's still our principle assignment at NIH to simply watchdog for regional PDV drops, and for individual cases of dreamlessness, anywhere in the network. Our system is monitoring a quarter million weekly uploads, with primary filters on failed imprints. It's our job to catch even the slightest slip. You can rest easy that we haven't seen it yet. We'll let you know if we do."

Sergeant was beginning to wear down, to the point where he was sporadically dropping into a waking daze. He became regimented in his eight or nine-hour home sleeps, but they were producing only half that much in normal sleep equivalency, and longer sleeps proved counter-productive. Making matters worse, he and Dr. Hriniak were spending many late nights in the labs, times when the two of them could do the more conspicuous work without causing a stir among their co-workers.

Sergeant no longer had the energy for full-court basketball. His exercise became casual biking along the river, Vanessa usually with him. He loved riding abreast with her, or just back, his handlebars aligned with her waist. And when the path got too busy he happily dropped all the way back, mesmerized for miles at a time by the sight of her pedaling. He was equally enchanted by the sight of her passing in and out of the shower, stepping into her jeans, walking barefoot across the floor, sitting across the dinner table. She was the perfect dinner date, smarter and hipper than he was without ever lording it over him, forever upbeat and full of life. And while his condition hung a bit of a pall over them, it couldn't snuff the vitality that marked their time together. A current flowed steadily between them, rarely a static moment.

Dream sharing was still an important connection, though in their altered world Vanessa's dreams had to do for both of them. Now, of course, she recounted them by simple narration, and most mornings found her doing exactly that. The exchange was surprisingly rich in the wake of the suspended injections. Vanessa's powers of dream recollec-tion had been greatly enhanced over the past two years, conditioned through repeated use and external prodding and reinforcement to be nearly on a par with her short-term waking memory. Sergeant's dream-lessness sharpened his thirst for her output, and his direct experience with both her REM world and her waking world gave him a better understanding of the characters who populated her dreams, the set-tings, the sensitivities. Their extended dream sharing had given them their own mechanism of color, a particular language that evoked images and tones, emotions and narrative flows that they understood so well in each other. In that way Sergeant held some place in the dream current, bathing his arid mind in dreams it could no longer generate for itself, and slowing the relentless bake of the killing sun that was dreamlessness.

REMEMBRANCES

It was the far end of Sunks where we met after school or on Saturdays. The most common pastime required only a football and could accommodate any number of players. The ballcarrier would run and dodge until tackled by some or all of the others, then give up the ball for another to carry. This would go on indefinitely, kids in bluejeans and sweatshirts mauling and piling on each other, smells of grass, leaves, dirt, leather and sweat until dark, or until the bells of the Dundee Presbyterian Church rang six o'clock and time for dinner, whichever came first.

The Grassford household carried its own bell, bolted firmly near the back door, that my mom would sometimes ring to try to end things a bit earlier for me. It carried easily throughout our small block, and the next. But it would have to be rung with extreme vigor, the wind carrying just right, to be heard at the far end of Sunks. And in that sense, though I would not normally dream of openly crossing my parents, a prompt response was more or less optional.

We sometimes organized more formal Saturday morning football games by telephone. We would arrive by Stingray wearing jeans, shoulder pads and football helmets, and play tackle four-on-four, or with whatever number we could summon. Sunks was just right for this. The field was maybe sixty yards long by twenty wide with the uphill banks running evenly on both sides to create natural sidelines, and the elm trees spaced perfectly along both boulevards to make natural first down markers. We imagined these contests to be hard-hitting run-oriented affairs modeled after the Nebraska teams who played in the rugged Big Eight.

It goes without saying that on Saturday afternoons we'd listen religiously to those Cornhusker games on the radio. "Man, woman, and child!" Lyle Bremser, the voice of Nebraska football, would exclaim. "Look at him go!" A bit more remarkable was hearing the football broadcast in muted tones through the velvet and wood-lattice window in the dark confessional at Saint Martyrius church. On a fall Saturday, Father Dawkins, man of the cloth, was a man of the gridiron as well.

For the big games on television, like the Huskers' epic win over Oklahoma in "The Game of the Century," we'd pile into the little TV room, my grandfather Roy crazed and forever enthusiastic even in the throes of the worst pigskin predicaments, my father like Eeyore, gloomy and quickly defeated as the score swung tortuously between good and evil. Sandy Kohanek, a Dundee girl, went big-time, making it as a Nebraska cheerleader and having her picture in Life magazine. She was flung over a boy's shoulder, her long legs and perfect backside facing the camera, with "NU #1" embroidered on her red cheerleading panties as she flashed a million dollar smile over her shoulder. My buddies and I were feverish about that picture, and we were feverish about football. The days we walked home from school we took to roll-blocking any sign we saw in people's yards. Fall election season was ideal – without political signs we were reliant on houses for sale. We flattened them in broad daylight, snapping the wooden stakes, bending the metal ones at right angles, leaving them twisted and prone on the grass. If homeowners straightened the metal ones back up or restaked the wooden ones – sturdy as ever, though grossly truncated – we'd roll them again the next day. In Nebraska, it was the patriotic imperative.

PLAGUE

For two full months Dr. Hriniak did everything in his power. Having concentrated on the CTC levels in Sergeant's blood stream for the first month, and having seen no beneficial effect when the quantity had reached zero, Dr. Hriniak began a program of targeted dream intervention. He tested Sergeant both in wakefulness and in sleep for his quantities of cortisol, the stress hormone generally found to be increased during REM. Sergeant's quantities proved to be above normal in his waking hours, but not rising at all during sleep, suggesting a perpetual state that was not entirely of either realm. Dr. Hriniak prescribed a drip to boost Sergeant's cortisol levels during sleep, a dicey procedure requiring precisely calibrated and incredibly minute quantities of a highly controlled substance. After ten days of intensive trial, Dr. Hriniak concluded that cortisol supplements, at least in quantities he deemed safe, did not stimulate dreaming.

Dr. Hriniak then turned his attentions to the hippocampus/neocortex interaction, which is normally decreased during REM. This was an area of particular expertise for Dr. Hriniak, and he had little difficulty applying partial blocks to dampen that exchange during Sergeant's sleeps. These sessions produced a side effect similar to what is commonly experienced as hangover. Sadly, Sergeant's morning misery was all for naught. None of it produced the slightest trace of REM sleep or a pod imprint.

Throughout the process Dr. Hriniak was consulting with as many of his colleagues as he could, fishing for ideas, disclosing only as much as he needed but more than he liked. The window for independent research was closing. Sergeant's condition would soon be exposed, perhaps as an inevitable consequence of his and Dr. Hriniak's prominence within Protocol, and perhaps because both men were beginning to drop their guards. As innovative and dedicated as their prior work had been, this task, wandering alone in such uncharted terrain, seemed somehow too daunting. A sense of futility had seeped into them.

Sergeant's line between wakefulness and sleep continued to blur. He was never certain as he drifted off that the coming sleep wouldn't be the long one, the sleep of many weeks. Working as if in a dream, drifting from one passing thought to another, grasping at ideas that wandered in and out of focus, he pulled up the telephone directory for Omaha, Nebraska, and was pleasantly surprised to find an entry for Wesley Grassford.

PALM TUNNELS

A feature story on Henry Cleverby in *The Wall Street Journal* sparked a new wave of customers from both coasts. The article also reconfig-ured Henry's standing in Omaha, where the local media, beyond the early opinion pieces that had criticized him so robustly, had largely ignored him. His low local profile had been largely of his own making. Despite his successes, he'd maintained a simple lifestyle. He'd stayed in his original Dundee home, a modest brick-and-stucco American Foursquare on a tiny lot. To the extent that he spent free time with anyone, he spent it with his old grade school buddies. Most Friday nights he could be found in the field, watching crucifixions like any commoner in the Rabble, keeping anonymous tabs on operations. A 1957 Pontiac Bonneville in near-mint condition was his only conces-sion to luxury, and even that spent most days tucked inside his cozy one-car garage. No one would call him a bastion of health or fitness

– he was puffy and pasty – but like that Bonneville, and uncommon among Chief Executives, Henry was remarkably well-rested. He slept like a dwarf – ten hours, deeply, every night of the week. He dreamt like a prophet. And his work was no more stressful than a stroll through a palm garden; he was made for it.

But Henry was far from content. He was perfectly aware that his enterprise was built on a most unusual fad; and to a businessman a fad is a footrace, a rush to fill out the existing model, consolidate, and diversify before the market is splintered among competitors, or dries up completely. There was still a lot of geography to be covered, and he knew that well-financed competition had to be coming. And still he was finding the time to shepherd in a quirkish new initiative. He had quietly assembled a team of orthopods. They were still in the developmental stage, but, by all early indications, metatarsal tunnels – or sole tunnels, as he would soon call them – were perfectly feasible.

PLAGUE

Sergeant usually preferred the aisle seat, but he found himself drawn to the window as his plane made its approach into Omaha. The brown and turgid Missouri River wound its way and doubled back, splitting and rejoining itself in a tangle aggravatingly obstructed from view by the wing, leaving him wondering exactly where Iowa ended and Nebraska began. He landed ten minutes late on a cold clear October afternoon, rented a car and headed north, away from the city. Twenty-five minutes of driving put him at the Grassford residence, an unpainted wooden assemblage tucked in a canopy of autumn-yellowed maple.

Behind the screen, the front door was wide open. Sergeant knocked and heard Grassford's immediate response: "Coming, Mr. Sergeant." Sergeant watched Grassford's approach, surprisingly quick-footed for a man of his age. Before any time had passed, Grassford had poured beer into two frosted mugs and dumped a horde of peanuts from a large canvas bag onto the stout wooden table.

"I've done some inquiring," said Grassford, cracking a peanut and tossing the shells right onto the wood plank floor, "and I understand you are one of the bright stars at Protocol. I've been following Protocol's progress with great interest."

Sergeant was a bit distracted at the peanut decorum. They weren't on the porch. It wasn't a baseball stadium. They were in the house, which was actually quite tidy. How could he just toss his shells to the floor? "I really appreciate your allowing me this meeting, Mr. Grassford, taking the time, inviting me into your home."

"I trust you had no problems finding your way." He reached for another peanut.

"No problems, sir. It's a quick ride from the airport as you suggested."

"I'm hoping you'll see a bit of Omaha before rushing back to Boston." Shells again to the floor.

"I wanted to come a couple years back when the NIH made Omaha our third Dreamtracking site."

"I was happy to see Omaha picked in the early stages. Some of the press took an interest in my reaction, which was uniformly positive. Unfortunately I haven't been able to participate in your study. I'm outside the range of your demographic – I'm afraid I'm not much of a dreamer."

"We're under the impression that virtually no one is outside of our demographic. Surely you have REM sleep, Mr. Grassford. Isn't it just a question of recall?"

"I thought maybe so, although my case has always seemed a bit extreme. The fact is, I don't recall any dream I've had, ever. I understand that to be an abnormal condition, but it has been absolutely consistent with me – I've never really known if I'm not remembering dreams or not having them at all. It's been like that for as long as I can remember. To tell you the truth, I hardly know what people are talking about when they talk about dreams. I have waking dreams I guess, remembering things from when I was younger, way back when I was a boy, things so far in the past that I don't know how much in them is even true. But I did try sleeping with one of your headsets. I followed the instructions to the tee and didn't imprint a single pod over a period of several nights. I assume that would indicate dreamlessness rather than amnesia."

"Mr. Grassford, we have over a quarter million participants in our study and not one of them has ever recorded a blank, given some minimum duration of sleep. Are you sleeping through the night?"

"Yes, yes, sleeping like a baby."

Grassford was surrounded in peanut droppings. Sergeant dropped his first shell purposefully to the floor. "Your account of not recalling any dreams ever is astounding to me, but I'll be way more surprised if you've actually never had them. Amazing, I came here to discuss your article and your research on the Plague, and within ten minutes we are off on a completely different tangent. Mr. Grassford, it's very important to me to understand your dreaming, or rather the extent of your dreamlessness, for reasons that go beyond general research. Would you mind giving the kit another try under my direct supervision?"

"Meaning what, I have to report to some sleep lab?"

"No, no, I can do it here. I'll get you fitted out with new pods, get the kit installed properly, and make some observations during the night if you don't mind me creeping around a bit. I can sleep on your couch between checks."

"Mr. Sergeant, I haven't had an overnight house guest in fifteen years. But if you don't mind the couch, I don't mind having you here for a night or two."

REMEMBRANCES

The fourth grade girls, like all the girls at Saint Martyrius, wore identical uniforms – white blouses, plaid skirts and blue knee socks – but I would instantly pick Eileen O'Neary out of any crowd of them. Fantastic auburn-red hair poured out of her head in bedazzling Barbie-doll volume, hair that was remarkable in both color and profusion. It maintained an irresistible shine in the light of day, and seemed somehow to carry sunlight into the dull fluorescent haze of the classroom. Her complexion was the most exceptional Irish blend, charmingly fair and yet receptive to fine golden coloring in the sunny seasons. She was also the fastest afoot, and the quickest with figures, of any girl in the class. Sister Mary Helen would often pit the boys against the girls, one of each gender marching sequentially to the blackboard, mathematical gladiators grappling at long division, chalk clacking away, first to finish correctly deemed the winner. Eileen was the only girl we feared.

She was so well loved at school that year that – encouraged, prodded and harassed by Jeremy Cleverby – she would publish rankings of her favorite boys and update them weekly as we moved up or down in her favor like college football teams shifting up and down in the polls. She was able to do this with great charm and good nature, without a hint of arrogance, but rather with a quick smile and an easy laugh that made her sparkling eyes squint almost shut. I was somehow undaunted by the competition, and actually worked myself into the number one slot for a period. This honor was highly symbolic; there was no tangible benefit to a number one ranking. We didn't kiss or hold hands – nor, to my knowledge, did any of us want to. We didn't really even hang out.

I called her on the phone only a time or two during my reign at number one. I walked down Happy Hollow across Underwood to the O'Neary house once or twice if I had Mikey or Jeremy to go with me, but I was terrified not only of Eileen, but of her family's gargantuan German shepherd, Schultz, who roamed the grounds freely as most dogs did in those days. Eileen would just laugh and say, without a shred of credibility, "Schultzie would never hurt anyone."

I would see Eileen occasionally at the swimming pool, sitting in a beach chair during swim team practice. I would look for her every time I turned my head to breathe when I was swimming in the right direction (I could only breathe one way), and in her presence I would strive to look like an earnest swimmer with great form and promise, despite my rather labored approach. But truth be told, I hated swimming. I would often be drafted to fill out a relay spot among the younger boys or to flounder in an individual butterfly event. I would bring home the desultory white and yellow ribbons indicating third or fourth place, pinning them to the bedroom wall under my brother's blue and red ribbons for first and second.

Once the early thrill had worn thin I didn't much like being an altar boy either, having to leave an hour before my Stingray gang to make the early morning weekday masses only the elderly would attend, nodding off during "through my fault, through my fault, through my most grievous fault," awakening just in time to tinkle the handbell at just the right liturgical cues, bearing the indignity of pouring the water over Father Dawkins' warty hands and clearing his handwashing linen. But we all liked the spotlight masses, the big crowds at 11:00 on Sundays or on holy days of obligation. Incense duty at the high masses, the gold chain held high in the left hand, the pungent smoking urn swinging in the right, made me want to throw up; but this was more than offset by the spiritual rapture that flooded my beating heart when Eileen would kneel to take communion, my patin just touching her milky white throat.

PLAGUE

Sergeant and Grassford sat near the river, pleasantly glutted with steak and vegetables. The host was settled in his stump chair, Sergeant on a thick cross-section of a maple trunk they'd rolled into place. A three-quarter moon was up over the bluffs. The great river was nearly silent, even at this proximity, but Sergeant could feel its presence, even as it faded into darkness. The air was crisp, the autumn night coming on with purpose. Sergeant was grateful for the old-school foam sleeve insulating his hand from the frigid can of beer.

"I apologize for taking the more desirable seat, Mr. Sergeant. I'm afraid it's custom-fitted to my anatomy."

"You carved it yourself?"

"Yes, in stages. It started as just a jagged stump, but it had a little flat section that faced the river just right. I sat there a time or two, but there was a bump that bothered me, and one day I brought the hammer and chisel down from the shed and chiseled it out. And then a week or two later I chiseled some more to make the seat a bit bigger. Then I hollowed and flattened out the back. Every time I came out here to sit I'd chisel a little more. After a time I realized it was damn near perfect – fit me to a tee. That had to be twenty-five years ago. Then I figured, what the hell, I'll weather-treat it so it lasts as long as I do. I've kept up with that ever since. Weather permitting, I sit out here most evenings. And mornings."

"I have a little woodshop myself — got into it fairly recently. Not ideal for apartment living, but I do love woodwork."

"I'm no woodworker, Mr. Sergeant, but I cut all my own firewood. I live in a hardwood forest, as you saw today, mostly maples. I don't take down live trees, but there's no end of dropwood and stringers. I use a pole-saw to drop the stringers, a two-man handsaw to cut the lengths, and a maul to split. Beyond the cutting and splitting I like to bicycle for exercise — the city has put in some nice bikepaths along the river which are good for riding maybe eight months a year."

Sergeant reckoned Grassford to be at least seventy years old though his body had the bearing of someone fifteen years younger. "I do a lot of biking too," he said, "mostly just to get around Cambridge."

"I've got an extra bike that's in decent enough condition. We can oil the chain, pump the tires, and, by the looks of you, raise the seat, and I can show you around the bikepath in the morning. If you want an upper body workout you're welcome to split some wood too."

"Outstanding. I do appreciate your cooking for me." After a pause Sergeant continued: "So you're comfortable with the plan for tonight? I picked up the fresh pods and a new Podreader this afternoon. Once you're asleep I'll be checking in as quietly as I can, frequently at first to identify your sleep cycle and less frequently after that."

"That's all fine, Mr. Sergeant."

"In the morning we'll go over your dream results, or lack thereof, and then maybe you can tell me about your Plague research. I'd love to take you up on the river ride also."

"Excellent."

They gathered up the dinner plates and the cooler and walked back to the house. Sergeant settled on the screen porch. Grassford lingered inside for a moment. Sergeant expected him to return with two more beers, resolving to buy some himself in the morning. Instead, Grassford carried three heavy binders.

"Are those the transcripts from the victim interviews?"

"Nope, I assume you've already read all those. What I have here would constitute exclusive and original research material." He winked. "No one has ever read any of this. I thought you might want to look through it tonight between your shifts of watching an old man sleep. It should give you some feel of Omaha at the time of the Plague."

Sergeant glanced at the binders. They were standard three-hole punch, each stuffed two inches thick with manuscript. The top book was inscribed simply: *Remembrances.*

"I write them down exactly as they come to me, and it seems to settle me, to offset what I assume is the effect of my perpetual dreamlessness."

PALM TUNNELS

The advent of sole tunnels made the Calvary Enterprise productions all the more compelling. In the earlier stages of the operation, when feet were strapped onto a support wedge, crucifees could last indefinitely. They could suck water from a sponge on a spear (always a crowd pleaser), and if they were willing to urinate and, in the most dire of circumstances, to defecate in such an immodest and public position (and this was a bit of a troublesome legal point for Calvary in its ongoing skirmishes with the city), then time on the cross was there to be had, albeit at a hefty hourly rate. Sure, their hands and shoulders would ache like hell, particularly if they'd carried their cross for any distance. But before sole tunnels there had never been any serious health risk, never any question of anyone's passing out, and, if left unattended, actually suffocating to death.

Henry Cleverby had by now seen dozens, if not hundreds, of crucifixions and had carefully assessed the onlookers' reaction to each of them. He awarded Matthew Leverage the high honors, not out of any sense of personal sentiment, loyalty or indebtedness, but because, plain and simple, Leverage made for the best theater. Cleverby ordered a promotional blitz unprecedented in Calvary's short history, properly setting the stage for Leverage to repeat his original groundbreaking trek over the Missouri – this time to become the first man nailed through all four flesh tunnels.

Threatening weather could not dampen the size of the crowd, or its enthusiasm. The new risk profile had forced Calvary to completely rethink its medical approach, and dedicated monitoring was in place for this event, as it would be for every such event to follow. This proved providential when Leverage, after exhibiting substantial distress almost from the beginning, lost consciousness at two hours and seventeen minutes, just as heavy rain began to lash the onlookers, and well before anyone on the event team had anticipated. The large Friday night crowd, Cleverby included, was disappointed when the spectacle was cut short. But they couldn't help but feel they had seen something groundbreaking, if somewhat troubling.

Leverage was quickly revived. He refused hospitalization, and reported himself back up to snuff after two days of bed rest.

"Not so different from ultramarathoning or the extreme iron man events," said Cleverby in response to a reporter's challenge regarding deleterious health effects. Leverage had a ghastly look to him, but he seconded Cleverby's benign appraisal, while also speaking quietly of the powerful visions he'd experienced on the cross. Leverage described those visions further on his website; they elicited fervent streams of reader commentary; and, to some devotees, they became the gold standard of the crucifixion experience.

PLAGUE

It was a cold night along the riverfront. Sergeant had never operated a woodstove before, but Grassford had shown him how to load the wood and tweak the airflow. Grassford had poured in the load of swept-up peanut shells, and the fire had consumed it greedily. The cabin was basically a one-room affair, what Sergeant knew in the city as a large studio – not quite a loft – although in this case it was made of logs and set on thirteen acres of maple forest. Sergeant had not called Vanessa, oddly overcome by the notion that cellphone use was unsuited for this setting. Now that he was past her bedtime he regretted his failing, settling instead for a brief electronic message she'd pick up in the morning.

Grassford himself installed the new pods into the headset, correctly and with so little effort that Sergeant began to suspect that human error had actually not been a factor when Grassford had originally failed to imprint. Grassford then strapped the headset into place as naturally as he untied his shoes. "Good night, Mr. Sergeant," he said, then dropped almost immediately into sleep.

Sergeant opened *Remembrances* and began to read. It was written in small chunks, contained anecdotal episodes offering Sergeant frequent breakpoints to observe the sleeper, consult his watch and make the normal notations. Grassford did not appear to be a snorer. Sergeant wondered if, barring an initial pod failure – a one in ten thousand occurrence – Grassford really would prove to be a non-dreamer. And then the strangest thing began to happen.

Sergeant had installed a small self-powered fixture on the mantle. It was of a type used widely in sleep laboratories, casting a bluish light that gave observers a perfectly illuminated look at the sleeper while not at all impairing the sleep process. Sergeant's reading light was similarly non-intrusive. Grassford's first signs of REM sleep were brief – a normal observation since REM periods typically grow longer later in the sleep cycle. The pods showed no perceptible illumination, again not inconsistent with the faint imprints typical of early REM. Sergeant was finding himself interested in *Remembrances* – he had to force himself to make his clinical sleep observations at the narrative breaks rather than diving immediately into the next bits of reading. As he was rebuking himself for this slackness – "Focus, Sergeant!" – a faint green glow caught his attention. Grassford was in a REM state; that much was clear. Only it wasn't a pod that glowed; it was Grassford's pillow.

Sergeant had noticed that Grassford slept on a pillow without a case, which he'd dismissed as a small point of eccentricity. But now the whole pillow cast an odd glow of neon green, understated and yet indisputable, insistent and quietly emphatic. Sergeant leapt up and switched off the mantle fixture. The green glow was enough to illuminate the room. Sergeant scrambled for his camera and began to snap away. But no matter what setting he tried – night, flash, no flash, automatic, manual, video – the green light simply wouldn't register photographically. After a short while it was gone.

Sergeant contemplated this for a few minutes. He reviewed the photos, confirming the disappointment of having no visual record of the glowing pillow phenomenon. He checked his watch and sat quietly in thought. He made some notes, and after a long while he settled back into *Remembrances*.

Dreamtracking had swiftly become part of the national fabric. Protocol quickly followed the Dream Tones release with an expanded analytical spectrum that most notably included profession metrics. This added a whole new wave of sensational findings. Dentists tended toward Dismemberment and Entrapment. Attorneys exceeded the statistical norms in Striving, Slogging, and Debasement. Schoolteachers led the way in Slogging and Disquiet.

Protocol introduced a social media site to complement the official NIH URL. Dreamtracking donors could connect with others who'd established similar Dream Tone profiles, post blogs in reaction to the latest announced trends, and, most importantly, post their own dream narratives. These would be added to the thousands that had been quickly amassed and made available to the public, neatly sorted by tone type.

Pseudo-sciences began to grow around the twelve Tones. Horoscope enthusiasts were greatly disappointed when Dream Tone tendencies did not correspond to the astrological signs based on the birthdate of the dreamer, nor to the real time phases of the moon at the time of the dreaming. Their disappointment grew all the greater when regular Dream Tone columns began to replace horoscope columns in publications across the country. Pop science Dream Tone books provided simplified and generally unsubstantiated dreamer profile analyses, tenuously linking the dream science with the slightly more established sciences of personality.

Celebrity magazines began to feature actors, musicians and others by their personal Dream Tones. Politicians made themselves more real, more accessible to the voters, by openly discussing their Dream Tone tendencies; one hotly contested California senatorial race pitted a Conservative tending to Slogging and Entrapment with a Liberal espousing Disquiet, Dismemberment and Eroticism. Speculation abounded as to what Dream Tone tendencies lent themselves to optimal performance in the arts, in athletics, in business, and in statesmanship.

Christopher Collins steered the Protocol ship in the flow of these gale force tailwinds with a practiced and steady hand. He resisted the call from his Board to capitalize more overtly on the sensation of Dreamtracking, to charge new participants a one-time or monthly fee for the kits, or a subscriber fee for the web service. Collins was open to a different fee structure in any move overseas, but he insisted on retaining the original model in the States, holding to the scientific high ground, working through the aegis of the NIH and on the basis of federal funding.

There was, of course, no shortage of the latter. While the usefulness of such an expanded monitoring program was debatable, the public enthusiasm was politically impractical to resist. Both parties advocated universal participation opportunity throughout the country. Twenty more major urban markets were approved for Dreamtracking. Existing population centers were re-opened, expanded to accommodate the backlog of waitlisted donors. And for the first time, rural areas began to join the network, at a rate averaging fifteen counties a month.

PALM TUNNELS

Four-tunnel crucifixions quickly supplanted their palm tunnel predecessors as Calvary's showcase events. Friday night crucifixions were becoming as ingrained as high school football, in Omaha and in all of Calvary's markets. As spectator counts began to dwindle for the traditional palm tunnel events, so did the demand for that mode of crucifixion; Cleverby found himself slashing prices and relegating those to off-hours. But four-tunnel crucifixions brought bigger crowds than ever before. Eliminating the support wedges seemed to add just the right touch of squirm and writhe, though to some this soured the Mardi Gras atmosphere that had given the events their more general appeal. In any event, four-tunnel events carried huge price tags and superb profit margins. The cost of medical supervision was not cheap, and Calvary marked up these services quite liberally. The events, in their many excesses, called to mind the televised holiday parades of yesteryear. Processions down municipal streets, props, crowd control, concessions, hired extras – they all made for a costly undertaking.

PLAGUE

"Good morning, Mr. Grassford. I've taken the liberty of putting on a pot of coffee."

"I don't suppose you got much sleep standing sentry all night."

"That's true, but real sleep has been an elusive concept for me anyway. And night watch was most interesting. Your REM sleep provided nothing for the pods, just as you noted in your first trials. But your pillow – that's a different story. Your pillow lit up like a green lantern. It happened three times, concurrent with REM sleep on each occasion. I've never seen anything like it. Are you aware of anything special about your pillow? I did notice you don't use a case."

"Funny, I noticed that glowing pillow thing as a kid on occasion. It was one of those unsubstantiated memories – no one else ever saw it. After a long while you're not quite sure whether it actually happened or not. So now after all these years someone else has finally seen it. I'm pretty sure the pillows are referenced in the *Remembrances*. Did you do any reading?"

"Yes, I made good progress, and I very much enjoyed what I read, including that bit about the pillows. It was unclear from the text whether the glow you saw was coming from yours or your brother's."

"It happened both ways, I think. Mine would always fade out fairly quickly while my brother's might last several minutes longer – long enough to light my path to the bathroom and back, and then some."

"If REM sleep was driving the illumination then that would make sense, since he was sleeping away while you were up and out of bed." And then, "Surely you're not using the same pillow now that you did as a boy."

"No, but the same make. As you probably read, my grandfather sold foam products; he'd bring pillows home every Christmas, carloads of them. We had boxes of them in their original packaging, enough to open a small pillow shop if we so chose. When my mother died and we sold the house, the supply ended up with me. I've been breaking a new one out every couple years for decades."

"If you don't mind I'd like to send the one you used last night to the labs – and maybe one still in its original packaging. And tonight maybe we can try the headgear again with a new store-bought pillow."

REMEMBRANCES

One September school day my dad didn't come down for breakfast. The bacon and toast were already on the table and going cold. "Wesley, go upstairs and rouse your father," said my mother.

I ran upstairs and found him still in bed.

"Dad, Mom wants you to come down for breakfast." He didn't stir. I shyly grabbed his shoulder. Still nothing. I hollered downstairs: "Mom, Dad's not waking up!"

I ran back downstairs. My mother was alert but still standing at the sink. "Mom, Dad's not waking up!"

She held my eyes in a look that betrayed no emotion, rinsed her hands, and before she had taken more than a step I was already out of the kitchen, sprinting back up the stairs, looking back over my shoulder like a dog to make sure she was following.

She sat at the side of the bed and said "Andy, Andy," softly at first, as if awakening a child, and then firmly, like she'd speak to a misbehaving child or pet, like I'd never heard her speak to him before. She shook him by the shoulder. No response. She felt for his pulse, took note, and dropped his wrist.

She turned to me and said: "You need to get to school." Then she picked up the phone and dialed 911.

PLAGUE

Sergeant had great difficulty executing the simple tasks he had for the rest of that morning. He threw Grassford's active pillow, along with one of the many Grassford held in reserve, still sealed in its original Sandman & Sons packaging, into the back seat of the rental car and headed downtown. The light off the river bothered him, and the glare off passing cars forced his head away and his car nearly off the road. He struggled to stay on task – when the GPS announced his arrival he hardly knew where he'd been headed. Inside the shipping center he agonized over picking the right box for the pillows, fumbled and tangled the packing tape, and struggled with the labeling machine.

When the pillows had finally been shipped he sat in his car for a full ten minutes, alternately contemplating his just concluded bout of spasticity and trying unsuccessfully to remember his remaining chore. It occurred to him that he had pre-entered his second stop in the GPS, so he started the car and let it lead him, on the theory that arriving somewhere would spur the memory of what he was supposed to do there. The GPS dropped him in a Target parking lot. He walked into the store, past the food counter, past the line of red shopping carts. Somewhere in those 150,000 square feet was just what he was looking for. He began to wander the aisles. And then he remembered the new pillow.

PALM TUNNELS

Henry Cleverby was at the extreme edge of the entrepreneurial spectrum. He was somehow able to run what had become a considerable operation while maintaining specialty expertise within each category of endeavor. He was well-versed in every aspect of both of his enterprises. He knew the workings of his studios inside and out, knew the key personnel in each location on a first-name basis. He understood his balance sheets like a farmer understands his fields; bankers took special comfort in dealing with a top man so well versed in the numbers. He would immerse himself in every prospective real estate market, spending days or weeks as needed in new cities to familiarize himself with traffic patterns, demographic data, and market conditions before moving forward on any new deals. Through doggedness, intellect, and the simple force of his personality he became thoroughly versed in fields that had been completely foreign to him.

By the time Calvary Enterprises bought its first cable television and web-streaming operations, Henry had made himself a virtual expert in both fields. He personally drove the programming presentation, the distribution rights, the revenue strategies. Reality show formats served to profile tentative New Stigmatics working themselves up to crucifixion, chronicling palm and sole tunnel procedures, personal fears and doubts, and compelling dynamics involving family and friends. For the more hardcore enthusiasts, crucifixion action videos with interactive spectator input streamed to five continents, with production standards equivalent to those in use with the major sports networks – state-of-the-art graphics, top-quality video, professional commentary, proprietary soundtracks. Viewership was high, already on a par with some of the minor sports.

Henry would not waste his time discussing any further geographical exclusives with the deep-spool supplier; he bluffed replicating the operation in-house, and then, at a hefty discount, bought the company outright.

PLAGUE

"Decades later I still feel like such a dope putting on these ridiculous bike helmets," said Grassford. "They'll actually give you a ticket if you don't wear them. We never had them as kids, or seat belts either. It's all taken some getting used to."

With Grassford in the lead, they wheeled down the hard-packed driveway, then veered without warning into a nearly invisible opening into the woods – not more than a meter wide – without giving up any speed at all. They barreled through the underbrush, with mottled light and branches passing within a foot of Sergeant's face on both sides, charging into blind curves and naturally ramped bends in the path. Sergeant was aware of impressive trees overhead, but dared not take his eyes off his immediate route. He wondered at Grassford's pace – "Can I really be having a problem keeping up with a guy that age?" He noted that the path was more pristine than unaided nature might suggest, no rocks, relatively smooth, only the occasional root breaking through the surface.

Then they were through, shooting out of the woods onto a generously proportioned paveway. And there was the river, massive and brown, like molten mud half a mile or more across, swollen with rains from the endless plains upstream, rippling like a muscled beast as it made its southerly way. Its surface was layered with eddies suggesting untold obstructions beneath, and differing patches of current, and the occasional floating mass, logs and tortured branches on the long and incontestable run to New Orleans.

The path wound with the river and was flat like the river, requiring no changes of gear, no surges of leg strength, just a steady pumping in perfect pace with Sergeant's heart. Each bend brought a new vista, a leisurely slideshow of foliage and riverscape. At certain exposures he felt the sun warm on his face, watched it color his arms. He thought of Vanessa and longed for her dreams, thought of coma and longed for real sleep.

REMEMBRANCES

About a month into my father's sleep, my mother dropped me off in front of Grandpa Andrew's, helped me lift the mower from the car, then drove on to the hospital. I walked in through the front screen door. "Hi Grandpa Andrew," I hollered, bolting up the maroon-carpeted stairs to his study. But there was no one at his desk, so I poked around the corner into his bedroom. And there he was, flat on his back, arms folded across his chest like a president lying in state. I could see his arms moving slightly with his breathing. He was fully dressed, in his gray cashmere sweater vest and signature blue bowtie.

"Grandpa Andrew, I'm here to do the lawn." Still no response.

Thora wasn't due in for another several hours. I sat on the bed and watched his breathing and thought about nothing for the longest time. Then I remembered a conversation we'd had some time ago, maybe as part of some school assignment I'd been given. I'd asked him the biggest change he had witnessed in his long life. His answer had been immediate: "Cement!"

An hour and a half later I saw my mother's car through the window. I figured she was wondering why the grass still wasn't mowed. I sat for another moment, then ran to the stairs and charged down, taking them by twos.

PLAGUE

"Mr. Grassford, with all the research you did on the Plague, all the interviews, all the transcriptions, did you come away convinced that the dreamlessness caused the comas? You presented a strong case linking the two in your article, but I didn't sense you as the author arguing strongly for cause and effect."

"I thought they were definitely related. I still think that. How could I not? All twenty-three talked about it. Either dreamlessness caused the comas, or dreamlessness was just one stage in a progression leading to coma. But I have to tell you that my own prolonged dreamlessness, coupled with my persistent wakefulness during the day – and, granted, some would interpret my entire adult life as a type of protracted comatose state – has to make me believe that the connection between dreamlessness and coma is not a given, does not necessarily occur in all cases. If not, then we have to face the inconvenient question of why I haven't succumbed to the long sleep."

"Your dreamlessness is still a question mark in my mind. And by the way, from what I've seen in my two days here, if you dropped into a coma, living alone in these woods, you wouldn't get any care – you wouldn't live to see the other side of it."

"That prospect is singularly unterrifying, Mr. Sergeant."

After a pause, Grassford continued: "Mr. Sergeant, you've taken a great interest in my dreamlessness, and that would be perfectly consistent with your professional pursuits – I understand that outlying subjects need to be understood. But you knew nothing of my dreamlessness before you arrived here, which piques my original curiosity as to your motives in coming. I know you had a poor sleep last night on account of monitoring mine, but that doesn't explain the hollow around your eyes I noticed when you first appeared at my doorstep. You also mentioned some problems getting real sleep. Is it possible that you too are dreamless?"

Sergeant was silent for a moment.

"I was going to bring that up, Mr. Grassford, and I'm sorry I haven't. You are very observant; the truth is I haven't recorded a dream in eleven weeks. Nothing like your streak I suppose – and we may find some dreams in you yet – but this recent dreamlessness is taking a toll on me for sure. The bike ride today was enlivening, but I've felt increasingly sluggish and lethargic, a flood of malaise as you described it. Sleep seems to have lost its restorative power, and I am constantly in what seems like shadow or mist, a middling place between sleep and wakefulness. I'm worried about coma, and I'm worried about my partner..."

Sergeant excused himself to read a message.

"Zack: Both pillows contain an extremely high concentration of a compound very similar to Zamprotocol. This is a remarkable development, especially if they date as far back as you believe they do. More later. Hriniak."

141

Sergeant contemplated a response to Dr. Hriniak, and then a call to Vanessa, and then he lost his train of thought altogether.

PALM TUNNELS

With the *Wall Street Journal* piece, Henry Cleverby had consented to his last interview with the press. For one thing, he couldn't stand the thought of giving trade secrets to potential competitors – all that stood between an open playing field and a sudden and costly dogfight was a light going on in one capable person's head. But beyond that, Henry was increasingly concerned with his personal privacy, becoming almost obsessively so. In perhaps the most extreme incident, he engineered an elaborate – and completely fabricated – sale of his house. He formulated graphics for a fictional real estate company, staked a For Sale sign in his yard, and replaced it after three weeks with a Sold sign of similar design. A moving van appeared. Furniture was lugged out of, and then back into, the house. A transaction surfaced in the listings; it was a sham purchase by a corporate shell, but to the casual neighborhood observer it was all convincing enough: Cleverby was out of the neighborhood, and just as well. From this point on the shades on his modest American Foursquare were forever drawn, and he was not seen at home by light of day.

He took a similarly anonymous route in expanding his businesses to new regions. Concerned with southern coolness toward northern operations, especially those of a spiritual nature, and occasionally besieged with pickets on the theme of "No Crosses for Corporate Cash," he created a new entity for his expansion into Texas and the cotton belt. Calvary Enterprises entered those markets on its own, but with a marked lethargy easily outpaced by Gethsemane's Gates, a brand newly launched under a complex layering of holding companies. New Stigmatics and others took comfort in the perception that they were not yoked to a single corporate provider, though that perception was, of course, farcical. Cleverby had actually considered hiring a recruiting agency and charging it with luring away his current number two man, to run what would be presented as a competing start-up. He'd abandoned the notion on further consideration, but followed through on another initiative in the direction of anonymity and privacy; he took an individual office in a different building to run his network of holding companies. He spent the majority of his days working there alone, powering through business checklists and video games, peering through his palm tunnel or beating a rapid four-four.

PLAGUE

Grassford awoke with a stiff neck. "Mr. Sergeant, this new pillow you bought me is horrible."

"Good morning, Mr. Grassford."

Grassford sat up and rubbed his head. "Where's my headgear? You removed it while I was sleeping? How did you do that?"

"Lots of practice."

"Why did you do that? Have you already thrown in the towel on my dreaming? I certainly don't recall anything I would imagine to have been a dream."

"You don't remember anything about an ice cream shop? Pogosticking?"

"What are you talking about?"

"Mr. Grassford, I've given this some thought, and I'm going to tell you something I've told very few people. If I liquefy an imprinted pod, and then inject that liquid into my own bloodstream, the dream on that pod plays back in my head. It doesn't matter whose dream it is. After the injection I drop into a sleep, and I dream it as if it were my own."

He paused a moment for Grassford to take it in.

"I discovered this on a hunch in the lab a couple years ago. Protocol made the conscious decision to bury the discovery on the grounds that it wasn't a useful technology, and that it reflected poorly on our scientific methods. But to this day, and after huge amounts of effort, they still haven't found any other way to recover full-bodied dream content. Sure, we can track dream frequency and intensity and even the emotional tones, all of which has been very interesting and very useful. But I can go much further. You lit up a pod like a Roman candle last night, and, well, the fact is I thought it would be better to ask forgiveness than permission. I injected your dream early this morning. Believe me, the dream was real, highly stylized, with a compelling narrative thread."

Grassford snorted.

"Mr. Grassford, I re-imprinted the dream, and if you're willing I can give it back to you this morning. After all these years you are as far removed from remembering dreams as anyone could ever be, but if we do it soon enough I can almost guarantee you'll have the first dream you've ever remembered, and you'll have enough familiarity with it the second time through to know it's really yours. I know it sounds crazy, but if you trust me on this I think it can change the whole way you look at sleep. You've forgotten your dreams for so long – with this prompt I think you'll begin to remember, or at least be on the path."

"I've been doing nothing but remembering for decades, Mr. Sergeant." And then after a pause: "This involves an injection?"

"Yes, it does."

Neither man spoke for a full five minutes. And then Grassford said: "Alright, Mr. Sergeant. Let's give it a shot."

WESLEY GRASSFORD — October 28, 2029

At the ice cream store with my family. I am preoccupied with thoughts of the upcoming introduction. None of my family seems to be wondering what my girlfriend is like, or even seem aware of the rendezvous at hand. This is strange, but fortunate in a way, for they do not notice my tension.

My last sister in line looks on hungrily as the lady behind the counter goops hot fudge generously over her banana split. As we prepare to leave I notice that I have only a giant bowl of vanilla ice cream. Panicking as my party files out, I rush back to the counter, begging the lady to convert my order. "At least make it a hot fudge sundae," I say, "I'll pay the difference." The lady shakes her head coldly.

"We don't have any hot fudge."

As I stare open-mouthed, she turns away and begins to wipe the back counter. I also have a runny chocolate milkshake and I pour it in a thin long line along the length of her front counter before leaving.

We wait by the elevator on the main floor of the crowded summer Saturday afternoon department store where my girlfriend will meet us. My oldest sister holds a crate of purchased candy bars. My older brother pages through a Playboy while we wait, and my mother and sisters crowd around him to look. This is strange, but fortunate in a way, for they do not notice that my girlfriend is late.

Finally she wanders in, just as the elevator arrives. She is wearing ugly clothes, including a grubby T-shirt without a bra. She doesn't need a bra though, for her breasts are strangely missing today. I am sure she has made a horrible impression until she pulls her hands out from behind her back, producing a cute baby chicken in each. Not surprisingly, one is a little blue balloon with spindly cartoon legs; the other is yellow. My family fusses over these chicks as we ride up one floor. They seem content in our care, far from their mother hen. Minutes and minutes pass, and I ask no one in particular what the elevator's problem is.

We begin our journey with me at the wheel. Miles and miles along, the blue chick tragically pops. All eyes leap to the yellow chick, which is pathetically roasting on the back heater. It has wilted to a third of its size. It withers, folds and dies.

The journey is long and treacherous. Driving is pogo-sticking, and I am embittered.

(Isolation, Striving, Disquiet)

REMEMBRANCES

Later that fall, when my father and Grandpa Andrew had both awoken, I had an offbeat football trip with Grandpa Roy. He'd overslept that morning, something almost inconceivable on a game day, and rather than bursting into the kitchen bellowing "Go Big Red!," he leaned through the door, holding his glasses in one hand and rubbing his head with the other. Without the familiar black glasses his face seemed colorless, and the dents the glasses left on either side of the bridge of his nose were implausibly pronounced, cavernous, as if he'd been wearing them since childhood and his flesh had grown around them.

We were latecomers to the Cornhusker Hotel lunch, the cold-cut trays depleted, the mayonnaise and mustard bowls congealed and crusted. We arrived at the stadium much later than usual, well past Grandpa Roy's comfort zone, at the time when the less devoted hordes would crowd in just to make the kickoff. He lost his composure on the up ramp, throwing elbows and fighting his way up through the red-clad mob in a manner that was somewhere between aggressive and insane. There were a few angry comments, but people seemed more or less willing to pass this off as an older man's eccentricity. I trailed behind at some distance nonetheless.

PLAGUE

VANESSA JONES — October 28, 2029

I notice animals coming out of a room, so I wander down the hall to see what is happening. They are coming either directly out of a sausage machine run by a deranged-looking man, or they are somehow sustained by his sausages.

The house belongs to my oddball aunt and uncle, and their two daughters are sitting along the opposite wall. The mood is unsettling, but we begin conversation, and the discomfort begins to dissipate. Their dog, an enormous short-hair, saunters in with a bristling, muscular gait. I recognize at once that he is an imminent menace. No one else seems to notice. The dog runs at Zack. I half expect that someone will do something to intervene, but no one does, so as the dog leaps I put my arm in its path and am ready to accept the bite. The jaws begin to close on my arm, as if in slow motion, but at the last instant my uncle pulls the dog away.

The party moves to another room where my aunt and uncle sit at the table but we stand. My cousins leave the room and I am filled with revulsion and relief — it has been a chore visiting with them.

(Disquiet, Entrapment)

REMEMBRANCES

Grandpa Roy never used cruise control on the way home from the games since we always left immediately afterwards in heavy traffic. It was nearly dark when we crossed the Platte, but I could see his head nod forward just as the car lost thrust. As we began drifting to the right I said "Grandpa?"

One set of tires left the road, then the other. We were bouncing on the shoulder, still nearly at highway speed. Grandpa Roy's hands were at his sides, his chin bouncing on his chest. I thought about jumping out, and I thought about the brake pedal I couldn't reach on the other side. In the end I grabbed the steering wheel, turned it left, then over-compensated right. The corn had been harvested already, so rather than crashing through eight-foot stalks we bounced through a field of foot-long stover. I didn't try to steer any longer, but tried to keep Grandpa Roy's head from banging the steering wheel at every furrow. And then we came to rest.

PLAGUE

"That was one strange experience, Mr. Sergeant."

"Did you recognize the dream as your own?"

"I certainly did. That was definitely my family and my old girl-friend, though she was a lot prettier in real life than she was in that dream. Or at least I'd like to think so."

"I had that impression also, I mean that she was basically a beautiful girl but didn't happen to be looking her best when she met your family in that department store."

Grassford shot him a look. "I don't know if I like you running around in my dreams and leering at my women," he said drolly.

"I don't intend to do it again, Mr. Grassford. And I didn't mean to leer at your woman, but I couldn't help but admire her. The little balloon chickens were a nice touch also. Hopefully there's been a bit of a link established, and you'll begin to remember at least parts of your dreams on the first take now. But the important thing is the fact that you definitely are dreaming. My lab tells me your Sandman pillows are loaded with a CTC compound very similar to what we use in our pods. The load in those pillows is so great that it must have been overwhelming everything else, precluding your dream content from hitting either the pods or your short-term memory. My hunch is that you've been dreaming all along, but losing every trace of those dreams before waking, as a function of the pillows."

Grassford sat rubbing his head, his elbows on his knees.

Sergeant continued: "There's a lot more to digest here. First of all, how did those CTC compounds get in those pillows? They were manufactured in what – the sixties? We didn't invent CTCs until a couple years ago. I'm sure our CEO will be in a panic about his patents. What do you know about this Sandman operation?"

"Very little, I'm afraid. The plant was destroyed by fire in sixty-eight, and it put my grandfather out of work. A Mr. Sandman showed up at my grade school as a special science instructor the very next spring. I told him about my grandfather and asked him if he was that same Mr. Sandman. He said to pass my grandfather his regards, so I assumed he was the guy, but he wouldn't ever talk about the company. My grandfather died shortly after. I didn't see Sandman at the funeral, and I never pursued it any further. Sandman did have a mysterious air about him, and a bit of the mad scientist."

Sergeant digested this for a moment, then pressed on. "Secondly, while I'm happy you're dreaming, and presumably have been dreaming all along, that does not bode well for me. If you'd been dreamless for decades without passing into coma then I'd feel much better about my chances. But with you off the list I'm once again the only known living non-dreamer. Do you figure I'm headed to coma? I definitely feel like hell."

"I don't think anyone ever figured it out enough to really do much more than speculate. As I said, I was struck that all twenty-three victims I interviewed were so adamant about the dreamless malaise. And if I've really been dreaming all along, then the argument for an absolute connection between dreamlessness and coma is a lot more convincing, as you suggest. I've mentioned it before – you do have the look of someone who's only halfway here. Though I'll admit you're decent company for someone in the throes of a deadly malaise."

Sergeant chuckled and nodded in appreciation. "And lastly, Mr. Grassford, did I read in *Remembrances* last night that the whole male wing of your family – your father and both grandfathers – dropped into comas at roughly the time of the Plague? Am I correct in assuming that they were among the thirty-six? And if so, why have you never come forward with this?"

Grassford considered for a moment. "They were private men and proud men. They were embarrassed to have been taken. They thought it undignified. I tended to disagree. Maybe it was just me – I saw something noble in the state of the eternal sleeper. But they didn't want their names or their stories out there, and I had to respect that. Only my grandfather Roy even agreed to talk to me about it, and halfheartedly at that. I also thought if I were perceived as being a crusader on

their behalves then my research would be considered less objective –
although as it turned out nobody published the article anyway."

"Not for fifty years anyway. As it turned out you generated a hell of
a lot more interest by holding it back."

"I wish I were that smart. Sergeant, do you happen to play backgammon? Strange as it sounds, if there's one thing I've missed in the
solitude of my latter years, it may be board games."

"You're on. We'll play a few games of backgammon and then maybe
you can show me Wahoo."

"Excellent, although Wahoo is better in fours. After all that I'll be
ready for a siesta. Maybe I can work up another dream."

Vanessa Jones was struggling. She had a high counterpoint riff in
mind, but couldn't get up and down the fretboard fast enough without
its becoming a distraction to her. The bass parts she wrote for herself
were complex and challenging, but she wasn't out to make her mark
as a master bass technician. She was a writer and a performer; bass was
just her instrument.

The high counterpoint could easily be handed over to a guitar
player or overdubbed in the recording process, but to play it live herself without a herculean reach she would need a high C fifth string.
That posed a problem she had grappled with before. With the exception of the heavy metal guys who needed the extra lows, Vanessa found
bassists who played five-string instruments uniformly pretentious.
And she was wedded to her Fender Precision; she just couldn't see
investing all the time to integrate a second instrument to the level of
effortless familiarity she needed. When she wanted different sounds
she'd get them from her amp or her effects pedals. But playing a different bass guitar was like speaking a second language. The neck, the feel,
the distances – everything was different.

That kind of stubbornness had held her back — she knew that. Some bands function as dictatorships, some as democracies; she'd quit one promising version of each, finding the former too stifling, the latter too indecisive. She'd been recruited for a professionally packaged all-girl band — she had the looks and the voice and more than enough instrumental skills — but hated the material and couldn't work with the second-rate drummer.

Now she was on her own. She played out under her own name with a fluid mix of backing musicians. She did some studio work. She taught some at Berklee, where she had studied. And she did just enough stand-in gigs with other bands to earn some extra cash without quite committing herself.

On this day she was dead-ended, frustrated with the riff, thinking too much outside the music. She looked at her hands, something she often found herself doing in times of unsettled mood, considering them overdeveloped and ugly. She understood that this was the fate of the professional bass player, but she had to admit it bothered her. In any event, she'd had enough for the day. She put the bass on its stand, clicked off the amp, and locked the door behind her.

The weather was glorious, but she walked the Cambridge streets without noticing much of anything. A bass line played in her head, but it never surfaced beyond a backdrop. She knew those streets without thinking. She walked without any particular orientation, without consciously forming a route, until she found herself at the Protocol offices. She proceeded directly to reception.

"Vanessa Jones for Dr. Hriniak, please."

"Do you have an appointment, Ms. Jones?"

"No, but I'm a close associate of Zachary Sergeant's, and it's important that I see Dr. Hriniak. Can you please relay that message to him?"

"Please have a seat, Ms. Jones."

Vanessa sat on a leather couch that was so comfortable she was tempted to lie flat. The receptionist spoke on the phone; Vanessa could not make out the conversation. The bass riff continued to play in her head. She closed her eyes and listened for the beginnings of a melody. After several minutes she was interrupted.

"Ms. Jones, my name is Brian Markham. If you'll follow me I can take you to Dr. Hriniak."

PALM TUNNELS

Henry Cleverby was riding an incredible five-year streak, a ridiculous run of twenty-one quarters in which his businesses blew away even the most outrageous projections. The cable and the web streaming had made a geometric impact on the financial model. "The upstart midwestern body art and entertainment tycoon may soon become the wealthiest Nebraskan since Warren Buffett," said *Forbes* magazine. And indeed, Cleverby's personal net worth was nearing a hundred million dollars. The Senator's heir was not only a market visionary and an operational whiz, he had a financial acumen that far exceeded the scope of his own companies. He was an instinctive and fearless investor in other companies he found interesting. Like Buffett, Cleverby was a high-profile shareholder, not so much by reputation at first, but by his conspicuous approach. He had no regard for diversification. And once outside the sphere of Calvary, he abandoned virtually all concerns with maintaining his low profile. When he'd decided on an investment, and he decided on very few, he would buy large enough chunks of the company to demand attention, to be heard, to warrant at least some clout in its governance.

From the moment he bought into Protocol Products, Cleverby had shown a particular interest in its developing technologies. At first his keenness seemed the charming naivete of a new investor; he would wander through the labs, mingling with the technicians by special arrangement before and after the shareholder meetings. But increasingly his digressions began to derail those meetings. It was not malicious, or perhaps even intentional, but a simple reflection of Cleverby's formidable intellect, endless curiosity, and easy audacity. He began to ask more and more probing questions as to the science behind the business, questions that were increasingly out of place in those forums. Christopher Collins tried to remove this human nettle with pre-emptive phone calls, but they seemed only to sharpen Cleverby's intellectual appetite. Collins was an experienced corporate diplomat; keeping his exasperation in check, he offered to send one or two of his best science people to Omaha for more detailed exchanges. And with that they had an understanding.

PLAGUE

Sergeant sat in Grassford's recliner armchair poring through *Remembrances*. He was startled to complete Volume One; he'd hadn't noticed he was coming to the end, and then suddenly there were no more pages. He shut the book, took a look at Grassford – still sleeping soundly – and headed outside, where there were perhaps two more hours of light.

Sergeant felt a bit wobbly. The particularly short sleep on top of the compounded REM deficiency seemed to have had a particularly debilitating effect. The autumn sunlight stirred him to a vague awareness of a plan, but it was only faintly recalled, foggy like an unrecovered dream, until he saw, once again, the basket in Grassford's driveway, a sturdy wooden post with a backboard of two-by-sixes and a through-bolted metal rim with a nylon net. It looked like it was set at regulation height. And then he remembered. He headed to the woodshed where they'd tuned up the bike the day before; he'd noticed a basketball there on a shelf. A ball needle was taped to the base of the bike pump. Sergeant pumped up the ball, happily observing that it held the air and was pleasingly tacky to the touch. He stepped outside and began dribbling on the hard-packed drive. His first jumpshot felt surprisingly good. "Maybe my legs are back," he thought.

He had decent elevation in his jump, and when he knew he could stop worrying about his legs he began to find his shot. Fingertips gripping the seam, elbow straight to the rim, left hand to steady, full follow-through with the relaxed shooting wrist. Swish. He heard the screen door slam, and there was Grassford, crossing the driveway, picking the ball off the ground and snapping a fundamentally sound chest pass back to Sergeant. Clearly Grassford had some knowledge of the game. Sergeant elevated. Swish. Again Grassford snapped the ball back. Again Sergeant elevated. Swish.

"Nice shooting, Mr. Sergeant."

Swish. Swish.

"I'm used to chain nets in the city. This one makes a nice indoor sound."

"If there's anything I hate it's a basket without a net. I once bought a gross of nets, and I used to circle through the schoolyards all over Omaha, climbing on the roof of my pickup truck and installing one whenever I saw a bare rim."

Swish. Swish.

"Mr. Sergeant, I have laughably little experience at this dreaming thing – my lifetime remembered dream count is now two – but does anyone actually have happy dreams? Or sweet dreams, as my mother used to say. Don't get me wrong – I'm enthused and grateful to be dreaming – but it's not exactly fairyland, is it?"

WESLEY GRASSFORD – October 29, 2029

It is late afternoon, but being wintertime the sky is already dark. I'm on a train full of blank-faced people traveling in a strange land; I find myself sharing a bowl of soup with a nondescript but vaguely grotesque fellow, as if he is a fellow prisoner in some system of Stalinesque gulags. I am fascinated by the crescent-shaped cuts of the soup meat – so much so that I'm really not getting my share of the meal. I labor meticulously with my spoon to herd all the meat crescents to one edge of the bowl; left unfulfilled, I then begin to separate them from the soup altogether, lining them up on my napkin, the other fellow slurping all the while. Struck with the futility of my labor, I dump all the meat crescents back into the bowl, at which point the mixture becomes more of a stew than a soup. I am filled with disappointment, even bitterness.

The train howls along, its windows opaque with filth. Without warning, the nondescript fellow pours the mix evenly into a rectangular casserole dish and tops it thickly with whipped cream from a can. We share this cake in silence.

Somewhat rejuvenated for having left the train, I exit the platform and begin to run to my quarters. The night is crisp and dark, but light from the comfortable houses along the road shows the way; and though a thin layer of ice and crusted snow covers the streets, my footing is secure. My route is all downhill, so my exertion consists of simply flopping one foot in front of the other. Still I tire after some time, and in a gesture of lighthearted fatigue I flop on my belly, looking to slide impressively on the ice. But I stick like a sneaker on a fresh-waxed gym floor.

I am abashed at this failure, conscious of contemptuous stares from uncertain places. I pull myself to my feet and inspect the loosened buttons on the front of my rather expensive woolen overcoat.

(Failing, Debasement, Disquiet)

Dr. Hriniak was not a tall man, and his glasses were as thick as any Vanessa had ever seen. But as he gripped her hand and looked her in the eyes she knew that he was a man of presence. None of this was surprising to her.

"Dr. Hriniak, thank you for seeing me. I know you are very busy. But Zack has always spoken very highly of you, and I wasn't sure where else to turn. As you know, Zack has been dreamless for almost three months now. He told me you'd put a lot of effort into his case, and I appreciate that. As you also know, he flew out to Omaha on a wildass hunch to meet with Wesley Grassford. I haven't spoken with him since he got there. That may not strike you as much of crisis, but it is very unlike him, and given the possibly cumulative effect of his dreamless-ness I have to say I'm concerned."

"Zack has spoken very highly of you as well, Ms. Jones. My last several messages to him have gone unanswered, and I've begun to share your concern. I do know things have taken an unexpected turn in Omaha – not at all what Zack could have expected. Grassford himself claimed to have been dreamless over a period spanning several decades – for as long as he could remember – but Zack has apparently been able to remedy the situation. Which is all well and good for Mr. Grassford, but doesn't do anything to help Zack."

"Dr. Hriniak, I wasn't thrilled with his traveling alone in his condi-tion, but that's the way he felt he had to do it. I've called him several times now with no answer and no return calls. I'm a little wary of overstepping – don't want to barge in on him at what could be a critical stage..."

"You have my word: if I don't hear from him in the next hour or two I'll call Grassford directly and track him down that way. I'll let you know what I find. Oh, and Ms. Jones, as I'm sure you've considered, you and Zack may have some legal exposure on this. I'm doing my best to snuff it on this end. Beyond medical consultation, I've spoken to no one. My advice to you is to do the same."

PALM TUNNELS

Zachary Sergeant had another appointment in Omaha. He hadn't looked forward to this meeting, thinking the whole crucifixion movement very creepy, but he'd taken a good deal of heat off Dr. Hriniak by agreeing to it.

Henry Cleverby was a few years younger than Sergeant, but Sergeant couldn't help feeling a bit cowed by the mystique of the man as he waited in the thirty-eighth story reception area. There was nothing conventionally imposing about Cleverby; he was slight of build and pale of skin. As he rose to greet Sergeant their height differentials were greatly accentuated. But there was something offputting about Cleverby's extreme self-assurance. He was either supernaturally and perpetually certain of his judgment, or completely immune from perceived censure, or both. He was smartly and impeccably, though not formally, dressed. His hair was studied, perfectly imperfect. He looked Sergeant in the eyes and met him with an interested and slightly conspiratorial smile.

"Zachary Sergeant. When Collins mentioned you were coming I said there was no one in his company, including himself, that I considered as interesting."

Sergeant was put slightly off his stride. He offered a few pleasantries about the city and expressed an interest in Cleverby's panoramic office views, to the east toward the river, and to the south. Cleverby walked him to the windows and patiently described the sights. As they took their seats Cleverby moved the conversation along:

"I'm afraid you're a couple days too late for our inaugural Festival of the Crosses. We had them lined up all through Elmwood. It was a regular Golgotha theme park."

"I'll have to look that up."

"What, Golgotha?"

"Yes."

"You didn't grow up Catholic?"

"No."

"Well, you may have heard, we had forty simultaneous crucifixions. A hundred centurions could hardly get them all nailed up. There'd never been anything like it. Forty hired mules, a procession through the palms. It made for some very compelling television. And we had ninety-five hundred paying spectators on hand, many from out of town – filling hotel rooms and restaurants all around the city, by the way, for all the shit we get from the mayor's office. Besides the normal concessions, we sold fifteen thousand units of tossable filth at six hundred percent margins."

"Those are the bio-degradable exploding packets?"

"Yes, but don't ask me what's in them. Vegetable matter, dogfood, detritus from one of the meatpacking plants, I don't know. The spectators couldn't get enough of it; it was a feeding frenzy. I think the crucifees were a little surprised themselves – they hadn't really seen that kind of intensity from the crowds at their previous sessions. We had crucifees from twenty-one states, all repeat customers, by the way – we discounted the fees as kind of a loyalty rewards program, and to make sure the event was running on full throttle. The weather was perfect – heavy rainclouds rolled in between the second and third hours which gave us a nice dramatic effect without actually dropping any rain." Cleverby was on digital autopilot, poking successive fingers of the left into the palm tunnel on the right.

"I've been wondering – who exactly are your customers?"

"I have different groups of customers – entertainers and spectators. What's unique about this business is that BOTH groups pay for the privilege. I assume in this case you're referring to the entertainers, the people who sign up to be crucified. Between you and me, Zack, they are freaks. It's a bit of a mix really, a preponderance of spellbound and dimwitted fanatics, extremists – interspersed with some relatively intelligent if somewhat misguided thrillseekers. Most are believers, but a surprising number are not. The great majority are blessed with disposable income and a willingness to part with it, though some are sponsored by their church groups, or their own fundraisers – people actually do bake sales for this shit. But every one of them is an exhibitionist. And they all carry a serious predisposition for pain. I had the guys give me a trial run in the warehouse a few months ago, and I gotta tell you it hurt like a motherfucker. I was only up there for about ten minutes and I only have one tunnel." He waved his right hand. "My other three limbs were strapped. I said, 'Get me the fuck off of here.'

"But some people can handle that, and a lot more. I liked the business better in the early days, the two-tunnel days, when things were a lot more low key, more fetish than fanaticism. We couldn't vouch for our customers, obviously, but we always tried to take a theatrical approach, lighthearted, a bit tongue in cheek. This hardcore stuff is not so much to my taste; it's bordering on the worst kind of pornography. I'm the first to admit that – off the record – and I'm very much to blame for it."

Sergeant wasn't sure how to respond, but it was his turn to speak. "So you've been to Cambridge a few times?"

"Oh sure. I went to Harvard for three semesters. Did you know that? And since I got my Board seat I've been to every Protocol event – board meetings, investor meetings. I used to spend a fair amount of time poking around in the labs, talking to the engineers. I'm surprised I never ran into you – they must have been holding you back. Some of your products are fascinating, to be sure, and that's why I've bought so heavily into the company, but as I've said on the record, I find management a little too conservative. Take your personal case with the dream injection."

"What?"

"I'm referring to your very inspired injection test in the labs, and to management's immediately stifling the gem you'd handed them. You've got a lot of balls, putting yourself on the line, taking your own medicine, so to speak – a lot more than I showed in my five or ten minutes on a cross – I'm a fucking coward – and a lot more than the whole Protocol management team has shown with any of their products. I'm surprised you went back after that suspension, and it's a good thing for them you did – without the Podreader and the Dream Tones their stock would be dogshit. I shouldn't tell you this as a shareholder, but you've been grossly underpaid."

Sergeant was dumbfounded.

"Listen, with all due respect to your Dream Tones, we both know they're like silent movies compared to where the injection work could go. Protocol management has known from the beginning that you took a supply home with you, presumably for use in experimental off-hours injection work, but to my knowledge they've never pressed the point, never showed their hand to see yours. What's come of it, Zack? Can you reliably inject specific dream experiences into third party recipients?"

"I can't really talk about any of that."

"I didn't expect that you would, right off the bat. But listen to me, Zack. I'm in the business of delivering extraordinary experiences to people with endless appetites and the money to pay. I'm looking three, four, five years out. How do I deliver the next crucifixion enhancement? And when crucifixion is played out, what follows? These consumers want a head rush, and you, Zachary Sergeant, the individual, the innovator, the inventor, are uniquely positioned to deliver that. We buy a Zamaprotocol license from Collins, you come along with it, we're in business big-time. You'll make real money here. I'm an entrepreneur, not a bureaucrat, and I'm smart enough to know you don't pay your innovators on a corporate salary scale. We can make things happen. Your friend the musician – I've listened to her stuff. She's actually good, and if she doesn't get the backing she needs hardly anybody will even know her. We'll buy a fucking label, Zack, make sure she makes it big. Think about it."

REMEMBRANCES

Spitballs had been a longstanding grade school delight. It was common knowledge that pulling the ink apparatus out of the Bic pen tube produced a fine shooter. All you had to do was load, wait for the teacher to look away, plug the hole, aim and fire. I was always impressed by the accuracy of these simplest of devices; you could land a reliable headshot from half the classroom away.

Spitballing was a cyclical undertaking. Kids would get into it for a week or two, then drop it for a couple months. And then someone would tear off a piece of notepaper two inches square, mouth it into a round wet missile, and fire an inspired first shot. This would set off a week of classroom skirmishes. Normally one would target a fellow student sitting several rows over and several rows up in order to maintain some semblance of anonymity, or at least plausible deniability, as the shooter. But Karl Klosner changed the time-honored groundrules when he began a campaign of point-blank devastation, firing from four or five inches off the ears of Mikey Langston, who was sitting right in front of him and recoiling with each shot. This looked incredibly irritating to those of us who were taking it in, Klosner firing twenty, thirty, forty shots within a ten minute span, each one stinging off one of Langston's ears. Spent spitball rounds covered the floor at Langston's feet. We began to wonder how Langston would respond; his persecution could not continue indefinitely. He was a clever, if somewhat quiet boy, and we nodded in something between appreciation and awe when, holding his head steadily forward so Karl couldn't quite see, he shoved an entire sheet of 8x11 lined paper into his mouth. He chewed for what must have been five or six minutes, his jaw muscles flexing steadily as he endured unending volleys to the ears. Just as class came to an end and the beleaguered and aged Sister Mary Helen turned away, Langston stood, turned, and threw his sopping wad as hard as he could, landing it dead center on Karl's forehead. Even Karl had to laugh, one eye closed, wiping at the splatter.

This episode changed our notion of spitballs forever. The term was now "spitwad." Rather than shooting little balls around the classroom, we abandoned our bics entirely and began to throw huge globs of spit-soaked paper pulp, not so much at each other, but against the front wall and blackboard, where they would smack and stick, presented emphatically for the general admiration. Sister Mary Helen did not seem to possess a keen sense of hearing, the ravages of age compounded by the starched cotton habit covering her ears. She would turn away, just for a moment, and three or four students would rise in unison to heave their sopping wads at the clock hung high above the blackboard. By day's end, time could no longer be ascertained.

PLAGUE

WESLEY GRASSFORD – October 30, 2029

Our skyscraper sport drawing to a close, I peer down from my eighty-fourth floor game-perch with casual curiosity. The black streets are heavily freckled with neon citrus pinpoints, some stationary, but those inching about animating the whole, microscopic particles in search of molecular mates.

I'm tired from our game and gaze across at my fuzzy-haired friend who leans out my home window, eighty-five flights up the opposite skyscraper. It is time for me to go home. It seems like I could simply jump across to my place, such is the illusion of towering height, for I could never really leap a five-lane street. So my friend stretches across a bridge of two bedsprings, thirty feet square, joined feebly in the center.

I begin the delicate crawl, my knees gouging into the steely rectangles, my hands, monkey-like, clasping progressive sections of two-ply wire. Only this crafty iron twistwork suspends me as I grope far above the city. The bridge exists only in the pain in my knees, for my view down is horribly unimpeded. Approaching the middle mark, I ponder suspiciously, doubting the integrity of the center joint. Not surprisingly, it gives, folding and splitting.

I begin downward acceleration, plunging headlong, still clasping the useless bedspring. This is ridiculous, of course, so I release it, and it floats upward, or such is the illusion as I rocket streetward at an inexplicably faster rate. I consider my options and conclude that there are indeed none. "So this is it," I decide, floating weightlessly – another illusion – far above the concrete.

I feel my way about our sunny back yard in my novocaine-numb body. Only once have I experienced a lack of communication with my physical self anything like this – when my lips blabbered in foreign tongue after dental extractions

— and this is now my whole body. Things just haven't been the same since surgery. Surprisingly though, I did survive the fall. I am now left alone to my therapy, applying my full concentration to shuffling with my walker. Strangely, I am not as depressed about this falling out with my body as might be expected.

I grope on an undetermined route. My sport is craftily dodging the mounds of dog doo. I discard the walker, but this is not healthy sport like before. In the shadows of the scraggly bushes on one end of our plot, I come across a green plastic lawn bag. I plop to my knees to do curious battle. Summoning the dexterity to undo the twist-tie is unthinkable, so I tear primitively at the meat of the sac. It gives, and I rip away the plastic. Its contents are soiled bones that I recognize as my own; my entire skeleton is heaped before me, the vestiges of my skeletal transplant.

Marvelling at the surgeon's skill, I examine my arm. The scar runs full length, branching right up to each fingertip, but it is neat, subtle. I dig about in the bones, which nest in the soil of potted plants. I pull out my skull, crushed from the fall.

(Falling, Disquiet, Dismemberment)

"Mr. Sergeant, I think I want my old pillow back. This dreaming business is for the birds."

"Not a sweet dream, Mr. Grassford?"

"No. It was most unpleasant. I haven't had a dream anything close to sweet yet, thank you."

"Neither have I, that I can recall, and I've been dreaming a lot longer than you have, with all due respect. That said, there are some very positive aspects to dreaming. Or, at least there is one that I can vaguely recall."

"I think I prefer memories."

"Nothing is stopping you there, Mr. Grassford. Is *Remembrances* an ongoing work?"

"I'd done an entry every day for a period of some years until you got here. They've always just sort of come to me, but at this point I'd have to work pretty hard to come up with another entry. I'm not sure I could even do it, to tell you the truth. In my brief experience with dreams I'm starting to feel like it's one or the other – like memories preclude dreams, and dreams preclude memory. Or at least like there's some sort of an inverse relationship there. Seems like the natural aging progression would take a man from dreams to memory, but I appear to have just done the opposite. I assume you are still dreamless, Mr. Sergeant?"

"Yes, and feeling foggier by the day. I'm at the edge of what you called the malaise, Mr. Grassford. Did the Omaha men return from their comas in this kind of state, or did they come back as they'd been before the dreamlessness? Had they really shaken it?"

"You could use a change of scenery, Mr. Sergeant. With your permission I'd suggest we go for a ride and save that discussion for afterwards. It's a fine day for your tour."

Grassford led them out to the old barn. He rolled back the heavy wooden door, and there sat an antique gold sedan, facing forward, the letters B-U-I-C-K centered in chrome over the grill.

"It's a beautiful car, Mr. Grassford."

"1967 LeSabre. Runs like a top."

Sergeant settled into an interior that was like new. Grassford fired the ignition, slipped the on-the-column gearshift into drive, and they were off, down the hardpack, then right onto the road, joining the river on its southward path. The view to the river was alternately unobstructed and shuttered by trees that flickered across the window like pickets in a colossal fence. In time they passed the airport, passed Carter Lake, entered downtown and passed the ballpark. "This area held all the old Union Pacific rail yards," said Grassford. "Back in my day the ballpark was in South Omaha. Going way back you could smell the stockyards when the wind was blowing out to right field. The stock-yards, of course, are long gone too."

They passed by the Old Market and the site of Jobber's Canyon, now a cloyingly landscaped corporate campus. Grassford turned the gold Buick right, headed west. He doubled back past Central High School – "the old state capitol before it moved to Lincoln," he explained – past Saddle Creek and up through Dundee, turning north on Happy Hollow, past Memorial Park, across Underwood, and there suddenly was Sunks. Grassford had indicated it to his left, swiveling his head, talking steadily now, his words garbled into echoes. Sergeant heard "first down trees" and saw their sturdy trunks rolling by over Grassford's shoulder. He heard the bells of Dundee Presbyterian ring out the hour. He felt a wave of overwhelming drowsiness, this one peaceful and soothing in wel-come contrast to the nauseating and wretched fatigue of all the many weeks before. His head settled onto the gold Buick's fine and supple upholstery. He was gone, off into long sleep.

PART THREE

PLAGUE

It had been a good long while, more than five decades in fact, but Wesley Grassford had been through the drill. After a quick exploratory nudge he let Sergeant rest. He didn't poke or prod, didn't take a pulse, didn't try to slap him awake. He didn't even stop the car. He simply turned it right, heading east, out of Dundee, past Omaha Cathedral and Barat Academy of the Sacred Heart, past the Robert's Dairy plant, and on to Saint Joseph's hospital. Opting against the usual mayhem of the emergency room, he pulled up instead at the main entrance, where half a dozen wheelchairs sat vacant, intermittently spaced but all facing out, as if some miraculous group healing had occurred just earlier. Grassford set one of the chairs at Sergeant's door and locked the wheels, then undid Sergeant's seatbelt, grabbed him under the arms and hauled him across and into place. Securing Sergeant's head as best he could, he wheeled him to the front desk and waited patiently for a full five minutes, until a staffer finally accepted his eye contact.

"My friend Mr. Sergeant requires accommodations."

REMEMBRANCES

Mr. Sandman was an oddity to all of us. He was the only male teacher we had ever seen at Saint Martyrius, the only single-subject instructor in the school, and even stranger, he had arrived midway through the academic year.

From the beginning he established that he would be no ordinary teacher. Teachers stood at the blackboard, worked with chalk. But Mr. Sandman worked with overhead projectors and with dead animals, or animal parts, animals and parts that we were to slice open with exacto knives and pull apart for our scientific edification. These grade school dissections began with cows' eyes, progressed to whole frogs, and then to baby pigs. Since the school had no science facility, the lunchroom had to do. With one subject animal for each group of half a dozen kids, we'd pass the knife around the lunch table, taking our turns exposing yet another organ. The place reeked of formaldehyde.

At one point in the pig dissection Mr. Sandman stepped out of the room. Karl Klosner, who had certain porcine features of his own, most notably an oddly upturned nose and substantial fatty reserves, unraveled the intestines, gripped one end in each hand, and began quite unexpectedly to jump rope. This was shocking in itself, and his energy and his athleticism were further surprises to those who'd never seen him on his trampoline – for my part I half expected to see him break out the Thunderbutt. He jumped with great dexterity and with manic glee, the intestinal strand slapping the polished cafeteria floor in perfect percussive beats, his fatty front bouncing in time beneath his shirt. Karl tended toward bucked teeth, and now his labored breathing accentuated this trait, his upper lip curling up on itself to form an open triangle from which spewed a peculiar laughter mixed of spittle and whistles and grunts. Only after what seemed like an improbable span of uninterrupted lunchroom pandemonium did Karl collapse to a slumped position on the bench. And then, just as matters had run their most unusual course, did Mr. Sandman reappear, his eyes without expression and his mouth not visible beneath his prolific moustache. Could he have been completely unaware?

PLAGUE

Grassford had a call waiting for him when he got home from Saint Joseph's.

"Mr. Grassford, this is Dr. Hriniak from Protocol Products in Cambridge. I'm sorry to disturb you so late, but I've been trying to contact Zachary Sergeant for several days now. I understand he'd been visiting you and thought you might be able to help me locate him."

"I'm afraid your conversation with Mr. Sergeant will have to wait, Dr. Hriniak. I've just checked him into St. Joseph's hospital here in Omaha with a sudden and unexplained loss of consciousness. I assume it to be the onset of coma."

"I'm sorry to hear that, Mr. Grassford." And then after a pause: "You say 'unexplained', but am I correct in assuming you consider this a return of the Plague of Dreamlessness?"

"I think this is likely a case of that, yes. Mr. Sergeant, who to my knowledge was otherwise healthy, was complaining about an extended period of dreamless sleeps. He seemed mentally quite volatile, with periods of remarkable clarity followed by periods of extreme fogginess. He lost consciousness this afternoon – we're already several hours and counting. I understand he'd been injecting dream-imprinted CTCs over a long period prior to this, which may or may not have caused or exacerbated his situation and may or may not differentiate it from Omaha. So he may be unlucky enough to be the victim of an isolated case as opposed to the precursor of a larger outbreak. But Sergeant was with me when he dropped into sleep, and it was just like I remember it from sixty-eight. I'm no doctor, but I can't think of any other explanation."

"I tend to agree with you. I was working with Zack to try to restore his dreaming right up until his trip to Omaha. I'm afraid we were unsuccessful. Were his vital signs normal?"

"Yes, the medical people were happy with his blood pressure, his respiration – everything beyond the obvious problem."

"Are we going to be dealing with a Plague of Dreamlessness media circus in the morning?"

"I don't think so just yet. I didn't get into any of those conversations with the hospital people – I thought about it, but figured Sergeant might have some legal exposure on the injection front and deserved at least some effort to hold off the circus, as you call it. So I kept my opinions to myself. My guess is that as far as the medical staff is concerned he's just some random out-of-towner who has lost consciousness – a serious matter but not earthshaking in the context of everything that goes on at a city hospital."

"Assuming you're right and it takes a while for Zack to pop out of this, I imagine it will be a day or two before the medical people come to grips with the lack of a viable diagnosis. And a couple more before they start any discussions at the management level about going to one of the federal agencies with it."

"With all the Dreamtracking mania you people have drummed up you'd think the hospital would have to go to them at some point. But in reality I wonder if the Plague of Dreamlessness is all that high on anybody's watchlist. It's just been so long – it's become more fun and fantasy than actual medical threat. Assuming this is an isolated case, it could stay relatively quiet for a while. But this is Omaha, and my name is on record as the contact person; I imagine someone will piece it together soon enough."

"Zack has no living parents – we'll have to look into his larger family. At any rate we'll have support staff there tomorrow to relieve you, Mr. Grassford."

"I don't require relief, Dr. Hriniak. I'm happy to look in on him."

"Thank you."

"Dr. Hriniak, I know Sergeant had stopped the injections with
the onset of his dreamlessness. You should know that he had one
injection here, without my approval, trying to jumpstart my own
dreaming after what has been a long lifetime without. His methodology was quite effective – to my great amazement I have begun
dreaming, or, rather, remembering dreams. I do appreciate what he
did for me."

"When I last spoke with him he mentioned your situation, and he
sent us two of your remarkable pillows. I'd like to discuss them and
plenty of other things with you, but that's for another time. I'm glad to
hear you're dreaming. Oh, and Mr. Grassford, for what it's worth, his
injections here were all unknown to me until after the fact. All of them
were without my approval. As groundbreaking as his work turned out
to be, I wish it had never happened. I believe we have common ground
in wishing for his full recovery."

Dr. Hriniak contemplated things for an hour or two, then placed
a call to Christopher Collins. Collins was already asleep, and while he
always awoke to emergencies sharp and instantly coherent, it was a
dynamic that usually did not bode well for the caller. Collins willingly
gave almost all his waking hours to the company, but he did protect his
sleep.

"Chris, we've got a situation with Sergeant. I just got off the phone
with Grassford, who tells me he's fallen into a coma. Grassford was
with him when he dropped and personally drove him to the hospital
this afternoon."

"The Plague of Dreamlessness." Collins considered for a moment.
"Not entirely unexpected, of course, but still a little jarring when it
actually hits. We're still working on the assumption that this will be an
isolated case?"

"Sergeant's is the only case of Absolute Dreamlessness I'm aware of, and the CTC injection factor is a pretty obvious wild card in his profile – makes him a decided outlier in the general population to say the least."

"Does Grassford know about the injections?"

"Yes, he knows, though he seems to genuinely like Sergeant and is motivated to protect him from the media and any possible legal trouble. He claims to have avoided any mention of dreamlessness or plague during the hospital admission process."

"We're lucky for that. We need to keep him in that frame of mind. What about Sergeant's partner?"

"Ms. Jones came to see me today, as a matter of fact. She hadn't heard from Sergeant since he'd been to Omaha. I need to tell her about the coma."

"Do it in the morning – let's touch base beforehand. Did Sergeant sit with Henry Cleverby before he went down?"

"I don't know."

"Shit. See if you can piece that together – maybe through Grassford. I'd like to be able to deal with Cleverby without going in blind. Can we assume Sergeant will be out of it in a month or two and will make the same full recovery as the original Omahans?"

"I don't think we can assume anything, but, as you say, things worked themselves out in Omaha. I'm hoping that's the worst case here as well."

"You think about it, the whole time Sergeant was developing the Podreader and the Dream Tones he was basically mainlining Zamaprotocol. Now that he's laid up we need to get some of our other employees on that program instead of just dicking around in their lab coats every day." Collins laughed, somewhat awkwardly. "Alright, Anders, let me sleep on this, and we'll meet first thing in the morning."

"Chris, there's another issue with Grassford. He was having dreaming problems as well, something approaching a lifetime of dreamlessness apparently. Who knows why he's not in a coma too. Anyway, Sergeant did a workup on him. The pods failed to imprint, but, according to Sergeant, Grassford's whole pillow lit up during REM."

"What? The pillow? I assume Sergeant was hallucinating?"

"I was wondering the same thing. But he sent us the pillow samples. We checked them up, and, sure enough, they're loaded with compounds very similar to Zamaprotocol. We have no clue where those pillows came from, but the really odd thing is that they seem to date back to the 1960s."

There was a ten-second silence.

"The other odd thing is that Grassford began a normal dream pattern once Sergeant replaced the pillow."

"Anders, I'm going to hang up now. Be ready to sit tomorrow at 8:00."

PALM TUNNELS

To the surprise of no one, Henry Cleverby least of all, competition did spring up in the South. And when it came, it came hard and fast. Operating as "The True Cross," the company was well financed and professional, driven by Christian investors and managed by fervent New Stigmatics. Its approach was decidedly reverential — early customers loved the knowing encouragement and the gentle counsel they received. Branding was subtle but effective: each cross was inscribed with a parchment over the head inscribed "SASE," representing the Latin "Sequor acerbum et sublimum exemplum," or "I follow the harsh and noble example."

The True Cross quickly converted aura to market share; waves of follow-on stigmatics flocked to the experienced hands that could guide them, the tunneled hands of staffmembers who were true advocates, fervent participants themselves. The company enjoyed an easy facility with the Christian media. In one noted gambit, the top management team – CEO, CFO, and COO – submitted to a group crucifixion in Memphis. It was a laughable stunt in the eyes of the cynics; but it was much publicized and became a landmark event for the true zealots.

Henry Cleverby was a realist. He was well aware that his business model was in for a flogging. Spectator revenues, and, more importantly, the sacred cow of broadcasting revenues, lay squarely on the foundation of the "entertainers," the crucifees. The earnest and solitary pilgrimage had been the core of the business at the beginning, and even now those individuals fueled the rest of the enterprise. A mass defection would ultimately bring down the house. It had already begun, and begun in earnest. There was only one way to compete; his operations would have to be repositioned, restaffed, and reoriented to a more sincere, sympathetic and supportive customer approach. It would have to start at the top.

PLAGUE

Christopher Collins was more than ready the next morning at 8:00.

"So Anders, you're telling me that CTCs very similar to what we spent millions of dollars developing have turned up in somebody's bed pillows? From the 60's? How the hell did that happen? Who made the pillows?"

"One of the pillows Sergeant sent was in its original packaging. I have no idea how a pillow that old was sitting there in mint condition,

but it's a break for us. The packaging refers to a Sandman & Sons out of Omaha. I've only checked around enough to know they've been out of business for a long time – several decades at least. As to how the CTCs got in there I have no idea. We don't know if Sandman manufactured its own foam or had a supplier."

"How similar is their stuff to ours?"

"The CTC we found in the pillows is in a reticulated foam state with porosity levels at ninety-seven percent. The quantities they used were crazy – the whole pillow is essentially a soft block of CTC. Obviously Porosity-97 is a much less dense application than we've used here. But the root polymer is nearly identical to that in Zamaprotocol."

"Close enough to present a patent problem?"

"Any patent from that era would be long expired by now. And consumer cushioning products are a far cry from Dreamtracking – it would have been a shaky claim to say the least. But the compound is similar enough that under different circumstances we might have had a problem."

"I'll have legal start a search on this Sandman operation. They'll get as much information as they can without calling too much attention to themselves. As you say, we need to find out if Sandman actually produced the compound or simply bought and applied it. The latter seems more likely to me, in which case we need to track down the source. I don't know who did the internal labwork on those pillows, but you need to close the loop with those people in our building."

"There's no loop. I did that work myself."

"Good. But that's just one containment issue. The bigger problem, obviously, is Sergeant. We can't have a star Protocol employee becoming the poster child for the return of the Plague, especially when he's been illegally injecting a proprietary substance from our labs for a couple years. He's in a 400-bed teaching hospital in Omaha, of all places, and checked in by Wesley Grassford, of all people. Way too many people with access, way too fat a story, way too easy for someone to put this together and go public. We need to get him out of there. The fact is, we never should have let him out of Boston."

"We can't just yank him, Chris. He needs hospital care."

"I mean we get him care-flighted to a medical facility up here where we can keep a lid on things. He doesn't have much of a family as I recall. What kind of signatures do we need?"

"I'd be more curious about where we'd put him."

"We own a big piece of the Sanborn. We could put him in there, handpick and orient the staff, chalk it up to coma care research." Hriniak shrugged. Collins continued: "The more I think about it, that's definitely the way to go. I'll look into the care-flight and Sanborn logistics through my office. You track down whatever family is out there and see what signatures we need. I doubt they'll object to our pulling him back here. He's got nobody in Omaha."

"I don't disagree he's best out of Omaha, but won't we be creating a bigger scene by moving him?"

"We've got to get him out of there. It's up to us to make it quick and keep it low-key. It's a completely logical and defensible move. We're obviously in a lot better position to give him support here. You still have to tell his girlfriend, right?"

"Yes, I'm planning to call her as soon as you and I are done here."

"Perfect. You can tell her we're bringing him back at our expense. And make sure she understands it's in her best interest to keep quiet. Tell her you're trying to keep both of them – Sergeant and Jones – out of the spotlight and out of trouble for illegal injection of stolen substances, or something to that effect."

"Already done. She seems like an intelligent woman."

"And how are we going to keep a wrap on Grassford?"

"I'm working on that."

Vanessa had released three singles to two independent radio stations in Boston. They had quickly run up the playlists, generating a local buzz and word-of-mouth sales that were beginning to make a financial difference for her. They were also, as intended, putting pressure on the labels to step up and finalize a deal. On some level she was dead-on; she knew those recordings were the best work she had ever done. But on another level she was alarmingly unfocused. Her show at the Paradise was less than two weeks off and she hadn't even finalized her band personnel. This was not uncommon for her historically – she was accustomed to ensembles. But it was very uncommon for someone who now had recognized music, music that an audience would expect to hear played in a certain way. And that audience would include half a dozen music executives.

Phil Guy was drumming, that much was certain. He was the only musician from the recording sessions who wasn't strictly a studio guy. He and Vanessa had formed the rhythm section in more than one band over the years. Guy was technically superb, a human metronome behind a kit that reflected his six-foot-six-inch wingspan and sprawled over half a typical bar stage. He was always deferential and apologetic about crowding the other musicians in that way. But there was nothing deferential about his play. He started songs in studio-perfect time and carried them with transition signatures that put his distinctive stamp on everything he played. But for all his technique he performed with a feral edge, played like a savage; in most bars he had to be walled in with plexiglass so as not to blow out the room.

Guy was also a diabetic. He was well-loved on the Boston music scene, often playing out as Phil Guy and the Fellas, and his insulin breaks had become legendary. Initially he'd been shy about it, injecting himself demurely behind his kit. But a series of frontmen had realized the entertainment value inherent in the process, and Guy's injections were now spotlighted events. He wouldn't say a word, but while depressing the plunger with his right hand through his jeans and into his right thigh, he'd drive into a left-footed and left-handed solo that just didn't seem possible with two limbs. The crowd always loved it.

Dr. Hriniak flew to Omaha to personally coordinate Sergeant's transfer. The chartered jet was fully outfitted with medical staff and equipment. The whole operation, Lexington's Hanscom Field to Omaha's Eppley Field, the transfer itself, the flight back, would take seven hours.

Dr. Hriniak checked in with the hospital administrators an hour before the transfer was scheduled, looked in on the patient, then headed to the cafeteria for a coffee date with Wesley Grassford. The two sized each other up like newly assigned roommates, but the conversation quickly turned to Sergeant.

"Are you sure he's OK to fly, Dr. Hriniak?"

"Perfectly safe to fly, and he'll get a lot more medical attention where he's going than they can provide here. I understand you've kept an eye on him. That was kind of you."

"I come in once in the morning, once in the afternoon, just to make sure they're keeping up with everything. A patient in that condition needs a persistent advocate."

"When Sergeant comes out of it we'd love to fly you to Boston for a stretch. Everything on us."

"I think I'll take you up on that, Dr. Hriniak. I've never been to the Northeast. Thank you. In the meantime we'll keep our fingers crossed that he does come out of it."

"The medical people will be updating you every day, Mr. Grassford. I've promised you that."

"I appreciate that, just as I appreciate your coming out here personally to make sure things are done right."

"By the way, there've been a few developments with your pillows. We've been able to duplicate the glow phenomenon in our sleep labs. It's definitely a REM-driven process, very much like the imprinting of our CTC pods. The pillow materials are quite similar to some of our CTCs. From what we've been able to establish, Sandman was brewing his own foam right in downtown Omaha. Not a lot of regulation in those days, probably a sloppy setup – not a big surprise that a fire wiped him out. I just can't imagine how his foam ended up loaded with CTCs. Either it was completely by chance, or he was some kind of genius working way ahead of his time. Neither scenario makes any sense to me, no matter how much I turn it over. I don't see how reticulated foam circa 1965 makes that kind of quantum leap, by accident or by design. And if the latter, why would Sandman or anyone else even bother? What would have been the relevant application in the 1960s?"

"I haven't given it any thought in that way," said Grassford. "I'm not a science person or a business person. Did Sergeant mention to you that Sandman taught me grade school science after he lost the business?"

"No. Are you serious?"

"Yes, he showed up the spring after the warehouse fire. He looked a little like Einstein – big moustache, wild white hair – and he didn't mind the comparison. But he was no Einstein. My hunch is you're barking up the wrong tree worrying about Sandman being some kind of genius."

REMEMBRANCES

Saint Martyrius girls carried their schoolbooks by cradling them with both arms to their chests. Boys carried theirs stacked neatly under one arm against a hip. The irresistible play was to come up from behind and bat the back corner of the boys' books so they'd all splat onto the sidewalk, splayed open with their pages snapping in the wind, looseleaf sheets scattering like mice into the street. This game had an endless attraction, and went on for several months until the school-issued volumes were mash-cornered, scraped and mangled.

The Parent Association, oblivious to the real cause of the textbook defacement, responded to this crisis with a generous distribution of protective, rubber-lined, canvas drawstring bookbags, all in Saint Martyrius Spartan green. Kids actually took to the bags, used them almost uniformly, which solved the book-dumping problem but had other unforeseen effects. Before school, when we'd gather on the blacktop, we began to swing the bags by their drawstrings, spinning like Olympians with their hammers and occasionally whacking our fellow grade-schoolers with the mass of books whirling around at the far end. Accident evolved into intent, as it so often does in schoolyards, and book-swinging brawls began to break out around the blacktop. This swelled quickly into all out class conflict; hordes of fourth-graders in pitched battle with mobs of fifth-graders, all swinging their green canvas bookbags like lunatics, staggering with dizziness, and fatigue – and with considerable blunt trauma. Kids took the brunt of the beatings flush to the crania, filing into school at the sound of the bell with red swollen ears and big welts on their noggins. Those lumps of combat, on open display up and down the aisles of two classrooms, were oddly unremarked upon, and with no resulting intervention the hostilities raged on every morning for several days. Such was the maniacal fervor that, to their parents' astonishment, kids flocked to school half an hour early, to enjoy the full fracas. The durability of the bags was truly impressive; not once over those many days did a drawstring pull loose, not once did a bag split and disgorge its academic content.

PLAGUE

Without warning or intent, we had become a nation of dreamers. While the value of sleep seemed quite obvious, it fell well below diet and exercise on the health meter of the public psyche. We had repeatedly shrugged off the reports of our grossly sleep-deprived college students and our chronically over-tired workforce. But now there was social commerce in dreams. Young people especially placed a value on building their dream profiles and posting consistently high dream volumes and the occasional wacky dream narrative. That demographic group was particularly faithful in uploading weekly to the NIH, and equally eager to track the corresponding personal profile updates on the Protocol site.

This "oneirological ardor," as the Wall Street Journal called it, was in full flush at the close of October, 2029. So the surprise was all the greater when Washington dream volume suddenly dropped four percent in a single week. It was completely without precedent. Weekend staffers made tentative calls; figures and methodologies were checked and double-checked; and the matter of the deviant readings moved steadily up the chain of command.

NIH Director Nate Howard placed an urgent Monday morning call to Dr. Hriniak. "Anders, this is the first statistically significant drop we've ever recorded, in any population center. And four percent is way beyond what we would consider significant. It's a huge red flag. Our postings are due on the site in just over an hour. I want you to know you're the first person I've dialed."

"I appreciate your calling me right away, Nate. I suppose the first question is, can we buy a day or two to review the data before we go live with it? We'll be on this with everything we have, and I can have a team down there by noon to work directly with your people. I think we'd better be certain before we post such alarming figures."

"I've thought about that. Send your people by all means, but my position is that we have to post the data on the regular schedule. I think it would be more alarming if we didn't. It's how we respond to the posted data that matters. We can buy time by simply acknowledging the irregularity without comment. We'll just commit to a scheduled statement for later. But I don't think we can hold off on that statement for more than a day, maybe two."

Dr. Hriniak was silent. He was clearly not pleased.

"Anders, we've run our preliminary checks on the data – the obvious quick overview stuff – and it appears to be sound. Nothing has changed in our collection mechanism. We see no reason to believe the data is faulty beyond our not liking what it's telling us. I would rather be in a position to publish a corrected or adjusted data set than to explain why we withheld information, especially given our agency history with the Plague, something I don't need to remind you of. I'm going to be adamant on the point of full disclosure. This type of swing, unfortunately, is the downside of posting the data in a real-time format."

"What do we actually know right now about the data?"

"I'm told the number of downloading participants is slightly up against last week and against the twelve-week average. The weighted dream volume is off four percent against both of those periods, and essentially against any historical period we can access. Our tracking history is obviously not long, but while participation numbers have shot through the roof, the weighted dream volume numbers have been very, very consistent – in Washington, where we've been tracking it the longest, and in all our more recent population centers. Until now."

"Do we have a gender breakdown?"

"No, not at the level where we need it anyway. And that's the obvious need given the Omaha history. I'm hoping we'll have those numbers before your people have landed."

In the car to Sanborn, Dr. Hriniak had been on the phone with the NIH: the gender reports that Nate Howard had hoped would take just hours to generate were still not ready two full days later. The NIH system, with substantial input from Protocol executives, tracked several gender differentials, but due to a peculiar software structure could not easily apply gender metrics to overall dream decline. This was, of course, insane. Dr. Hriniak had been pushing the point since the beginning of Dreamtracking. To put it charitably, the NIH Information Technology team was not particularly adroit in that way. "For god's sake, count them by hand," said Dr. Hriniak with uncharacteristic irritation.

Despite the dream decline issue, Dr. Hriniak still managed his daily trips to Sanborn. Sergeant had been seamlessly settled and looked completely at peace in his tangle of monitors and tubes. Dr. Hriniak fussed over his care, immersing himself in the clinical details and running through huge chunks of the literature on coma, familiarizing himself with its various forms and stages, the nuances of care and recovery. He began to form his own notions; after a few days he began to discuss strategies with Sergeant's caregivers as if he were part of the team. Toward the end of the first week he sat again with Christopher Collins.

"How's the patient?" Collins inquired.

"He's stable. The Sanborn setup is solid. You definitely made the right call. Though coma care is, I'm afraid, still quite primitive, even in the most favorable surroundings."

"What did you think of Nate's statement on the DC dream decline?"

"He was a bit more dismissive of the data than I'd expected. 'We're watching it carefully, no immediate cause for alarm' – but I suppose that's about all he could say, really."

"That's a good approach from our point of view. Assuming the dip was a glitch and doesn't get any worse, I don't think there'll be too much fuss. But people are paying attention now, and we're week-to-week on this thing. If Monday's release shows more decline, the press is going to be riding posse, and Congress will be right behind them. In that case we're going to need some answers. Do your people have any theories we can work with yet?"

"No, nothing."

"Of course it's not our fault if dreaming starts plummeting across the board. Hell, we should be commended for setting up the warning system. But the point is that a lot of money has been spent without really figuring this thing out. I know I'm catastrophising here, but we'll be caught up in a heavy backlash if the Plague actually resurfaces and people start dropping the same as if we hadn't done any of this monitoring. At least the Feds would have had time to set up the coma centers. That's a strong argument in our favor – all that preparation with the centers will take the pressure off the hospitals, and provide centralized, specialized and efficient coma care."

"You've been rehearsing."

"Our PR people are relentless. What would the coma center staff have to do for these folks anyway? Turn them over once in a while? Change their diapers?"

"They wouldn't be in diapers, Chris. They'd have urinary catheters for one thing. There are concerns with nutrition and fluid balance, pressure area care as you mentioned, physiotherapy for the muscles and joints, and a host of other issues around ventilation, circulation, infection control, and so on."

"Even if the victim count got big, like in the thousands, they'd come out of it in a month or so, right?" Silence. "Alright, I know you can't answer that."

It was probably for the best that the Washington gender reports had been slow in coming. When they did surface late in the week, they showed precisely what Dr. Hriniak had feared: the weighted dream volume shortfall was completely on the male side of the spectrum. Men were off an average of eight percent. Women were flat. All completely in keeping with a hypothetical return to the Plague of Dreamlessness.

Dr. Hriniak stewed privately all weekend, but Monday's dream volume report, in conjunction with the delayed gender announcement, was enough to produce a more general alarm. Weighted PDV had dropped another four percent, doubling the two-week total. This decline was also presumed isolated to the male population, indicating an aggregate sixteen percent decline in that group. Worse, certain individuals were down more than half; and this was morbidly clear to them as they tracked themselves on line in weekly real time. Nate Howard was under fire, facing the aggressive national media he'd been fortunate to dodge the week before.

"Mr. Howard, do you have any idea why Washington is the only population center showing a dream decline?"

"We don't have an answer for that."

"Is it expected to spread to other population centers?"

"We have no indication that this phenomenon moves in that way. Assuming the Omaha model is relevant here, which is by no means certain, the original cases never expanded out of their initial and relatively contained geographical base. As has already been mentioned, everything is perfectly normal everywhere else we monitor, and our network in this country is quite extensive thanks to the aggressive growth plan we've executed in less than two years, and to strong support from both Congress and our volunteer base from coast to coast."

"What advice are you giving those individuals who are showing the most dramatic declines?"

"We have hotlines set up and web-based chat centers available. We have reports of slightly increased levels of fatigue that seem related to REM sleep deprivation, which we are equating to dream decline, though we have no way to quantify fatigue beyond the numbers of people reporting it. We believe that more sleep may be only slightly helpful, that the decline in sleep equivalency is only superficially offset, if at all, by increased sleep volume. But this is all very preliminary. We are advising those in dream-decline to continue with their lives more or less normally, but to be diligent about getting a full night's sleep and to endeavor to minimize stress and stress-producing activity."

"If the weekly decline continues at a four percent rate, with men declining at double the overall rate, Washington men will be dreamless in just over ten more weeks. Will the centers be ready in that case?"

"We will have some centers ready, yes."

"Do you have any indication as to how many people are undergoing substantial dream decline, and how many of those might be expected to drop into coma?"

"Let's be clear that it's only speculation at this point that anyone experiencing dream decline is heading to coma or any other health degradation. To answer your question, twenty-four percent of our monitored Washington-based males are experiencing dream decline. The breakdown by percentage decline is included in your press notes."

"Mr. Howard, if twenty-four percent of the males are responsible for all of the decline, doesn't it follow that those individuals will reach Absolute Dreamlessness far sooner than ten weeks from now? I see in the notes that a substantial sampling is already over fifty percent degraded."

"Yes, that follows. We are moving as fast as we can."

"The population of Washington, DC is roughly 600,000. If we eliminate minors we're down to just under 500,000. That would indicate almost 250,000 adult males. If, as you say, a quarter of them are affected, that would potentially make for over 60,000 people headed to coma, just with the current infection numbers. Could the centers possibly handle that?"

"We're getting a little ahead of ourselves here. First, it's just not valid at this point to call this dream decline an 'infection'. Second, the Omaha Plague put only thirty-six men into coma, a statistically insignificant percentage of the adult male population of that city. The answer is no, we are not going to have capacity for 60,000 victims in our initial care centers. But we will have a rapid expansion capability if and as needed."

"The population of the Washington Metropolitan Area is over 6,000,000. Has a quarantine been considered to protect that larger base?"

"Let me repeat: We have no indication that this phenomenon is spreading out of the District or that it is an imminent threat to do so. We have seen no incidents of dream decline outside of the District itself. Zero. We are nowhere near certain that this wave of dream reduction even entails any substantial health problems. We are monitoring this diligently and preparing for multiple scenarios, but anything as dramatic as a District-wide quarantine would be extremely premature at this point."

"Do we have any idea why only adult males were affected in Omaha, or are being affected now?"

"No, we do not."

"Mr. Howard, do we really know anything more about the Plague of Dreamlessness today than when your agency first disclosed it almost four years ago?"

"Look people, there are a host of diseases and other medical phenomena that we haven't solved. The Plague of Dreamlessness is just one of them. No one ever claimed to have fully understood what happened in Omaha, and certainly no one ever claimed to have a cure, or even a plan to prevent a recurrence. What we signed on for was a system of monitoring, and perhaps that system is serving us well right now. Let me stress that we don't know that this dream decline will continue to worsen, or that it will lead to incidents of coma or other serious health problems even if dream volume drops to zero for some individuals or groups. What we're seeing resembles Omaha in that it appears to be regional and gender-based; no one is denying that. If there is an outbreak of comas we will be prepared with specialized care centers with specially-trained staff. Keep in mind that Omaha carried a one hundred percent recovery rate." If the Plague of Dreamlessness is really what we're looking at, history indicates that it simply runs its course. That's all for today. Thank you."

Something akin to panic was tangible in the halls of Protocol. The more the various department heads pressed Dr. Hriniak, the more he retired into himself. Given his beloved and revered status in the company, this had a damaging effect on the group morale. He resisted management pressure more forcefully than he had done before. "I don't have any answers for this. We can sit around the conference table all day long and we won't come up with anything beyond speculation. None of us have been through it, and there's only a smidgen of historical data. Every day now is an education, brings us one step closer to real knowledge. The best way to learn at this point is to simply observe."

From management's point of view, his protégé's coma had taken something out of Dr. Hriniak. "He was closer to Sergeant than any of us had imagined," said one member of Christopher Collins' inner circle.

When Dr. Hriniak wasn't at Sanborn he was badgering the beleaguered NIH Information Technology department. He ordered increasingly thorough sorts for the Washington victim data, and as the reports streamed in, he read and charted them in seclusion, more office-bound than had been his established style. Beyond his NIH communications he sought no consultation. He initiated no meetings, attended very few. He left calls unanswered and unreturned. But late one afternoon he picked up the phone and called Wesley Grassford.

"Wes, it's Anders Hriniak here. Hope I'm not disturbing you."

"Hello, Anders. I just got off the phone with our friends at Sanborn. Sergeant seems to be resting comfortably."

"As a matter of speech only. The truth is, I've got the staff working him practically around the clock -- physical manipulation, deep tissue massage, electrostimulation. I'm afraid it's not a very restful sleep."

"More power to you, Doctor. They've mentioned that you've been quite regular in your visits."

"With only one patient in their care I don't think it's too much to expect them to keep him moving. I do think he may be the most well-exercised coma victim in history. Listen, Wes, the reason I called...I could use a little consultation up here, a little perspective, a sounding board. I know we discussed your coming up after Sergeant awoke, but is there any way you would consider moving that up some? I'd like to have you here now."

"And I'd like to be there. But I've been having a problem with stomach pain and would be a little worried being away for too long."

"Persistent problems?"

"Yes."

"Have you had it checked out?"

"No."

"All the more reason to come out now, assuming you're well enough to fly. I can set up all the tests for you here."

Grassford considered for a moment. "Yes, I'm fine to fly. And that would probably be helpful."

"I'll have my people book you for tomorrow."

REMEMBRANCES

None of us were quite sure why the impending sacrament of Confirmation called for so much fuss. Baptism, of course, was for babies. First Communion and Confession had required a bit of instruction certainly. But this was on a completely different level. We each had to pick a confirmation name based on a particular saint, and to be prepared to explain the choice with a testimonial as to our inspiration. The Archbishop of Omaha would be personally administering the event, which meant that we had to look particularly smart, and actually had to practice, like a football team. In the afternoons we'd line up and scale the stairs from the school to the church. There we'd run through our entry march, our cues, and our sequential processions to the altar where we were to become Soldiers of Christ. These practices were monitored not only by our own Sister Mary Helen, but by other nuns who somehow managed to leave their classrooms to be available for us at these moments. Sister Mary Catherine, a fifth grade teacher, would always appear, standing tall and bristling with vigilance.

The sacrament was to be punctuated with a symbolic slap to the cheek, delivered as one knelt at the altar rail. The nuns were extremely thorough in this part of our preparation. Sister Mary Catherine, playing the archbishop, was particularly vigorous in this regard, slapping our little faces with a zeal that could be heard throughout the church. We all vied to take our slaps in silence, except for Karl Klosner, who liked to reel back and voice an overpained exhalation – "Ooooh!" – to the muffled delight of all. Sister Mary Catherine took note of this, and would give him something extra in each of the next several practices.

The sacramental day arrived some weeks later, pews packed with uncomfortably dressed parents, grandparents, and siblings, special family lunches to follow. We filed in on cue, executing our marching maneuvers exactly as we'd drilled, and poured flawlessly into our designated pews.

It was the first time most of us had ever seen the archbishop. We sized him up as he began to celebrate the Mass; he was resplendent in the dazzling vestments of his station, but beneath them he displayed a languid manner, and he spoke in unsettling wispy tones. We sang:

> Sons of God, hear His holy word,
> Gather round the table of the Lord.
> Eat His body, drink His blood,
> And we'll sing a song of love.
> Hallelu, hallelu, hallelu, halleluia.

At the appointed sacramental moment, as the first of us took our places at the front kneeler, all eyes were on the archbishop. He paused, then opened with a feeble two-fingered tap on the cheek, and then another, moving down the aisle without delivering a single righteous blow. We felt shocked and betrayed. He was taking untold liberties with symbolism, shirking his sacred duty. "What a fag," hissed Karl Klosner, audible through several rows of pews.

PLAGUE

Dr. Hriniak picked up Wesley Grassford personally, and they headed directly from the airport to Sanborn Critical Care Center. They passed through security and headed down the hall toward Sergeant's room. Grassford noticed that their strides were in unison – not military style, but as if they'd been strapped together in a three-legged race. Then he heard the raspy tones of amplified music. He thought he had to be hallucinating. What would a live band be doing in a health care center?

It wasn't a live band at all, but rather a single bass guitar in the hands of a striking woman standing near the window. Her eyes were closed, her body undulating almost imperceptibly while her fingers ran up and down the fretboard, sending a wave of complex but gentle rhythm through the compact practice amp and flooding the otherwise sterile hospital room.

"This is Sergeant's good friend Vanessa Jones," Dr. Hriniak said by way of introduction. Vanessa's eyes popped open without losing a beat in her fingers. "And this is Wesley Grassford, just arrived from Omaha."

"It's nice to meet you, Vanessa." Grassford noted a flash of internal irony – he had just evened the score with Sergeant for having leered at his dream woman. Vanessa was an irresistible presence, filling the room as much with her person as her music.

"And you, Mr. Grassford. You probably think this is a little weird. Dr. Hriniak was kind enough to prevail on the Sanborn staff to allow music in the room."

"The dedicated live music does seem to stimulate some activity in Sergeant's brain," said Dr. Hriniak. "You can see some movement on the monitor there. In fits of optimism I imagine it is a happy place for him, and I think it may provide a nice change of pace from all his muscle-group work."

"I'm sure you're right," said Grassford.

"How was he toward the end, Mr. Grassford?" Vanessa asked.

"I found him to be a delightful young man, but I could see he was struggling. He was drifting in and out. As I said to Dr. Hriniak, he had moments of tremendous clarity interspersed with moments of profound confusion. His backgammon and his basketball were both impeccable, however."

Vanessa smiled. She continued to play, modulating up a step.

Grassford continued. "We had a nice afternoon biking along the Missouri. I think he liked that. He spoke fondly of biking along the Charles with you."

"I wish we were there right now. They're doing a good job of keeping him exercised, but I can already see him dropping muscle mass. He looks peaceful and relatively healthy, but, from what I've read, if he's out too long his prospects aren't good."

"His prospects may be better than those of any coma victim who's come before him," said Dr. Hriniak. "None of us know how long it will take Zack to come out of this, but there's been a lot of progress in keeping comatose patients physically viable over longer periods of time. Keep the faith. What do you say the three of us get lunch?"

PALM TUNNELS

Much of Henry Cleverby's to-do list was now consumed with repositioning his companies. With every passing day he was losing the grassroots business. The more spiritually-oriented customers were pouring like kernels of grain into the True Cross hopper. And the data indicated that customers whose profiles identified them as primarily "spiritual/ mystical" as opposed to "thrillseeking/theatrical" made up almost ninety percent of the market. Worse, The True Cross was making disturbing gains on the broadcasting side, recruiting and landing oustide talent, and availing itself of the well-established Christian broadcasting network. That network had been historically factious, loosely affiliated at best. But it was fully unified in this case, in its collective eagerness to grab viewership while rejecting the vile approach of both Calvary Enterprises and Gethsemane's Gates.

The adjustments required were obvious to Henry, and their execution was more or less elementary – tedious but relatively straightforward matters of personnel realignment, protocol revision, training, and marketing. But Henry's personal restructuring, the reorientation of his leadership, seemed to stagnate on the list, always carried forward, never scratched out – a to-do list eyesore.

PLAGUE

Midway through the meal Wesley Grassford cleared his throat. "Well, Anders, I imagine all these dream decline headlines have thrown quite a twist your way."

"You're right about that. And you'd think a budding national public health crisis and a co-worker in coma would be enough. I'm also dealing with the mystery of the magical pillow. How the hell did CTCs get into a 1960s bed pillow? Who went back in time with my patent?"

"At the risk of inserting myself where I'm not wanted..."

Grassford paused, as if waiting for permission. Dr. Hriniak gestured for him to continue.

"It's clear that Sandman's pillows are a point of heavy consideration for you. As an inventor you are naturally curious and proprietary, and I'm sure that's the overwhelming sentiment at Protocol. But maybe you need to let that one go for now. I don't see that the question of how CTCs got into our pillows sixty years ago, if you could ever even answer it, helps at all with the two main problems – Zack's coma and the Washington dream decline. It seems to me that what's important to consider is what impact the CTCs had when they got there."

"What do you mean?"

"Well, you and Sergeant both assumed that CTCs were the cause of his problem – a case of extreme exposure obviously, but the assumed cause nonetheless. And now you've identified compounds of a very similar makeup in pillows circulating around Omaha just prior to the outbreak."

Vanessa suddenly popped out of her silence: "And, by definition, all the Washington men that we know are in dream decline are using CTC headgear. Jesus, Anders. Are you guys tracking the problem or causing it?" This was met with a stunned silence – they were left with the clinking and the echoed conversation of a quiet restaurant.

Dr. Hriniak finally spoke: "Hold on, everybody. A common denominator should not be confused with a cause. Let's get back to Omaha for a minute. Wes, you're correlating the Omaha morbidity with Sandman customers? So is it your position that every victim was using the pillows?"

"We'll never know. But I can tell you for certain that three of them were."

"How do you know that?"

"They were family members. My grandfather sold for Sandman, brought the pillows home by the dozen. We all had them. That's how I had such a supply that I'm still going through them fifty years later."

Jones: "And Zack slept on one when he stayed at your house?"

Hriniak: "You had three family members with the Plague?!"

There was another silence while everyone regrouped. Again Dr. Hriniak was the first to speak, and did so very softly:

"If the pillows were the cause in Omaha, and, again, all we have is a circumstantial correlation, why do you think the victim count was so low? We think the thirty-six number is pretty accurate. The NIH has done historical searches of the area hospital records just to be sure, and they didn't find any other unexplained coma admissions at the time of the plague, or immediately preceding or following. Was Sandman's distribution that sparse, or is only a fraction of the population susceptible?"

Jones: "We know only males were affected in Omaha, and that's been consistent in Washington too. So we automatically assume that the exposure pool is reduced by just more than half. And not all of your Washington male donors are showing declines."

Hriniak: "More like a quarter of them."

Grassford: "Did you happen to notice the Sandman packaging before you worked up the pillow? It always seemed to me they were playing up the 'Sandman' theme in a way that seemed catered to children. My guess is that they marketed that product primarily that way. That would reduce Sandman's reach among adult males."

Hriniak: "Interesting. That would add even more fuel to the theory that children were somehow immune from the Plague."

Jones: "Maybe because they are the most instinctive and resilient dreamers."

Hriniak: "And theoretically they could have built a CTC immunity that they carried into adulthood. That would explain Wes's history."

Grassford: "I hadn't thought of that. Before he brought back my dreaming Sergeant and I were scratching our heads over why I hadn't ever gone the coma route. Or perhaps it was really only me who was confused. He's the smart one."

Hriniak: "Don't sell yourself short, Wes. You and Vanessa may well be the smartest people in the room." He took off his glasses and rubbed at his eyes.

There was another long silence before Vanessa spoke again: "Anders, have you been able to sort the pool of declining donors by seniority? I mean by how long they've been on the Dreamtracking program, how long they've been wearing the headsets. I'm wondering if you'd find that the men showing the dream declines have all been with the program since the beginning and have therefore had the longest periods of exposure to the CTCs. If that's the case it might explain why Washington's rate of effect is only twenty-five percent right now, and why no other population center is showing a problem just yet."

REMEMBRANCES

Mr. Sandman encouraged independent science projects that spring. Mikey, Jeremy, and I fell in with Chris Carmen, whose father was a dental surgeon and took an outsized interest in our enterprise. Dr. Carmen was more than happy to outfit us with medical supplies that were completely out of line for fourth-graders – scalpels, syringes, even anesthetic drugs. Somehow the idea had arisen for us to perform skin grafts on white lab rats. This seemed like an outrageous plan to me, but sure enough, when we met on a Saturday a room in the Carmen house had been cordoned off for surgery. Supplementary lighting had been installed; a glossy waterproof mat covered the table; and implements were professionally arranged.

Two rats paced nervously in the kind of glass tank where I was used to seeing fish swimming around underwater houses, or turtles crawling on unnaturally colored pebbles. I had always hated rats – my domestic chores included taking out the garbage, and lifting the lid off a can always bore the risk of uncovering a big gray rat, both of us airborne before I'd had a chance to holler and slam the lid back down. But these rats were so clean, bright white really, with cute little whiskers and twitchy little noses. I knew this project would prove nothing the least bit scientific; it was nothing more than sanctioned mutilation.

Chris did all the work, really; his father offered the rest of us roles in a halfhearted way, which we were all more than happy to decline. Dr. Carmen put on his rubber gloves and pounced with both hands into the tank, gripping a rat, lifting it out, and pinning it forcefully to the mat, one hand around the head and front legs, the other around the tail and rear quarters, exposing the midsection so Chris could shave off a patch of fur. He used an electric razor of a type I'd seen Joe Namath plug on television commercials. He then inserted the needle, anesthetizing each rat; and when they were motionless he shaved each rat more carefully, cleanly exposing the left side of each. Taking up the scalpel and tweezers, he snipped a patch of skin the size of a postage stamp out of each of them. He and his father then sewed the skin of one rat over the hole on the other, making crude black sutures and tying simple square knots.

None of us could wait to ride our Stingrays back home, which we did without much conversation. As I pulled up to Cuming Street I saw Mr. McGroarty in his usual station, watering his lawn with a hand-held hose, standing utterly motionless. But he happened to look up from under his hat as I pedaled by, just the slightest move of his head, and for the first time in my life I gave him a wave. Since I was riding uphill I had to grab my handlebar again pretty quickly, so it was kind of a half wave. But I'm pretty sure he saw it that way and gave me a half a waggle of the hose back.

Over the next couple days Mikey, Jeremy, and I dutifully checked in at the Carmens' house after school. The patches on both rats had turned brown, and they weren't moving much beyond their chests heaving for breath. Mercifully, both were dead within the week.

PLAGUE

Christopher Collins was in a lather when Dr. Hriniak entered his office. "We just got off the phone with Sergeant's sister, the one who signed off on his transfer. She'd just gotten a call from a hospital official in Omaha. They've become aware of the Grassford connection, and they know Sergeant flew to Boston, but they apparently haven't connected him, or you, with Protocol as yet. Sergeant's sister is a tough woman, and we'd coached her up. She told them she wouldn't comment on her brother or any family issues, and that if any confidential medical records were released to the press or anyone else without authorization they'd be staring down the barrel of a big-time lawsuit. I assume they've been trying to contact Grassford as well."

"He's not taking any calls from Omaha."

"Are you feeling alright? You look like hell. Anyway, I think we're going to have to give Sergeant up at this point. The Plague story is getting way too big – there's no way you and I can take on this kind of exposure. We need to go on record as having voluntarily come clean on Sergeant, and we need to do it before Monday, in case the reports show a third straight drop and this thing really gets ugly. We call Nate Howard, tell him we couldn't believe what had happened to Sergeant, we brought him here to see for ourselves and to give him the best care. We tell him that Sergeant had been suspended once for unauthorized injections, and that he had recently admitted to a long string of subsequent injections, and that we assume those injections to be the cause of his current health problem. We tell him we initially considered it an internal employment issue and a private health matter, but in light of the recent public health concerns we thought it our duty to lay it all out."

As Collins had feared, the Monday reports indicated a third consecutive weekly decline. The other shoe had dropped, resoundingly. Nate Howard didn't dare handle this one on his own. His announcement was held for consultation with several layers of superiors, and when it did come it had been carefully scripted. An additional six percent drop brought the three-week weighted PDV decline to fourteen percent, double that among males. Worse, over eight hundred men had generated at least two consecutive nights of zero dream volume by week's end, indicating a probable shutdown of their dream function.

With these stunning revelations Plague of Dreamlessness planning expanded quickly beyond the NIH, to more powerful forces within government. The Pentagon took several pre-emptive steps, many of them pertaining to military command-and-control contingencies. Congress began similar early stage preparations for emergency relocation.

Howard's subsequent discourse with the media grew more frequent, but far terser, shifting to a more logistical aspect, the race to establish care centers on a much faster pace than had been originally projected. Three mid-sized facilities had already been requisitioned and were being fitted with beds, and with monitors and equipment suited for coma care. The fallback plan focused on the Washington Convention Center, which offered over two million square feet in the heart of the city on 7th Street, N.W. Plans showed a capacity exceeding ten thousand beds, nowhere near sufficient for the worst case scenarios, but a heavy contingency for an outbreak that was purely theoretical. Convention organizers received notice of possible government-ordered cancellations.

Federal authorities commandeered the entire release of a new generation of Robocorp products that were particularly suited to coma care. These robotic units, manufactured under the brand name Robo-Stim, delivered regular electro-stimulation to various muscle groups, one application targeted to respiration, with the effect of making coma victims more viable upon awakening. Military personnel, medical reserves in particular, mobilized for Robo-Stim and conventional coma-care training. RoboCorp announced the pending introduction of another related product, the Robo-Cycle, which would add a recumbent cycling feature; directed and robotically coordinated stimulation of the lower body muscle groups could deliver a cycling workout to a strapped-in coma victim. "Forget muscle atrophy – they'll come out in better shape than they went in," claimed bombastic CEO Judy Jenkins, a competitive age-group cyclist herself.

Jenkins later apologized for the flippant tone of her remarks, but her slightly disrespectful and opportunistic manner reflected a national split in public opinion on the issue. Huge clumps of the population considered the oncoming of the Plague to be dead real and a serious threat to the country. Equally huge clumps refused to take the matter seriously, considered it an intellectual construct that had been milked for profit and allowed to run amok, representing everything that had gone wrong with a government that had simply lost touch. Geographic splits were roughly along traditional red state/blue state lines, with Nebraska perhaps serving as the exception.

There was no split in the capital. Panic in the District was both tangible and universal. Never before had medical victims been able to track their afflictions on-line in a reliable, government sanctioned, and precisely quantified format. Hundreds of seemingly healthy men took what they claimed as medical leave, many in positions of prominence or promise within government, business, or the national media. Many dozens left the city in direct contravention of the official guidance, sacrificing the prospect of specialized care in favor of reducing exposure to possible infectious or environmental causal factors. Morbid office pools speculated as to who would be the first to drop.

The media criticized Nate Howard, and perhaps rightly so, for over-investing in monitoring and under-investing in researching a cure. Howard fiercely defended his course of action. "We haven't even had access to this thing. How can we even begin to cure it if we don't have it among us to observe and to study? It is an absurd notion. This phenomenon, or Plague, or whatever you want to call it, has been out of circulation for fifty-plus years. I'm not saying we can fashion a quick cure if it does pop up again, but at least in that case we'll have a fighting chance, employing established methodologies with real samples and real patients."

Privately, Howard complained that "this really should have been a CDC (Centers for Disease Control) problem. That's what the CDC is for. But they sit down there in Atlanta and don't do a goddamn thing while we take the beating."

PALM TUNNELS

Henry Cleverby found himself wearing down. He'd been driving his brain like an old prairie plow mule, all day, every day, for months and years on end. Snared in a perpetual stream of work and video, he'd had no down time beyond sleep. Now the lines of sleep were blurring; it had all become more than he'd bargained for. He'd gone into business in the simple quest of personal cash flow, but he'd passed that milepost so long ago he could hardly recall it. It had even been fun, he had to admit, when he'd had open field in front of him, great swaths of market frontier to survey and claim at his convenience. But now he was playing defense, and doing so on several fronts.

The True Cross was feeding on his corporate flesh, swallowing market share faster than Henry had ever developed it. He found this disturbing, but, in isolation, essentially manageable. The personal attacks, on the other hand, were increasingly difficult to compartmentalize.

He'd been a human pachyderm for years, an elephant facing steady small caliber fire, and he'd dropped now to one knee. More and more he was looking at life through his palm tunnel. He'd taken to driving that way – oncoming drivers were horrified to see a man operating a vehicle with his hand over his eyes.

Henry had never claimed any moral high ground – nothing even close to that. But now he was being villainized by offenders who, in his mind, were far worse than he. "Hell, I'm the one who won't allow anyone under eighteen into these events," he complained privately. "The True Cross sells tickets to kids, holds this sadistic shit up as an honorable and holy pursuit, and somehow they're the good guys."

To those good guys, Henry was not only irreverent; he was a fraud. True Cross spokesperson Tracy White had this to say: "He's never been on the cross, doesn't even advocate it. Treats the noble Stigmatics with no respect whatsoever, takes their money, makes his obscene and cynical profit."

PLAGUE

The staff at Sanborn was under no illusions. From the beginning of Zachary Sergeant's stay – the shrouded circumstances of his admission, the very private nature of his care, the otherwise inexplicable nature of his coma – all signs pointed to a rogue case of the long-dormant Plague in a facility whose parent company was Protocol Products. To a man, the staff believed that Protocol was handling a classified case in quiet cooperation with the NIH. This assumption of government oversight, subtly encouraged by Dr. Hriniak, ensured that they maintained full confidentiality, a policy not strictly followed in other cases.

So they were caught a bit off guard when the NIH, from their point of view, completely altered its approach. Two NIH officers rolled in early one morning, without warning, their roles unclear but their attitudes unmistakable. It was still a classified case, but no longer a case being managed in quiet cooperation. The NIH agents interviewed Sergeant's caregivers one by one, grilling them on their backgrounds, on clinical procedure and on security protocol. Wesley Grassford and Vanessa Jones were also called in for wandering interviews, sessions that didn't seem to go anywhere beyond imparting a slightly threatening nudge in favor of complete confidentiality. The questions seemed so random as to suggest a deeper professional purpose, possibly to elicit a self-implicating mistake. There was mention of a possible quarantine, a scenario involving Grassford and Jones on the basis that they had visited or tended to Sergeant. But by the end of the day the notion seemed to have been shelved; it was said that only Sergeant was officially quarantined. "A moot point, to say the least," said Grassford.

He and Vanessa were a little worse for wear as they sat in the doggedly non-institutional chair and table set in Sergeant's room. There was a decent view out the window, a nice stand of maples out beyond the parking lot. But the chairs were oriented indoors, toward the bed, putting Sergeant's left foot in close focus as if propped for a sketch in a perspective class. Vanessa half expected to be handed a charcoal and a pad.

"So much for keeping the NIH out of Zack's case," she said.

"I was just thinking the same thing."

"I never liked hospitals in the first place. I like them now even less."

"I never got comfortable in hospitals either," said Grassford, "though I spent quite a bit of time in them during the Plague."

"Your grandfathers and your dad – they all went down one after another, within a matter of months? Your whole family must have been in shock."

"Yes, each drop was as much a surprise as the last. My father came out of it two days after my first grandfather went down, so we never had three down at a time."

"And they each came out as they were before? No aftereffects?"

"You know, Vanessa, that was the last question Zack asked me before we went for our last drive in Omaha. I put off answering – I don't know why – but I'm glad now that I did. He didn't need to know my answer, but you do. I was just a kid, trying to piece things together as best I could. Officially, as you know, all three of them came out with full processing function. The medical people were convinced of that on the strength of whatever tests they had at the time. Apparently they were very enthusiastic with the results – they described the recoveries as being much quicker and fuller than expected after such long comas. I'm pretty sure before-and-after IQ tests would have matched up. All three of them could probably do figures and calculations and chores at least as well as before. My dad went right back to his crossword puzzles, and his job, and I wasn't aware of any dropoff in either case. I went along with everyone else's proclamations, assuming they were completely back.

"But as time went by I came to the impression that a lot of life had gone out of them, not just at the beginning, but for good. My mother never agreed with me. Maybe it was simply the aging process, but I thought my father acted like he'd already cashed in his chips when he came back, like he'd lost the fight sometime during the sleep. My grandfathers were suddenly acting their ages, old men, crabbier, more resigned to fate, more prone to complaint. They'd lost their spunk. For one thing, none of them seemed particularly interested in what had happened to them. My mother was making a lot of inquiries, trying to drum up some medical attention, and I remember my father really discouraging it. In fact none of the victims I interviewed ever really seemed that interested, which may be one reason the Plague stayed just below the radar all those years."

Vanessa said nothing, so Grassford continued.

"It definitely took me a while to come around to that way of thinking, and I still wonder about that. Maybe it was just too shadowy to get my arms around right away – I just bought into what everyone else said at first, and didn't notice until later. Or I just imagined the whole thing, and any decline on their part was just part of the natural aging process. Or maybe I just got a little bored with them as time went on because I was getting older and they just didn't seem as engaging as they had before. Or maybe they just couldn't muster as much interest in me anymore. Maybe some combination of any or all of those things. There are just so many ways to think about it. And then they're gone and you wonder what you actually were thinking because nobody really talked about it."

Dr. Hriniak had managed to wrangle one more set of reports from the NIH Information Technology team without having to directly engage Nate Howard. This was a cross-check of the declining Washington dreamers with their Dreamtracking initiation dates. He dreaded seeing the results, but as fate would have it, the NIH techs garnered some manner of revenge for all his historic haranguing by exceeding expectations; this time they delivered the reports within just a few hours.

The data showed what Hriniak feared most: those suffering dream decline were, to a man, all from the group of earliest dream donors, throwing a good bit of credence to the theory of cumulative effect from prolonged CTC exposure. None of the subsequent donors, those initiated when the NIH had waived its regional caps and reopened to all comers, had shown any decline. In conjunction with the Omaha CTCs and Sergeant, it all made terrible sense. Hriniak's head slumped to his desk. Of all the myriad scientific and engineering advances since the dawn of the modern age, weaponry excluded, his creation would be among the few particularly condemned as not only unhelpful, but deadly harmful, relegated to the heap of shame with the likes of mercury dosing, asbestos, diet pills, and lead paint.

He knew at some level that with these revelations he was done as a commercially viable scientist, possibly even as an academic. He'd be ruined financially as well, with eighty percent of his net worth tied up in Protocol stock and options. But it was the hit to his reputation that he dreaded most. He had no illusions about his ego; he'd developed an image of himself sitting squarely in that rarest class of innovators, those whose contributions had merged science with art and entertainment, and he'd become heavily invested in others holding him in that same high esteem. He'd become a celebrity in his own right. After all, in the cause of medical advancement he had produced a smash cultural hit. And yet, even with all of that on a sudden precipice of obliteration, he maintained an ability to observe himself in a detached and scientific manner. Already he understood that he was headed into the stages of grieving; he'd need to clear Denial, Anger, Bargaining, and Depression before he could swallow the new reality. And he didn't have long. Interviews with federal agencies were pending, only days away. Within weeks hundreds or thousands of Washington men could drop into coma.

When he could get beyond himself, beyond contemplating his own personal tragedy, he waded into another wave of cost calculations. He mourned not only the undoing of years of his own labor, but that of the thousands of Protocol and NIH employees and hundreds of thousands of dream donors, and the waste of so much cash and material. More than anything, he mourned the bitter end to such an endearing nationwide lark. The world was a tough enough place without the dispiriting news he was about to inflict on it.

Dr. Hriniak could recall only one case of a professional having to blow the whistle on himself with anywhere near the personal damage he was now facing. It had occurred in the late 1970's and involved an engineer by the name of William LeMessurier. He had designed Manhattan's Citicorp Center, the fifty-nine-story stainless steel tower gleaming a distinctive white on the East Side Midtown skyline, its signature crown sloped at a rakish forty-five degrees. It stands on four stilts, one centered in each side of the building, allowing the structure's four corners to float, freakishly, seventy feet in the air. It was fully built, tenanted, and occupied when LeMussurier, prompted by an engineering student, realized that errors in his wind load calculations coupled with construction shortcuts – the contractors had cut costs by using bolted joints rather than welded joints – had left the building almost certain to topple over in certain wind conditions. Those conditions were projected to occur not once in a millennium, but once in fifty-five years, a near surety over the life of the building, and a reasonably probable occurrence within LeMussurier's own expected life. (He would, in fact, live for another thirty years.)

A building of that magnitude collapsing on the streets of Manhattan was, of course, unthinkable before religious lunatics toppled the World Trade Center two decades later; it would represent a specter of destruction and death unprecedented in the history of modern construction. LeMussurier's errors were inexcusable by the standards of modern engineering, which operated on huge margins of safety, with buildings generally overbuilt by a factor of nearly two.

LeMussurier agonized for some time before going to the building owners with the calculations. After several rounds of heated internal discussions, the parties declined to make a public disclosure. They opted instead to launch a quiet fix, rewelding the joints over the course of several months, including the hurricane season. Business within Citicorp Center continued as usual, its occupants completely oblivious to the purpose of the work. Public disclosure came nearly twenty years later, in the form of an article in *The New Yorker*. LeMussurier emerged as a reasonably sympathetic character, commended into posterity for his forthrightness in coming forward, although in Dr. Hriniak's estimation the secretive nature of the joint response should have tempered that legacy.

There was, of course, no chance of Dr. Hriniak's launching a secret fix. As he saw it, there was no fix, only dismantlement. On the other hand, there was no certainty of a problem either, nowhere near the conclusiveness of an engineering calculation, only what seemed a circumstantial probability without much backing science. Taken one step further, with no certainty of a coming wave of comas, and no certainty that his CTCs would be the cause in any case, then how could he, in good conscience as Chief Science Officer, act now to effectively bring it all down? And, make no mistake, that's what he'd be doing by presenting the case. Once the bureaucrats got wind of it they'd be covering their asses at the speed of light, disbanding a national program that had awakened the world to the social and scientific potential in dreaming, and leaving him on the island of blame and disgrace. What if no comas came at all? And what liability could he face if he didn't come forward and they did come? He'd been trained as a scientist, and there was no real science here to finger CTCs. It was only the speculation of a couple of lay people, and not particularly distinguished lay people at that.

If his goal was to navigate the stages of grief quickly, before hundreds or thousands had dropped into coma, he was off to a good start. By the end of that first sleepless night he was already well into Step One: Denial.

Vanessa spent a lot of time looking into Sergeant's unstirring face. Sergeant had lost a quick twenty pounds and looked gaunt – not at all the robust man she had known him to be. "He's getting awfully thin," she'd say to Dr. Hriniak and the attending physician. "Shouldn't we be cutting back on the exercise routines? Can't we add calories?"

She was equally a spectator to Sergeant's state and to her own thoughts, hearing her internal dialogue as if it were a conversation in the next room. "I can handle anything physical," she heard herself contemplate on many occasions, "but not brain damage or personality shifts." She imagined the struggle of walking away from a compromised man, a man immersed in fog but just lucid enough to know he was being abandoned. She knew anecdotally that the Omaha men had recovered "fully," but she now had Grassford's qualification on the point. Worse, she knew the prevailing medical theory that, after a point, victims of comas generally emerge with permanent cognitive degradation, in rough proportion to the length of the coma. She tried not to think about it, but it wouldn't seem to leave her.

She had learned to respect and trust the small full-time nursing crew. In what was essentially a private Protocol hospital wing, there were only five nurses circulating through Sergeant's rotation. They were a vigilant and dedicated group; one was a bit of a musician, and they all seemed to enjoy the novelty of her bass sounding on the ward. After the first few days she had earned their friendship and trust. She was free to lift and flex his legs, working his hips and knees, promoting circulation and continuing the vigilance against pressure sores. From what she'd been told, no amount of that manipulation was too much. The arms were a little tougher to access given the medical tangle around his head and upper body – the drip line, the breathing circuit, the nasogastric feeding tube, the arterial line, the ECG, the oxygen saturation probe – but she worked his hands in her own, kneading circulation and warmth into the end of each finger.

With no life playing on his face, she would often turn her gaze to the monitor as she poured out her bass lines. She took what satisfaction she could from the green squiggles that were presumed to reflect musical recognition in Sergeant's head. In that hospital environment she was limited in volume, but she experimented with different tempos, different genres, different keys, taking note of which combinations produced which patterns on the screen. She soon realized that pedal-driven effects such as compression, distortion, and reverb were contributing factors, and her gigging effects kit became a fixture at the foot of his bed.

Dr. Hriniak encouraged her science with these alternative Dream Tones, prodding her to define the variables and to form records indicating their relative effects. He taught her to distill those records into more sophisticated charts as the data grew, to form primary and secondary sorts, and to systematically assess other possible variables, integrating or eliminating such non-musical factors as time of day, interval from exercise, and direct or partial sunlight.

That kind of distraction, he thought, was good for Vanessa, and — who knew? — honing the application could actually end up being somewhat helpful to Sergeant. The thought he tried to whisk away was that his pedantry was primarily a diversion from the constant tug of war in his head, and a passable way to interact with Vanessa, whose presence was a droning and unspoken remonstration. Four days had passed since the trio had sat for lunch, and still Dr. Hriniak had not resolved to come forward, if not publicly then at least internally, to Christopher Collins.

Grassford and Vanessa queried Dr. Hriniak individually, once a day. They hadn't overly pressed the point — they knew he was grappling with it, and he'd put them off with reports of more scientific query. But he'd hinted that the initiation date reports had shown what Vanessa had suspected, and it seemed fairly obvious, even to non-scientists, that there wasn't a lot more science to be had. In a way, their silence was worse than badgering would ever have been.

Dr. Hriniak was inclined to retreat further into his office, to reduce his visits to Sanborn in order to avoid his two comrades from the lunch-table think tank. But, to his credit, he carried on with his established patterns of visitation. And, silently, they began to wear him down.

REMEMBRANCES

Part of the steady climb through Saint Martyrius was the transition to more formidable nuns in the classroom. Our fifth-grade teacher was Sister Mary Catherine, a tall, broad-shouldered woman in her physical prime. Her robes, habit, and eyeglasses could not conceal her bristling athletic tone. You could see the veins in her well-defined forearms and sinewy long-fingered hands. She had the eyes of a hunter, burning with the fires of vigilance. She was a different breed than we'd experienced in our earlier grade school years, when the teachers we'd faced were not only less intelligent than a good many of us, but elderly and physically unimposing as well.

Sister Mary Catherine was the sharpest teacher of all the Saint Martyrius nuns – she could challenge even the more gifted kids academically – but even at the beginning there was something slightly edgy, something just off-center in her approach. Other teachers had lumped us together as a single entity; we were forty kids from the countless Catholic hordes that had come before us and were sure to follow, forty head from an endless prairie herd stretching past the edge of both horizons, corralled at random and sent trudging through the well-worn elementary school curriculum. We were another in a series of schoolyear ablutions, another class, another cross to be borne. There was some measure of comfort in this anonymity, in the purely vocational nature of the nuns' interest. They sought no particular congress with lay people; they certainly did not invest themselves in individual schoolchildren. Their gaze was fixed upwards, their affinity with others of a similar bent, and with higher and more ethereal beings.

But Sister Mary Catherine brought a strikingly forthright and imposing presence to the classroom. There was nothing bland or dispassionate in her demeanor. Her reactions were highly-charged, adrenalized, emotional, right there on the surface. Her personal aversion to certain children was tangible, menacing and unmistakable. She took an immediate and profound disliking to Jeremy, whose air of defiance smacked not so much of entitlement, but of superior intelligence, something she absolutely could not stomach. It would drive her berserk.

She also disliked the pretty girls, girls who showed even the slightest manifestations of sexual blossoming, or who acted the flirt or coquette. She would grab them by their hair and make them kneel on the floor, not so much to measure their skirts, but more to produce the pain wrought of rock-hard tile. With sharp little slaps of a thick wooden ruler, she'd enforce the erect and upright posture that crushed the most vulnerable points of the knee, minute after minute, until the girl's eyes began to water and we, in turn, began to squirm in our seats. This was the first hint of the physical presence she quickly established within the confines of our second-floor classroom. As the weeks went on she showed no hesitation to simply slap the boys, hard, right across the face, as she'd done in the run-up to Confirmation. But now her own face would flush red, her hands tumescent and quivering for the kill.

For the first time I really took notice of the cathedral glass in our heavy wooden classroom doors. The large glass sheets were figure-rolled and thickened, patterned into high relief, as if they had been poured over an internal chicken wire skeleton. The result was an opaqueness that barked of confinement and isolation. No one would be looking in.

PLAGUE

When the following Monday's report showed another eight percent decline, Dr. Hriniak passed quickly and decisively through the final stages of Denial, directly into the throes of Anger. He jumped up from his chair, and, after a quick look to make sure his door was securely closed, fired his C7-403 Mobile Device against the wall, where it punctured the sheetrock and exploded into pieces and shards. He began to stomp around the office like someone who'd just smashed his finger in a doorjamb, swearing like a sailor in only half-muffled tones.

Twenty-two hundred Washington men were now carrying streaks of dreamlessness.

Dr. Hriniak stormed and raged, actually picking up his chair with the intent of heaving it through the window before reconsidering and setting it back down, more angry than before. He was red-faced and agitated; he could feel his pulse accelerating through his neck and head, could feel his eyes watering, noticed his vision deteriorating through fogging glasses. His feet hurt from stomping on the poured concrete floor; in one fleeting moment of clarity he wished he'd worn better shoes. He tossed the whiteboard eraser in the air and punted it across the room – there was none of the puff-of-chalk satisfaction he remembered from the old school erasers – he was too old for this – then chased it down and punted it again.

And then, as abruptly as he'd begun, he stopped, sat quietly on the edge of his desk, and began instinctively to measure his pulse. It was the first time he'd lost his composure in many years. His head drooped to his chest but lifted rhythmically as he began to stabilize his breathing. He had begun to pull himself together. It was time to go upstairs and strike a Bargain – with Christopher Collins.

"Chris, I had an interesting brainstorming session over lunch with Grassford and Jones the other day. They have a perspective I can't get here at Protocol, and they make a perfectly logical but alarming case. It's pretty simple: if we assume, 1) that Zamaprotocol caused Sergeant's coma, 2) that some form of CTC was encased in Omaha bed pillows at the time of the Plague, and 3) that Zamaprotocol has been a common exposure to all the men we know are in current decline, then we have at least a theoretical common denominator. Extending the logic, it's possible that Zamaprotocol may not just be monitoring for dreamlessness. It may actually be causing it."

Collins opened his mouth to speak but found himself on the inhale rather than the exhale. Dr. Hriniak continued before Collins could sort that out: "I've done some cross-checks on the compromised Washington dream donors, and as I feared, those who've been negatively impacted are all from the original startup group. In other words, they've all had the full period of exposure to Zamaprotocol. None of the newer donors are exhibiting dream decline. Yet."

"Slow down, Anders. Sergeant's exposure was intravenous, extreme and habitual. We don't know that all the victims in Omaha were using the pillows. And we don't know that all those affected in Washington are our dream donors."

"Grassford claims to have first-hand family knowledge of three of the original victims, all of whom were using the pillows. As to the current bunch, there's no way to know until people start dropping."

"If they start dropping. We don't know that any comas are coming. And if they are, you can make just as convincing a case that Dreamtracking is providing a perfectly viable warning system to the country, which, by the way, is the generally held opinion in the medical and science communities. That is my position as CEO until proven otherwise. We're not committing corporate suicide on a hunch by two completely untrained lay people, Anders. It's an unsubstantiated idea, and that's all it is. I'd keep this between us, and in fact, as far as I'm concerned, this conversation didn't even happen. Oh, and by the way, I've got a Board call scheduled for tomorrow afternoon to bring everyone up to speed on Sergeant."

Vanessa was beside herself at the one-month mark. From the start of Sergeant's ordeal she'd carried that timeframe in her head as an internal do-not-exceed mark. Something in her, not particularly science-based, and theoretically inconsistent with the Omaha cases, insisted that some level of cognitive dysfunction was certain beyond a month of coma. She called for a general state-of-the-union meeting of the medical staff at which she was the first to openly cite the Plague of Dreamlessness, to query as to what kind of care the government was planning in its Coma Care Centers, to press for more proactive measures. The time for monitoring and maintaining, in her view, was nearing its useful end.

The medical team, without acknowledging that the Plague of Dreamlessness was even in play here, assured Vanessa that the Coma Care Centers, if called into play, would rely on the same care techniques, but without the boutique environment Sergeant enjoyed at the Sanborn. The care was to be of the same passive ilk – maintain the vital processes, introduce movement, protect against pressure sores, and hope for the best. Sadly, that was the extent of the science. Furthermore, Sergeant was as thin as he'd get – after the initial weight loss no further deterioration was expected. The Robo-Stim Dr. Hriniak had been able to secure – bitterly enough, as it had come from a despised Protocol rival – had done its job. With its help, Sergeant had been spared the gross loss of muscle mass that had sometimes produced horrifying gauntness in prior coma victims. (Dr. Hriniak, perhaps in another attempt at escapism, had flirted with the idea of syncing the Robo-Stim's muscle stimulation tempo with input from Vanessa's amp, but quickly abandoned the idea when Vanessa objected in no uncertain terms – she would not have Sergeant dancing like some kind of marionette.) The team further assured her that there was "no certainty" of cognitive decline, even past six weeks. None of this sat well with her.

The meeting died its slow death, and the participants trickled away. Grassford was the last to go, looking more slumped than Vanessa had ever seen him as he trudged down the hall. He seemed to have aged in just the short time she'd known him. She went back to Sergeant's room and picked up her bass. She'd developed her science of music and coma to the point where she, like a seasoned snake charmer, had no difficulty enticing the desired response from Sergeant's monitor. But this time she activated the looping component and laid a second track over the first, looping that as well. And she laid a third track over that – wishing now for the elusive fifth string to provide complementary treble. She put down the guitar, the tracks still looping, and, for the first time during Sergeant's hospital stay, worked her way carefully through the cables and tubes and nestled alongside him in the bed. Within a few minutes, she joined him in sleep. As she drifted into REM she dreamt only in sound, only in music, as if she'd been born blind.

REMEMBRANCES

I doubt that any of us knew the word "eccentric" at that time, but, if we'd been introduced to it, Jeremy Cleverby would have come immediately to mind. He was definitely a bit different. His father's being the Mayor of Omaha was one thing; his being an only child was another. He was the only member of our gang whose Stingray had gears and handbrakes. That bike was also banana yellow; and it carried a preposterous stickshift, a black eight-ball on a six-inch chrome peg, mounted on the top tube of the frame, right between his legs. It was the most outrageous bike any of us had ever seen, and to this day I've never seen another.

Jeremy subscribed to several specialty magazines, most of them focused on either sportscars or his more unusual passion — city planning. His parents imposed no curfews on weekends, so on sleepovers we'd stay up until three or four in the morning, he regaling us — eleven year-olds nodding with sleep at uncharted hours — with the latest statistics on the tallest buildings in the world, sneering at Omaha's ineptitude until, in 1969, we finally put up something reasonably respectable for a smallish city — the thirty-story Woodmen Tower.

Eileen O'Neary's boy list was Jeremy's brainchild; he prodded her for her weekly release even though he rarely rose above number four. He was not a natural athlete but was a spitfire devotee of Nebraska football, with an encyclopedic knowledge of not only the current roster, but that of the projected recruiting classes one or two years out. He was also the first of us to have a favorite baseball player who was a black man. We would follow suit with players like Omaha's own Bob Gibson, or Lou Brock, or Roberto Clemente, but Jeremy was the first, with Henry Aaron. When we all began to collect baseball cards, buying the five-cent bubble gum packs with whatever change we could muster, Jeremy was right in the thick of it. The gum sticks were powdery white with sugar, and hard, almost to the point of cutting our gums. We would cram five or six pieces into our mouths at once, but Jeremy would throw his gum haughtily into the bin, complaining that it had stained some of the cards. He bought the fewest packs, perhaps because he lived furthest from the store and didn't like long bike rides, but he had possession of the only Sam McDowell card in the group. Try as we might, none of us could work it out of him by trade, despite offering packages of players far more valuable than McDowell, a fine left-handed pitcher for the Cleveland Indians but no Hall-of-Famer. If we were offering doubles, even of players he desperately needed, the trade wasn't actually costing us anything of value, and he wouldn't do any deal that didn't involve some pain to both parties.

We all had our mischievous streaks, but Jeremy would take it to a different level. We, of course, would back down and repent when caught and confronted. But Jeremy would venture into an area of fla-grant defiance, an area none of us would touch. During one spelling test that spring Jeremy began to parrot Sister Mary Catherine – as she called out the spelling word Jeremy would simply repeat it, as if pondering it to himself, not loudly, but loud enough to be heard. She let it pass, but it was clearly a point of tension building with each additional word. When she announced "gnat" I had an instant and terrible premonition, and Jeremy did exactly what I feared, repeating the word in two syllables, clearly enunciating the gee, giving away the correct spelling to anyone in the class who might not have known.

Sister Mary Catherine exploded out of her chair, pirouetting around the desk and practically sprinting down Jeremy's row. I heard Jeremy say, as if slightly offended, "I don't know why I can't enunciate the words before spelling them." He was seated near the rear, but she was on him before he could say anything else, grabbing his left ear with an awful twist of her left hand and jerking him out of his seat. I was sitting in the last row, and I could see both of their horrible grimaces as she marched him toward the back door, she behind him, maintaining the death grip on his ear, her wrist bent unnaturally, his head contort-ing down and to the side. As they passed my desk and reached the door, moving awkwardly and at speed, she released Jeremy's ear to turn the handle with that hand; and, as his head came up, her free hand, the dominant right, clasped over the top of it, her fingers spread in his hair, and smashed it right through the window. Thick cathedral glass shattered all over the floor, where it mixed almost instantly with blood.

She had missed with the handle, and the door had never come unlatched. Huge shards of glass hung in place. Jeremy slumped to the floor with his upper body pinned awkwardly against the bottom of the door. Sister Mary Catherine stepped over him and jerked the handle open with both hands, the right one gushing blood. She pushed through the door and disappeared down the hall. In her wake the faint drone of the hydraulic door closer was the only sound in the room. None of us moved or said a word as the door closed slowly on Jeremy's head and shoulders.

After what had to be nearly ten seconds, Karl Klosner got up and pulled Jeremy's motionless body back into the room just enough to clear the door. It was free now to shut with its distinctive click; and somehow that made things feel a little less disordered, a little less disheveled, as if we had somehow closed the protective ring in our little herd. Karl returned to his seat. Jeremy lay quietly, blood from his head pooling on the floor just like we'd seen Bobby Kennedy's do on television the summer before.

PLAGUE

"Mr. Collins, I have Henry Cleverby on line three. This is his third call this morning."

"Oh, hell, put him through."

Christopher Collins took a big gulp of coffee and picked up the phone.

"Henry!"

"Hello, Chris. I apologize for my persistence this morning. I know I can be a real pain in the ass. We have the conference call scheduled for 2:00. I just wanted to touch base beforehand. What's this all about?"

"Henry, I'd rather present to the whole Board at once, rather than going through it piecemeal."

"Emergency conference call to the whole Board – sounds ominous. Would it have anything to do with Zachary Sergeant's lying comatose in Sanborn Critical Care Center?"

"What do you know about that?"

"You're aware I met with Sergeant here in Omaha. He was a mess, Chris. Apparently he caught a flight out, but not the one he'd planned on."

Collins had no response. Cleverby continued.

"I'm a pretty big fish in Omaha, Chris. Not much goes on here that I can't be made aware of. Sergeant was delivered to Saint Joseph's Hospital, in the throes of an inexplicable coma, and by none other than Wesley Grassford. Could it be the first Plague of Dreamlessness case in half a century? We can't be sure because he is whisked away two days later, careflighted to Boston. Protocol is nowhere on the docket, except for Anders Hriniak's personal signature on the hospital release."

Silence.

"Sergeant was subsequently installed at Sanborn. Sanborn is majority owned by Protocol, am I right?"

"I don't know where you're going with this, Henry, but we came clean to the NIH on all that already. Everything is above board."

"Except for the fact that Sergeant's coma is based on his REM being obliterated by years of CTC injection research. Research on behalf of, and with the complicity of, your company."

"Henry, we didn't sanction any injections. We suspended Sergeant for that injection in the lab."

"A bullshit slap on the wrist. You knew he'd taken product home after the first injection. You knew he was doing private injection research long after the suspension. And we all reaped the benefits. He came right back, gave us the Podreader and the Dream Tones, the latter completely the product of his ongoing injection work. We all made a bundle. But at what cost to him? And at what cost to you?

"What do you want, Henry?"

"I want you to support an agreement licensing Zamaprotocol to Calvary Enterprises. And I want Sergeant protected, because if and when he comes out of this I want him working with me."

"It may be out of my hands, Henry."

There was a pause. "What's on your hands is illegal, harmful, and possibly even fatal research methodology – off site, but fully known to you in real time as CEO. Unless you want me sharing my observations with the rest of the Board you'll put off the call. That'll give you an opening in your schedule at 2:00. I'll be in Boston by then, in your office shortly thereafter. Oh, and you might ask Dr. Hriniak to join us."

The big room at the Paradise was packed when Vanessa walked to her place on stage and strapped on her bass. She closed her eyes to the light and began to play. She immediately liked what she heard around her. She'd ended up prepping her guitar and keyboard players in a brusque and coldly professional sort of way – she'd handed them a clip of studio recordings and said "Play it like this." She hadn't seen them again until now, and she knew that she had come off as a bit of a prima donna. But it was unavoidable, and they didn't seem particularly put off. And at first blush they sounded good. The fact that she could hear them at all was also reassuring; she'd taken a chance and ordered no plexiglass cage on this night for Phil Guy. It was loud, but the balance was good. And then she stopped thinking.

For all that was going on, Vanessa was riding a strange musical high. Her dreams in the last week had veered out of anything she equated with the Dream Tones. She was dying to discuss them with Sergeant – such dreams were just not contemplated in their young science. But she'd felt it, and she'd even scanned it. She was competent enough with Sergeant's scanner, and her imprinted pods were definitely outside the established resonance range. Her dreamworld had become a wall of sound, audio only.

She had the same weird sensation on stage as she poured through the first set, seeing nothing through the lights, barely even glancing at the set list taped to the floor, but taking cues from Guy or launching out on instinct, not quite certain she'd picked the right song until she heard Guy and the band right with her. When Guy intoned, "We need some sugar," into the PA she almost missed it, but caught herself just before diving into another song.

"Sugar" was the stage name for insulin. The light people were on it before Vanessa, pumping the spotlight instantly onto the drum kit. Guy plunged the needle, the crowd roared, and suddenly, as if in a dream, Vanessa found one clear thought in the haze.

The immediate danger wasn't so much the coma; it was the fall. The most notable occurred in absurdly dramatic fashion when a twenty-nine year-old Congressional page collapsed at the top of the Capitol steps and rolled nearly to the bottom. News cameras on Capitol vigil were quick to record the scene. The victim was so banged up, with several contusions to the head, that it was unclear at first whether the fall had caused the coma or the coma the fall.

Three more went down on that first day. One simply didn't get out of bed, but two others suffered nasty spills, one a non-profit executive who fell on the Metro's long up escalator at Gallery Place. Only decisive action by fellow riders saved him from possibly catastrophic injury at the top grill.

Those first men fell on a Monday, coinciding with new NIH reports that showed an aggregate forty percent weighted dream volume decline among Washington men. Twenty-two hundred of them were in absolute dreamlessness. The Washington media had no problem grasping the significance. Video of the tumble down the Capitol stairs led all of the regional newscasts, and, within hours, the national newscasts. Tuesday's Washington Post led with the headline, "Four to Coma; Regional Plague Expected to Follow."

Dr. Hriniak was digging for the victims' names while trying not to appear frantic. He had to know if they were Dreamtracking donors. Nate Howard and Christopher Collins were under siege. Collins was basically in hibernation, not straying off the Protocol campus, huddling with his public relations people and sporadically browbeating his scientific staff. Howard gamely met the press, declaring with firm jaw that the first care center would be open within the week.

Stopgap measures were frantically discussed. If men all around the city could be expected to drop suddenly into coma, how could life in the Capital continue with any sense of normalcy? What if a Metro driver slumped at the head of a train, or at the wheel of a bus? For that matter, anyone on the road could cause mayhem, injury, death. Female cab drivers had never been in such demand. What about surgeons? Pilots? Air traffic controllers? A joint body of federal and local officials was hastily convened under the title Committee for Plague Management, concerning itself largely with just such scenarios.

Thirty more men dropped on Day Two, none, fortunately, in positions conducive to collateral damage. One powerline worker slumped high on a pole, hanging lifelessly in his safety harness and creating a national news sensation before a bucket truck could be secured to effect his recovery. By noon that day the Committee decreed that any Dreamtracking users showing decline were forbidden from working specifically identified "Jobs of Endangerment," and from operating any kind of motor vehicle or heavy machinery. Calls were made for the NIH and Protocol to make Dreamtracking records public; these were met with civil liberty arguments on behalf of personal confidentiality. But this was a crisis situation, and debate was cut short. By day's end it was decided that the records would be released in confidence to the

Committee, which in turn began to contact and to monitor the declining dream donors without releasing any names to the public.

The lack of common sense was decried; shouldn't these men have been aware of their dangerous dream declines, and shouldn't they have voluntarily discontinued that kind of work? But only a small chunk of the general population of men were in the Dreamtracking program. Public service announcements counseled men to register for Dreamtracking, and in the interim to begin to monitor their dream volume independently, using the crudest of methodologies. Oneirologists provided instructional dream-logging columns with tips like: "Use the technique you're most comfortable with — computer pads, pen and pad, dictation," "Keep your supplies at bedside," and "Do it first thing, before you shower or talk to your wife."

The Committee called for an immediate expansion of dream monitoring in the District. More than one official urged that it become mandatory for all Washington men. And in a very telling development, it was announced that the President and the next several players in the chain of political succession had complied with security requests. They had begun Dreamtracking.

REMEMBRANCES

On the morning after Jeremy had gone through the window, our Stingray gang, minus Jeremy, pulled into the Saint Martyrius parking lot. We ran into Mr. Sandman standing where we always parked our bikes, as if he had been waiting for us.

"Guys, can I see you in the lunchroom?"

"Right now?"

"Yes, right now."

We looked at each other – me, Mikey, Billy and Chris – and trudged after "The Sandman," as Jeremy used to call him. He had a key ring as big as a janitor's and selected the proper key at once. We had never seen the room so empty and so quiet. Mr. Sandman flicked a couple wall switches, just enough to light up one corner of the room, and we sat at a table there.

"You guys ride to school with Jeremy pretty much every day, don't you?"

We acknowledged that we did.

"I'm going to pay him a visit this morning and would like your help. I've got the good vibe hoodie here and would like you all to make a contribution."

"What's the good vibe hoodie?"

He pulled out a white foam hood, like something Jacques Cousteau might have worn on a dive, or a knight might have worn beneath his helmet, or a nun might have worn with her habit, or a mangle-eared rugby player might have worn in a scrum, or a little kid might have worn sledding at Sunks. If Karl Klosner had been with us he might have said something like "What are you, some kind of fairy?" But Karl never rode a bike, and none of the rest of us were quite that outspoken.

Mr. Sandman picked me to go first. The whole thing was loony, of course, but I slipped the hoodie over my head – it was thicker and more substantial than I thought, but pliable and form-fitting, rather comfortable once it was in place. I couldn't really hear when I wore it, but I could tell exactly what Mr. Sandman was saying:

"Just think good thoughts about Jeremy, whatever you like. Just close your eyes and get in a happy place with Jeremy in mind."

I didn't see any way out, so I shut my eyes and started pretending to concentrate, and then I realized that I wasn't that good of an actor and it might be easier to actually concentrate than to pretend. So I pictured Jeremy on his banana yellow Stingray, with his Sam McDowell card in his chest pocket, riding through a city of fabulous, gleaming, world-class towers of glass and stone and steel: eighty, ninety, one hundred stories tall; triumphs of innovative design and engineering; monuments to boldness, imagination and limitless optimism; lined up as if in procession on both sides of the street. He reached for the stick-shift between his legs, switched gears, and jumped a curb, all with his gaze fixed upward, taking in the colossal architectural wonders, pointing now and then at certain particularly compelling features, animated, talking steadily in a voice I couldn't hear. Things were going his way – I couldn't help but think that he might even have jumped to number one on Eileen O'Neary's boy list. But that bothered me a little, and I lost my train of thought. I figured enough time had passed, so I opened my eyes and pulled off the hood.

"Thank you, Wesley," said Mr. Sandman. "You can go on to class now. The others will be along shortly."

PLAGUE

Two days had passed without any sign of Dr. Hriniak. His afternoon visits to Sanborn had ceased. He had not returned calls. He was not in the office.

Vanessa Jones and Wesley Grassford discussed it at some length over hospital cafeteria fare. New coma cases in Washington had climbed from four and thirty in the first two days into the sixties and seventies in the next two, and had held steadily in that range in the days since. It was easy to imagine that Dr. Hriniak had been caught in a whirlwind of consultation. But it seemed unlike him to simply disappear. If their theory was correct, every day of delay was adding to the queue of future victims. And if Dr. Hriniak or anyone else at Protocol had come clean with the NIH, he would certainly have seen to it that Wesley and Vanessa had been told.

"I don't know what's going on over there," said Vanessa, "but I'm about done waiting for our friend the good doctor to do the right thing. It would be different if he actually disagreed with us. I swear if I could get anyone at NIH to take my call or to take me seriously I'd call them myself."

"What do you say we go ahead and try that anyway?" asked Grassford.

They exchanged a long and meaningful stare. And then Grassford made a call. "Nate Howard, please. Wesley Grassford from Omaha calling." But endless on-holds led to disinterested and dismissive live parties, more explanations leading to more on-holds. It was a timeless and terminal loop.

A full forty-five minutes later, an exasperated Wesley Grassford turned to Vanessa and said: "We can keep butting heads at the NIH from the bottom up. We can go to the press. We can storm into Protocol. But besides Zack lying here we don't have a lot of evidence – our case is pretty anecdotal. Nate Howard is the guy calling the shots, and he's the guy with enough background to grasp this all at once. Besides the IT guys, he's the only guy Anders ever talks to at NIH. He's the guy we have to get to."

"I'm surprised he wouldn't pick up. He has to know who you are."

"It's got to be crazy down there. It's possible I didn't even get close enough for him to make the choice."

"We'll never get to him by calling his office," said Vanessa. "We'd have the same problem if we went to the NIH in person. We need his mobile number. And preferably we'd call it from a number he recognizes so he'd actually pick up."

Grassford considered for a moment. "After Anders busted up his last phone I know he decided he needed a spare. I know where he probably keeps it, and I can pretty much come and go as I please at Protocol."

"I'd say go get it."

Vanessa dropped the pod into the metal quarter-cup and held it over the candle flame. The pod still held a slight glow, reflecting onto the inside face of the cup. It quivered a bit, then was suddenly sitting in a small pool of itself. Then it was gone. Vanessa dipped the syringe and thumbed the plunger upwards, drawing the liquefied pod into the chamber.

It had been the toughest musical choice she'd faced. It was always tough picking from your own work – whether forming a playlist for a show or forming the order for a CD, it required one's stepping out of oneself and struggling for the external point of view. What was the strongest cut? Which one should lead? Which one should close? When to go up tempo? When to drop it? In this case it was tougher still. The music was set in dreams, after all; transposing the melodies as best one could from waking memory, mimicking settings, playing them, recording them, gauging them against one another – it was a flawed process. A lot was lost in translation.

She thought she had a pretty good understanding of Sergeant's taste in music, but she couldn't be sure exactly what, if anything, he'd hear in a musical dream. Her dreams had always carried heavy musical overlays, but Zack would normally pick up more on characters, action, and physical props. Given that her recent dreams were exclusively musical, resonating well outside the Dream Tones, there was no telling if Sergeant would pick up on anything, even if he weren't in coma.

She had studied his monitored reactions to her bass lines at Sanborn. Over time she'd developed a general idea of the most promising keys, the most invigorating settings, the most restorative rhythms.

But this choice was, by nature, as instinctive as it was cerebral. The chances seemed remote that any of those dreamy tunes could stir him, even more remote that she could pick just the right one. Every injection entailed the risk of actually extending the coma. It was a ridiculous longshot, but time was running out. Windows were closing.

Much as she'd struggled sticking needles into herself, she'd never actually injected anyone else, and now she found that it was even more difficult. She half expected Sergeant to flinch, ridiculed herself for the absurdity, and sank the plunger.

PALM TUNNELS

By the time they were able to pull him down, Henry Cleverby had been unconscious and unbreathing for several minutes. He was catastrophically hypoxic, an obvious risk – almost a certainty, really – with any unsupervised four-tunnel crucifixion. But no one who knew Henry Cleverby considered it an attempt at suicide.

"He just didn't want to be watched up there," said Abraham Sanchez, the warehouse supervisor who had last spoken to Cleverby. Sanchez and three others had, on Cleverby's instructions, staked him and lifted him upright just after normal closing time. "He told us to leave him alone and not come back for an hour," said the visibly shaken Sanchez. "No one had ever passed out in the first hour, but we knew it was still dangerous without the medical monitor. So we ran in the second the hour was up, but we were too late.

"If it had been set up in advance we could have maybe gotten other people involved, maybe stopped it altogether. But he just popped it on us at the last minute, and anyone here will tell you it is very difficult to say no to Mr. Cleverby. We didn't even know he had sole tunnels until then."

A couple of the men had been trained in basic resuscitation techniques, and they'd been able to restore Cleverby's breathing, but not his consciousness. Emergency physicians at Saint Joseph's had done no better. Cleverby was off into coma.

PLAGUE

Vanessa huddled in the Sanborn parking lot several floors below Sergeant's room. She couldn't help feeling a little like Bob Woodward waiting for Deep Throat in 1972. Only this time Deep Throat was a seventy year-old Omahan with a stomach ache on his way to the airport.

The elevator light blinked, the doors opened, and out stepped Wesley Grassford. Vanessa smiled and stepped into the light. Grassford pulled the phone from his pants pocket and pressed it into her palm with a guilty look.

"I felt terrible, but it's the only way we're going to get through," he said.

"We're doing the right thing. I'll conference you in when I get him on the line." She gave him a long, tight hug.

"That's the best hug I've had in some decades," said Grassford. "To be honest, it's the only hug I've had in decades." Vanessa smiled, and they headed their separate ways, she to her car, he to his cab.

Vanessa drove away from the hospital for a minute or two, turned into a residential neighborhood and then into a park. She parked the car and walked into a grove of trees. She opened the C7-403 MD, scanned Contacts under "H", and placed the call.

A voice at the other end said, "Anders?"

"No, Mr. Howard, this is Vanessa Jones. I'm Zachary Sergeant's partner, and I've been working with Dr. Hriniak and Wesley Grassford. There've been a few developments I thought you should be aware of."

REMEMBRANCES

When I got to the classroom after finishing with Mr. Sandman's hoodie, everything had been cleaned up from the day before. The glass in the door had been replaced, but with standard translucent rather than the figure-rolled opaque. The cathedral glass must have been on order.

A substitute teacher was on duty. Someone said she was a really high-ranked nun, like the Reverend Mother in "The Sound of Music," and you could tell that from the way she conducted herself. She didn't mention Jeremy or Sister Mary Catherine or the window, but very pleasantly introduced herself and dove seamlessly into our first subject. Billy, Mikey and Chris filtered in over the next several minutes, and she let each of them pass without a word of rebuke. She brought a nice calming presence to the classroom, and we went through the whole day without any problem and without any mention of Jeremy.

Nobody ever told us anything, but apparently Jeremy woke up sometime that afternoon. He'd been unconscious for almost twenty-four hours. Somebody said anything more than six hours made it a coma, but somebody else said it had to be more than a day.

Jeremy's desk sat empty, and we had another reminder at the end of the week when they replaced the cathedral glass – the workmen were just finishing when we walked in. We only talked about it on the playground, and after a couple more days we weren't talking about it at all. I never heard any parents or teachers or priests discussing it. The only thing I ever heard that was even close to official was from Mr. Sandman, who stopped me in the hall one day and said, "The good vibe hoodie was very helpful. Thank you, Wesley."

There were only a couple weeks left in the school year, so it was no surprise that neither Jeremy nor Sister Mary Catherine made it back to our class. The Reverend Mother served out the term, and at length we heard the peal of the last bell and were set running into the dreamy days of June.

I called Jeremy's house a few times but never heard back from him. The heat came on and baked our skin. The baseball season ran through a hundred and thirty-odd games. The calendar turned to September, and, still, none of us had seen Jeremy. On the first day back to school Billy and I stopped by his house, just in case. And there he was, three months later, sitting on his yellow bike, ready to ride. He showed us the huge scar at his hairline – the big one below his eye we could see pretty plainly – but he didn't much want to talk about it. Sister Mary Catherine wasn't back that fall. We figured she'd been transferred for good to some convent or some school out of state. As far as I know, nobody sued anybody, nothing made the papers. It was almost like we dreamed it all up.

PLAGUE

Within an hour of leaving the Sanborn lot, Vanessa pulled right back in. She ran up three flights of stairs, took a left through the door, walked twenty-one steps and took the left into Sergeant's room – she could have done all of it with her eyes closed. He was, of course, just as she'd left him, but she wouldn't allow herself to admit any disappointment. She reached for the bass, powered the amp, slipped the strap over her head.

"You know any Kings of Coma?"

Vanessa looked up, not believing what she'd just heard. Sergeant held his endotracheal tube in one hand. He half-grinned and croaked again: "How long was I?" And then he fell back on his pillow.

Dreamtracking was out of business by noon of the following day. Nate Howard, his career passing before his eyes, confirmed the existence and the makeup of the Omaha pillows, and confirmed that every Washington victim to date was an original Dreamtracking donor. He consulted with the Surgeon General and key members of the executive and legislative branches well into the night. And in a noon conference broadcast nationally he stunned the oneirological community by ordering the immediate cessation of all Dreamtracking activity, citing "preliminary but quite substantiated ties between prolonged exposure to the CTC pods imbedded in Dreamtracking headgear and a decline in vital dream function." He shut down all Dreamtracking support on the NIH site, also effective immediately, and issued a recall of all Dreamtracking kits nationwide. There would be no more dream data uploads, no more narrative dream content blogs, no more individual dream profiles. Dreamtracking had taken its ball and gone home.

An hour before Nate Howard's press conference, Christopher Collins hosted a conference call with the twelve functioning members of the Protocol Board. He laid out the evidence against CTCs, summarized the call he and Dr. Hriniak had already held with Nate Howard, and advised the stunned Board members to tune in to the conference, which was airing within minutes. Just as the call came to an end, Collins resigned both his Board seat and his post as Chief Executive Officer. His next call was to his attorney.

It was a joy waking up to her after any sleep, the sensation of finding himself in his perfect place. But now, after thirty-seven days of the dark, this was like awakening from death and decomposition to bright life, and to an angel. Not any angel, but one created from the beginning of time, purposefully and perfectly for him. Sergeant was overjoyed, overcome; and yet words were suddenly an agony to him, vision and light a glaring headache. It was cerebral paresthesia, the unbearable progression of tingling and re-engagement that demanded utter stillness. He held her close, sensing the dawn of life in his arms and shoulders. He felt the return of breath to his lungs, the hint of a pulsing in his brain, the warmth of her breath on his throat.

Grassford wasn't sure exactly when his life had veered off track. He wasn't even certain it had veered off track – maybe his life had taken exactly the track that had been laid for it. But for as long as he could remember he had felt like something was ajar, heard an unsettled voice that was always there, sensed a body bobbing just at the surface. Being back home to the quiet and the solitude simply allowed him to confront it directly.

He'd found his physical place, in these woods along this river; that much he knew. Just now, centered perfectly over the bluffs, as if positioned just for him, a large single cloud stood out in an otherwise unbroken blue sky. It was dark in the center, brightly lit and fluffy at the edges, long and narrow and punctured oddly in the middle, like a donut flattened and stretched. Fingers of sun broke upward over the top of it and downward through the hole in the middle. He sat on his stump in admiration; it would only last a minute, and watching that cloud and those sunbeams seemed like his role at that particular moment, though he couldn't have begun to say why. Generally his course of action wasn't even that clear, and seemed to him even less sensible. Every day brought him closer to the end of his time, without his having even identified the mission, let alone accomplished it.

There was money to be had, and a good bit of prestige, in the wake of the Plague, but Grassford couldn't bring himself to show an interest. He'd been consistent that way his whole adult life. Money was not the mission; and if some other form of accomplishment was, well, he hadn't figured it out just yet. More likely, there was no mission at all, the notion being a half-baked construct of the semi-evolved brain. He was happy to pick up the occasional call from Sergeant or Vanessa – they were a delightful couple – but he ignored everything else. He preferred to spend what little time he still had in the fruitless and universal contemplation.

The recall was unenforceable. Only about half of the donors returned their kits. The others, it was assumed, stashed them away as collector's items, disposed of them outright, or put them in the queue with other gradually devaluing possessions – buried in bottom drawers, boxed up in closets, not to be seen or considered for several years until the next move or the next big cleanup when they would finally see the bin. As with handguns, the government would have much preferred the kits completely out of circulation, but it had no means to enforce requisition, and it lacked the political resolve to fund a buyback program, especially since the donors hadn't purchased their kits in the first place. New legislation did ban sale or transfer; so the kits and their components became a commodity limited to the underground. Pirated software began to circulate, software that supported uploads and classified dreams within the twelve Dream Tones. Unexplained quantities of Zamaprotocol began to surface as well; to those in the know, CTC pods became a renewable resource. And so, on the fringes of society, traditional Dreamtracking remained a lifestyle choice, albeit an unsavory one. Worse, rumors and unsubstantiated stories involving the injection of liquefied Zamaprotocol began to float, and then to rage, throughout the internet. Injection became all too commonplace, and there were sporadic recurrences of the Plague of Dreamlessness long after its second coming had faded into memory.

Dr. Anders Hriniak, cloaked in Depression, stayed on at Protocol, as he'd plea-bargained to do, consulting in the company's effort, in conjunction with the NIH, to track the Plague and mitigate its impact. Of the twenty-two hundred Washington men whose dreamlessness had been documented before Nate Howard pulled the plug, not a single one regained normal dream function before staggering through life for several weeks, then passing into coma and emerging from a Coma Care Center another six weeks later, to the man and almost to the day. Another three hundred men whose dreamlessness had not already been documented, the great majority of them in Boston or Omaha, also dropped into coma. In all, nearly twenty-six hundred men passed through Coma Care Centers. As had happened in the original outbreak, each of the victims resurfaced in a condition deemed consistent with normalcy, though, in the wake of the Plague's second coming, no one could be quite certain.

The news from Sanborn had not been good. Wesley Grassford's stomach ached for a very good reason, and it would soon be worse, far worse. There was no comfort, even in sleep; his dreams were malignant worlds, and deteriorating steadily, nightmares that hung on him like webs until mid-afternoon. He shelved his new store-bought pillow and brought another Sandman edition out of backstock. As he'd hoped, this ridded him of the dreams. But it didn't rekindle any kinder remembrances; the binders, untouched since Sergeant's visit, were apparently complete. Grassford had opted out of dreams, and he'd run plum out of memories. He felt the onset of the certain merciless end. It was upon him.

Grassford had counted the days until the moon was full. That night had come, crisp and starry along the Missouri. He sat on the stump where he'd so often sat before, watching the ripples of light on the surface, a sparkling and magical path across the water and to the moon rising rapidly in the east. The river was deathly quiet, and all the more menacing for it, ruthless and unsparing in its mission. Its waters were eternal memory, the relentless flow of uncounted millenia, a force of unthinkable power, bristling but somewhat muted, as if by choice. Its singleminded run, even in the silence of night, was awesome and unmistakable, unsleeping and infinite.

Grassford reviewed his life with a measure of regret, the wavering sort instantly overridden by the understanding that he couldn't have, and possibly wouldn't have, done anything different – the simple but hard-won knowledge that we are who we are. He looked back with a faltering hint of bitterness at the things that had gone poorly; he thought of it as a "halfhearted begrudgement" and dismissed it as he'd generally done, with a quiet smile and the simple sense of knowing better. Among the billions on the planet, his life had been far better than most; he viewed it with a genuine appreciation for the opportunity – and with the sadness of time, of inevitable solitude, and the passing of all things. He yearned for the forgiveness of those who'd known him; and he felt himself filled with that same forgiveness, for himself and for all who'd groped through the swollen and rudderless waters as he had.

And yet he couldn't help wanting another shot at all the things he'd shied away from, another shot with the fearlessness learned only too late. He wanted second chances – at small things, like walking the pipe over the creek, or racing a wagon down Nicholas Street – and at bigger things too. He wanted to talk to Grandpa Roy and Grandpa Andrew about what really mattered looking back at life, rather than fumbling for the commonplace. He wanted to speak truthfully with Eileen O'Neary, just as they had been then, to tell her that if she could spend the wonder of just one day with him, and then another, and then maybe another, nothing could ever really hurt or disappoint him. He rose from the stump, waded two steps into the river, then two more. He felt the cold as the current took him, sweeping him to the middle, bearing him weightlessly and forever to the south.

THE AUTHOR

M. Reese Kennedy was born and raised in Omaha during its heyday as the world's largest livestock market, slaughterhouse, and meatpacking center. He is the author of two novels – *The Plague of Dreamlessness* and *The Artist in the Pines* – and lives in rural Australia.